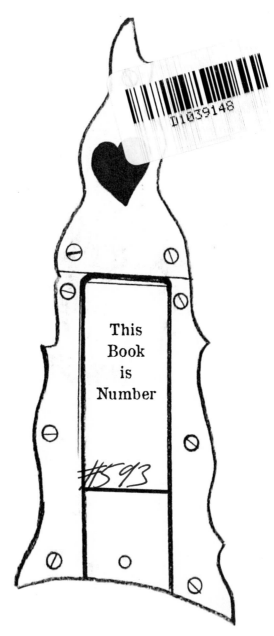

This
Book
is
Number

#593

One thousand copies of

The Fortunate Ones

by **FREDERICK W. NOESNER**
have been printed by
Masthof Press

*"Patience and diligence,*
*like faith, remove mountains."*

-William Penn

# The Fortunate Ones

## 18th CENTURY PHILADELPHIA
## AS SEEN WITHOUT SIGHT

### Frederick W. Noesner

# The Fortunate Ones

## 18th CENTURY PHILADELPHIA
## AS SEEN WITHOUT SIGHT

Artwork by Margarete A. Noesner

This book is printed in large
14 point type for ease of reading.

Library of Congress Number: 2010932522
International Standard Book Number:
978-1-60126-242-4

*Printed 2010 by*

Masthof Press
*219 Mill Road*
*Morgantown, PA 19543-9516*

This book is dedicated
to my wonderful loving parents,
Doris and Frederick M. Noesner,
who did everything they could to
help me become one of the
"Fortunate Ones".

# Author's Statement

I am a 63-year-old totally blind individual with a passion for colonial history. Seasonally for the last five years I have been employed as a colonial person by Historic Philadelphia, Inc. In this role I have lectured in Independence National Park on the history and development of flintlock weapons, as well as deomonstrating the skill of making by hand powderhorns.

As I walked the cobblestone streets of Old City Philadelphia, I frequently have pondered the question of how a blind person such as me would have lived during the 18th Century

How very different and difficult it truly must have been for the blind characters in my book over two-hundred years ago. They lived in a time before computers, before sound recording, before the development of Braille, before schools for the education of the blind, before society placed any genuine value on a blind person. We tend to glorify simplify and overlook the shortcomings of the 18th Century. However, for a person with a disability, it was for the most part a harsh and unrelenting time. More has happened to improve the lives of blind people in the last fifty years than has taken place during all history combined. Yes, it is true.

By reading my new book, *The Fortunate Ones*, join me now as we will explore the world of blindness during the 18th Century, for a very different world it was.

Frederick W. Noesner

# Contents

# Historic Map

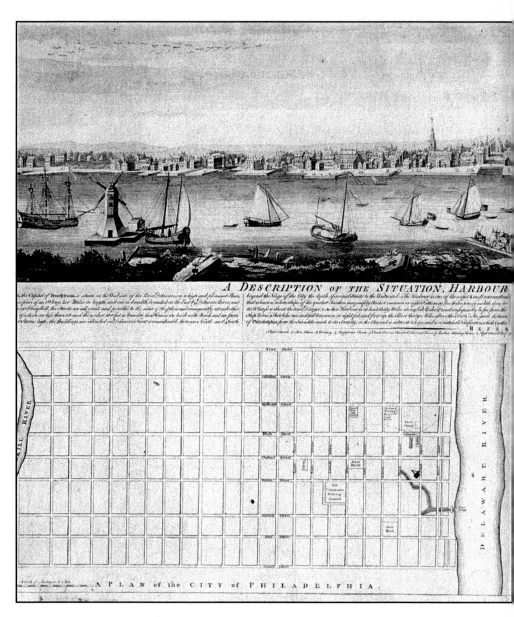

Philadelphia from 1756

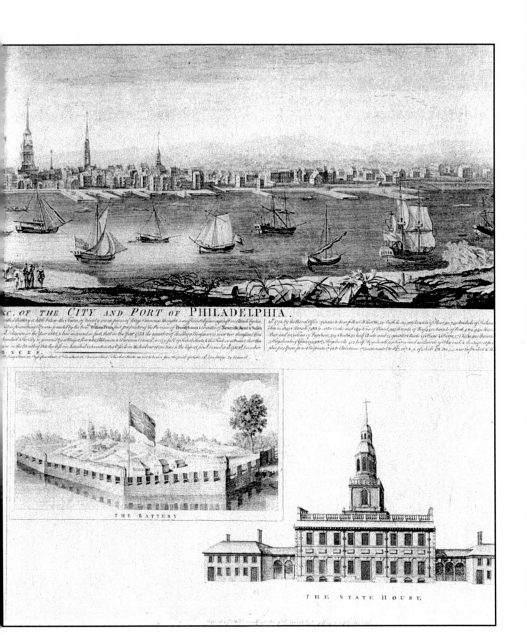

&c. OF THE CITY AND PORT OF PHILADELPHIA.

THE BATTERY

THE STATE HOUSE

# The Fortunate Ones Map

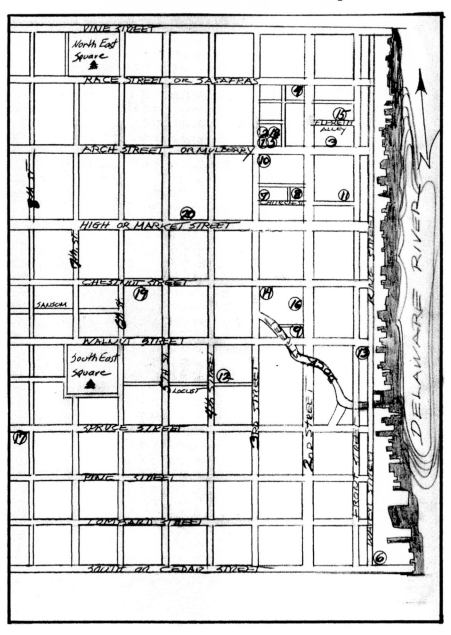

# Map Legend 1776

This simple map indicates the principle points of interest mentioned in this book. It depicts a portion of Philadelphia running west from the Delaware River to Eighth Street and from Vine Street on the north to South Street on the South.

1.  Annaler Gun Shop (Third and Arch Streets)
2.  Annaler home (Third Street)
3.  Home of Henry Annaler (Arch Street between Second and Front Streets)
4.  Henry Annaler's first Watch & Clock Shop (Second and Vine Streets)
5.  Allen's Upholstery Shop (Arch Street)
6.  Robert Bridges' Sail Loft (Water Street)
7.  Samuel Caruthers' Tool Shop (Third Street)
8.  Christ Church (Second and Market Streets)
9.  City Tavern (Second Street)
10. Coffee & Crown Tavern (Arch Street)
11. The Cooperage (Pewter Platter Alley)
12. William Fall's Livery-Stable (Locust Street)
13. Indian Queen Tavern (Water Street)
14. Abraham Kiessel's Shop (Third Street)
15. Daniel Mason's Home and Pottery (Elfreths Alley)
16. Masonic Temple (Lodge Alley)
17. Pennsylvania Hospital (Spruce Street)
18. Pump-Yard (Arch Street)
19. Pennsylvania State House (Chestnut Street)
20. Thomas Palmer Gun Shop (Market Street)

# Introduction

As I sit here at my desk, writing this book, my new computer speaks to me. Yes, I mean in a good clear intelligible voice. The new flat-screen is not of much use to me, but it does take up a lot less room than the old beastly monitor that it replaced.

I am totally blind and have been since early childhood. Although talking computer systems have been available for a number of years now, they have only been here for a moment of time on the stage of history.

People often ask me if it is hard not being able to drive. They act as if driving is the most important thing in the world. It has never seemed so to me. Not being able to have immediate access to the printed word, that is to say, not being able to read print in a timely fashion has always been the most significant and difficult issue about blindness for me. Growing up in a home that had many printed books, magazines, and newspapers, and not being able to read print always seemed to me to be the most troublesome bar.

From early childhood Mom would read to me for hours. In her loving voice, she made books such as *Peter Cottontail* come alive. Well over a half century later as I write this, vivid pictures flash into my memory of Peter in his little blue jacket with its brass buttons being chased around the garden by Mr. Macgregor. Thank you Mom! Still, I longed to read print. Around age five I came down with chickenpox. I was lying in bed being miserable. My grandmother came over to sit with me and read to me while Mom took several buses and spent all day traveling to the state office building in Newark, New Jersey, where she was issued a "talking book machine" for me.

In those days in the early 1950's the talking book machines were very large and quite heavy. The books that they played were long playing recorded records which turned at 33-1/3 revolutions per minute. Late in the afternoon, my exhausted mom returned home with both the machine and a recorded copy of the book *Pinocchio*. It was wonderful. Later I had large cumbersome volumes of Braille, but not everything was in Braille.

Dad read things onto a new device we obtained called a tape recorder. When this device was in recording mode, he would read or speak into a microphone and somehow his voice was magically and magnetically imprinted onto a very thin tape that would turn from spool to spool on the top of the machine.

The machine itself was the size of a small suitcase and was quite heavy and awkward to move about. He would drag this monster back and forth to his work, and, during his lunch time, or in the evenings at home, he would read either my school books or interesting articles from magazines that he thought I would enjoy. Often these would be articles from publications such as the *National Geographic* magazine. One that jumps out from memory described how they had discovered and raised a 16th Century ship called the "Vasa" from a harbor in Sweden. Another was about a family who were traveling across the country while living out of a trailer that their car was pulling. Later, when I was in college we obtained a small tape recorder for me to use in school. It was very compact for its time during the 1960's. It was about the size of a briefcase, but needed to use much smaller reels of tape.

In the early 1950's, our parents purchased a beautifully bound set of encyclopedias for my brother and me. They came in their own furniture-like bookcase, which further suggested the seriousness of the knowledge they held. I have many memories of sitting on the floor in front of this bookcase, with one of the volumes open in my lap. Running my young fingers over the smooth printed pages I yearned to be able to read them.

The wonderful parents that I was blessed with never said, "Oh, you can't read that because you are blind." The approach was that I should be able to do whatever sighted people could do although I might have to do it in a different way. There always had to be a way. During the 1950's it did not appear that there was a way for me to read print, but technology, like Mighty Mouse, saved the day. It took many more years, but today Computer scanners using special software programs have made it possible for blind people to read most printed books and magazines, as well as a wide variety of other documents. The same computers with speech translation software have opened the door making it possible for blind people to write as I am doing now.

This technology did not come fast enough to help me in school. In those days a typewriter was the best answer for a blind person to use as a writing tool. In fact, in 1847 a patent application was filed for a then new device called a typewriter. One of the claims made for this new device was that it could be used by blind people as a tool to write with. Today, typewriters can only be found for the most part in attics or museums. However, when I was in school typewriters were still an everyday tool in every school or office.

As I typed papers in college, I fantasized about having some lovely young thing that would sit in my lap while correcting all of my spelling mistakes, or possibly even just retyping everything for me when not occupied fulfilling more pleasurable fantasies. All of these wonderful things have come to pass within the window of my lifetime. Well, not exactly. The lovely young thing never appeared, but still, things are so much better than they ever were.

How very different and difficult it truly must have been for Andrew and Will and the other blind characters in this book over two-hundred years ago.

They lived in a time before computers, before sound recording, before the development of Braille, before schools for the education of the blind, and before society placed any genuine value on a blind person. We tend to glorify, simplify, and overlook the shortcomings of the eighteenth Century.

However, for a person with a disability, it was for the most part a harsh and unrelenting time. The first schools for the blind in this country were not established until the early 1830's. Although historic evidence exists documenting the fact that blind people did use dogs as travel guides as early as seventy-nine A.D. These dogs were in a limited fashion trained by the blind person himself. The Seeing Eye, (a school to train dog-guides to help blind people travel independently) was not established in this country until 1929. Braille was not developed by Louis Braille in France until the 1840's. Consider that before the last half of the 19th Century, people communicated in one of two ways. Either a person spoke to another face to face or wrote out their words by hand on a piece of paper, which then had to be physically transported to another person.

During 1861, the Pony Express was still transporting handwritten letters across the country as the fastest manner of long distance communication.

Today, we pick up the phone and are almost instantly connected with someone all of the way round the globe. Have a question concerning your computer, or phone service? Someone from India will be on the line to either answer or confuse you in a microsecond. Need the answer to an obscure question? A few keystrokes on your computer keyboard will connect you to something called the internet, wherever that might be. These things are advancements for the general public, but of even greater significance for those of us who cannot see is that we also have access to this information through the use of computers that speak, and scanners that will unlock the printed word from those smooth paper pages.

All of this has happened in less than one hundred and fifty years. In fact, I frequently tell people that more has happened to improve the lives of blind people in the last fifty years than has taken place during all history combined. Yes, it is true.

Join me now as we explore the world of blindness during the 18th Century.

For a very different world it was.

Frederick W. Noesner
Philadelphia, Pennsylvania

# Preface

# The Magic of the Colonial Experience

Antiques and their place in antiquity have always fascinated me. Not because of their economic value, but rather because they serve as a link to the past. A key that can open the doors of history. A connection that allows the past to come alive. While holding a flintlock musket, an antique watch, a long stem clay pipe, a silver tea pot, an old brass button, or carpenter's wooden plane I always listen to the item and try to hear its story. Is it only imagination or does one hear the drum-beat and tramp of military boots and a sergeant calling orders while holding the musket? Does one really hear the engine's whistle as the conductor closes the cover of his large silver pocket watch while swinging up onto the steps of the train?

The chunk, chunk, chunk of the steam engine coming to life while the clink, clink of the couplers clang together as the motion of the now slowly moving train begins to take the slack out? Does one smell the smoke and hear the background sounds of an old coaching stop tavern as one holds a long stem clay pipe? Can one be in the elegant Federal Period room while pouring tea from a silver tea pot? Can one picture the clothing one might have on simply by holding an old button? Is it possible to smell the freshly cut wood as the sound of an old wood plane slices a very thin curl of wood from a plank that will turn in to a fine desk, chair, or barrel?

I think one can. By physically standing at a given street address with the knowledge of what once was in that spot, can one enjoy contemplating entering a store that existed at that address several hundred years ago?

Can one wear the clothing of a given historic period, surround oneself with items from that same time and mentally go there? If you believe these things are possible join me now as I step back into Colonial America to contemplate how people of that day coped with life in that truly interesting time.

Several years ago, I was fortunate enough to obtain a seasonal part-time position as a Colonial person here in Philadelphia. This position has given me the opportunity to wear Colonial clothing, walk the cobblestone and brick streets of the old city and speak and interact with other Colonials.

As a totally blind person, I have often wondered what life would have felt like for a blind person of that time.

As a birthday gift in 2007, my wife gave me a beautiful antique silver hunter's case key wound pocket watch. Because one can observe the hands of a watch moving, and listen to the movement ticking out the seconds of time, one can have the illusion that a time-piece, whether it is a watch or clock, is a living thing. A thing that is not only measuring time moving forward, but might also allow one to move backwards through time.

One day last autumn while sitting at my desk here in my library, wearing Colonial clothing, I decided to try to think my way back into history.

Sitting there quietly wearing buckled shoes, knee-breeches, and a long linen shirt covered with a long weskit, with a brown woolen coat and tricorn hat lying on the desk in front of me; I drew out my large wonderful antique silver pocket watch. Springing the cover open; tick-tick-tick-tick-tick-tick-tick-tick-tick-tick. Slowly lifting the crystal, I quietly sat there gently touching the steadily moving hands; tick-tick-tick-tick-tick-tick-tick-tick-tick-tick-tick-tick-tick.

What time was it? ——
October 7, 1764.

# 1

# The Explosion

Headquarters at Fort Pitt were quiet as I finished writing my report. I was a Philadelphia gunsmith named Andrew Annaler under contract to the Crown serving as an armorer with the 60th Royal Americans. I sat staring at the report reviewing the columns of figures listing the small arms and gunpowder available for Colonel Henry Bouquet's impending expedition. In a few days, the Colonel along with some fifteen-hundred regulars and militia would travel down the Ohio River into the western lands to reclaim the several hundred Colonists who had been taken captive by various Indian tribes.

True, we had heard that many of these folks seemed not to wish to return, but those were thoughts for another day. At present, reviewing the long report stating the amount and readiness of equipment for the Colonel's expedition was the task at hand. As I looked at the number of barrels of gunpowder available, I had no idea that in a few minutes this number along with the lives and futures of many of us would be changed forever. Smiling as I dated and signed the report, for October 7th was my 28th birthday, I capped the small bottle of ink and closed the headquarters writing desk.

Earlier I had instructed several soldiers to open one of the barrels of gunpowder and fill the paper cartridges that had been prepared over the last few days. The round, 75 caliber lead balls for use in the Brown Bess muskets carried by the 60th Royal Americans had been cast from bar lead by the soldiers days ago. After they had cooled, they had been rolled by the men into paper cartridges. This was done by placing a piece of cartridge paper flat on a table and rolling it around a musket ball along with a stick of about the same size as the ball. When rolled it formed a tube. The end nearest the ball was twisted and secured with a tie of twine. Another tie of twine was rapped between the ball and the forming stick, separating the ball from the powder. The stick was then withdrawn. Now all that needed to be done was to pour a measured charge of gunpowder into the tube and fold over the top. These cartridges could then be easily carried in a leather cartridge box worn by each soldier.

Leaving Headquarters, I pulled on my brown wool coat and straightened my tricorn hat. Hearing laughter from the direction of the shed where I had left the lads making up the cartridges, I decided to check on them. On rounding the corner of the shed, a sight lay before me that filled me with dread. Gunpowder was packed and stored in wooden barrels weighing one-hundred pounds. The barrels were banded with copper hoops to prevent the chance of sparks. The lid was off one of these and stood against the wall of the shed. Private Joe Small stood laughing while dipping gunpowder out of the barrel. He had spilled liberal amounts of powder all over the ground. This would have been bad enough, but there sitting on a bale of hay was Private John Heart puffing away on his clay-pipe. Around him were several other lads passing a jug between them. "Get back and put that pipe out!" I shouted. Private Heart was startled and blew down the stem of the pipe. A shower of sparks flew up out of the bowl just before he dropped it. For an instant that scene was frozen in time. It was followed by a blinding flash and an explosion that destroyed the shed and rocked the air. I would know nothing more until I awakened in the post hospital.

The pain was intense. My face and head were completely wrapped in bandages. My hands were also bandaged, but much more lightly. I tried to lift them and touch my face and passed out again. Reawakening, I could hear surgeon Boyd's voice. He was changing the bandages on my hands.

"These are not so bad." I tried to move but he scolded me and told me to lay still. "We are trying to help you lad," he said.

"Your hands will be fine; you must have raised them in front of you during the blast. Let us now take a look at the rest of you."

As he slowly removed the head bandages I passed out again. I do not know how much later it was, but I could hear surgeon Boyd's calm voice saying, "Oh, good, you have decided to rejoin us. Can you hear me?" I tried to nod and groaned from the pain.

"Can you see my hand?"

"No," I mumbled.

"Can you see me at all?" asked surgeon Boyd.

"No!"

As he bandaged me he said, "Give it a few days and we will see what we see, but I think your sight is gone."

"Gone? What do you mean? I am a gunsmith. I have to be able to see!"

"Your hands will be fine, even your face is only burned a little, but some burning matter went into the eyes. I don't really think there is much we can do for you."

"Are you saying I will not see again?"

Boyd placed his hand on my shoulder and said, "Lad, you are the fortunate one. The other lads who were closer to the explosion are all gone."

"Gone?" I asked.

"Dead!" Boyd said as he stood and moved away.

# 2

# Healing

October and November slowly passed day by day while I healed. I had much time to review my life and think about what I might now do.

Born in Philadelphia in October of 1736, I was the fourth of five children. My father, Frederick Annaler was a Swiss gunsmith who had a very successful shop on North 3rd Street just above what had been called Mulberry Street. People were now calling it Arch Street. We lived directly next to the shop in a small but comfortable home. The first child, a girl named Alice, had died as an infant when she was but a few months old. The second child, another girl, named Susan, had married a cooper named Thomas Ward and had moved up to the Allentown area. My eldest brother Henry had been apprenticed as a clock maker to my mother's brother, Ebenezer Butler and now lived in Elizabeth Town in the neighboring Colony of New Jersey. Having always shown a great interest in my father's trade, I was apprenticed at age 14 to him and served a seven year apprenticeship. Our youngest sister Sarah was still at home when I left.

There had been a little deal of trouble over my leaving. Five years into my apprenticeship the French & Indian War had broken out. One day in the shop while Dad was heating a bar of iron and I was pumping the bellows for him, I asked him to allow me to end my apprenticeship and let me join the army. He had said he would not hear of it. "There is a war on son. There are guns to be made and repaired. Business is better than it has ever been and there is money to be made. You're needed here. It is no time to run off and let some fool of a general get you killed in the woods for nothing." Judging the iron to be the correct color, he placed it back on his anvil and continued the long and difficult task of hammering out a gun barrel. It was to be a barrel for a fine new Pennsylvania rifle. Focusing all his attention on his work, clearly the discussion was closed and there was nothing that would make him change his mind.

The years 1756 and 1757 were difficult and terrible years on the Pennsylvania frontier. After General Braddock's rout when he attempted to take Fort Duquesne, Captain Dunbar had withdrawn all of the remaining forces all of the way back to Philadelphia. This had left the western lands of Pennsylvania wide open and unprotected against Indian raids. These raids were encouraged by the French and they cost the Frontier people a dreadful price. England's focus had shifted to the Northern Colonies and Pennsylvania had been left to fend for itself. The Society of Friends, commonly known as the Quakers, were loath to form or fund any type of militia. Finally however, the Pennsylvania Assembly, which was at that time, largely controlled by the Quakers, passed a volunteer militia act. This was too little, to late, for many frontier people. Finally in early 1758 England sent Regular Army troops under the command of General John Forbes to open a road through Pennsylvania in order to lead a campaign against Fort Duquesne.

By the autumn of 1757, my apprenticeship had formally ended and when I learned that General John Forbes was gathering a force here in Philadelphia to be led in the field by Swiss born Colonel Henry Bouquet to open a road west and take the French Fort Duquesne I decided to go. Many soldiers and officers from the 60th Royal Americans had been into the shop. They looked grand in their new military uniforms with their red coats with dark blue facings, their black breeches and black tricorn hats. Their Officers spoke of vast forests west of the mountains. The wilderness and a chance for adventure beckoned me west.

I had read in the *Pennsylvania Gazette* that the Assembly had just approved a bill to fund one hundred thousand pounds to support the Militia, as well as offering five pounds to anyone enlisting for military service. This time when I spoke with my dad, he put down his work and looked at me for a long time. "Son, you are doing a foolish thing. You have now finished your apprenticeship and I cannot stop you. But why do you wish to go as a common soldier? As soon as you take the King's shilling, they will own you. You know you have never been good at taking orders! Have I trained you for nothing? You are a skilled gunsmith. There are not that many of us in the Colonies. If you must go, go as a gunsmith under contract to the Crown. Colonel Bouquet is a good

Swiss officer. I would rather you did not go, but if you must, speak with the Colonel and be proud of your trade."

Over the next few days, I thought about it a lot. Following Dad's advice I went to Colonel Bouquet's Headquarters and spoke with him. He was very busy, but he knew Dad as he had often been in our shop. He saw me and quickly agreed to contract for my services as an armorer. "Always glad to have another gunsmith along," the Colonel said while shaking my hand.

After leaving Philadelphia in the spring of 1758, we marched to Carlisle where I worked with Thomas Butler, the senior armorer. Although I had never met him before that time, he actually was a cousin of Mom's so it was good to be working with him. Mostly we were repairing brown Bess muskets. This often entailed a good cleaning, sometimes replacing locks, or at least lock springs, missing jaw cock or screw pieces, re-facing the frizzens so that they would give good sparks and often patching the wood of the stocks. Many of these muskets were older guns that had been reissued and in some cases had not been stored well. It was necessary to mark, or remark, the brass wrist plate with the regiment and soldier's number.

After a few months, life had become rather humdrum. I had not gotten to go as far west or see as much of the frontier has I wished. General Forbes had opened a road to the point of land where the Ohio River began. The French had abandoned Fort Duquesne after blowing it up. A new fort, located near the same site, had been constructed named Fort Pitt. General Forbes had returned to Philadelphia as he was very ill. During the spring of 1759 a dispatch-rider rode into camp announcing that General Forbes had died. As he reined his horse in before Headquarters, he was waving a copy of the *Pennsylvania Gazette* in his hand. We all wanted to read the paper as General Forbes had been a popular Commanding officer. After a bit it was posted on the wall in front of the Headquarters building. It read:

# The Pennsylvania Gazette

**PHILADELPHIA, March 15, 1759.**

"On Sunday last, died of a tedious Illness \*/JOHN /\*\*/FORBES /\*, Esq.; in the Forty ninth Year of his Age, ... Brigadier General, Colonel of the Seventeenth Regiment of Foot, and Commander of His MAJESTY Troops in the Southern Provinces of North America; a Gentleman generally known and esteemed, and most sincerely and universally regretted.

In his younger Days he was bred to the Profession of Physic, but early ambitious of the Military Character, he purchased into the Regiment of Scots Grey Dragoons, where, by repeated Purchases, and faithful Service, he arrived to the Rank of Lieutenant Colonel

His superior Abilities soon recommended him to the Protection of General CAMPBELL, the Earl of STAIR, Duke of BEDFORD, Lord LIGONIER, and other distinguished Characters in the Army; with some of them he served as an Aid de Camp, and with the rest in the Familiarity of a Family Man.

During the last War he had the Honour to be employed in the Character of Quarter Master General to the Army under his Royal Highness the DUKE;

which Duty he discharged with Accuracy, Dignity and Dispatch.

His services in America are well known. By a steady Pursuit of well concerted Measures, in Defiance of Disease, and numberless Obstructions, he brought to a happy Issue a most extraordinary Campaign, and made a willing Sacrifice of his own Life to what he valued more, the Interest of his KING and COUNTRY.

As a Man, he was just, and without Prejudices; brave, without Ostentation; uncommonly warm in his Friendship, and incapable of Flattery; acquainted with the World and Mankind; he was well bred, but absolutely impatient of Formality and Affectation.

Eminently possessed of the sociable Virtues, he indulged a cheerful Gratification; but quick in his Sense of Honour and Duty, so mixed the agreeable Gentleman and Man of Business together, as to shine alike (tho'truly uncommon) in both Characters, without the Giddiness sometimes attendant on the one, or the Sourness of the other.

As an Officer, he was quick to discern useful Men, and useful measures, generally seeing both at first View, according to their real Qualities; steady in his Measures, but open to Information and Council; in Command he had Dignity, without Superciliousness, and tho'; perfectly Master of the Forms, never hesitated to drop them, when the Spirit, and more essential Parts of the Service, required it."

After reading this notice, I went and found the post-rider who had brought the notice. He told me that he had witnessed the funeral procession. I stood there quietly with several others and listened to his description.

"Yesterday he was interred in the Chancel of Christ church, at Second and Market Streets in Philadelphia. It was a grand sight. First The Pioneers led the way. His own Regiment, the Seventeenth, as well as two Companies of Colonel Montgomery's Regiment followed, their colours with Crapes; the Drums covered with black; and the Officers with Crapes on their Arms. Two Pieces of Cannon trundled along with the Commanding Officer of Artillery. Next came the Engineers. This was followed by a led Horse, covered with black, conducted by a Groom. The Surgeons and Physicians, the Clergy, and Chaplains of the Army. The Corpse, and the Pall held by six Field Officers. The Mourners, the Governor; the Council, the Speaker and Members of Assembly, the Judges, the Magistrates and Gentlemen of the Province and City, two and two. The Officers from the different Garrisons, two and two. The Minute Guns were fired from the time the Corpse was brought out until the Interment was over; and the whole ended by a triple Discharge of the Small Arms."

Standing there listening, we were all touched by this description. I could well picture it as I had walked Second and Market Streets many times and had often stood there looking at Christ Church. It was a landmark of the city and was but a square or two from where I had been raised. A general and widespread sadness spread through the camp. However, after a few days, life seemed to have returned to its quiet routines. By the summer of that year, I was assigned to make regular trips back and forth over Forbes' Road, stopping at every fort along the way to clean and repair any broken weapons that needed attention. Most of the posts were a day apart, but some were more than that. We would camp in a meadow near a stream.

On one such trip late in the month of August we had camped in just such a spot. We had finished dinner when several Indians approached our camp. They appeared friendly. They had stopped to speak with a sergeant and I thought little more of them until the sergeant called to me. "They want you!" Wondering what he was talking about I approached this small group.

The Sergeant said, "The chief here wants you to fix a musket for him." I had no idea whether or not this Brave was a Chief, but I looked at the musket that he extended toward me. It appeared to be a French Charleville musket. The muzzle must have been clogged with something when it had been fired as it was burst. It was rusted all over and generally not in good condition.

The Chief sawed his hand back and forth over the barrel below the point where it had burst. I understood he wanted it cut off so it could still be used.

"Can you help the Chief here? They might rightly think it a friendly gesture if you could," asked the Sergeant.

"Sure!"

Taking the musket, I went to my wagon which held my tools. It did not take long to cut the muzzle square and round the edges. Next I cut the wood back a little below the muzzle. Finally I shortened the ramrod to the new length and threaded the end for a cleaning worm. I quickly cleaned off the worst of the rust and oiled the lock. When I handed it to the Chief, his face lit up. He mumbled something about giving me his daughter. I smiled and walked off toward the river to wash up after a long day.

It was a warm evening and the river water felt cool on my face. Suddenly the Chief appeared holding the hand of a beautiful young woman. He smiled at me and disappeared. I did not know their language, nor did this woman seem to know English. But there was no doubt in my mind as to what she was offering when she pulled her buckskin dress off over her head and stood there without a stitch on less than two feet from me. In a moment we were in the water and swimming to a small island that was only about twenty feet out into the stream. That was the beginning of the most amazing and wonderful night of my young life. She showed me things and did things that I never knew the human body was made for, or could be taught to do.

Returning to camp the following morning, I learned that we would remain here another day as a crack had been discovered in the axle of one of the wagons. As soon as possible, after helping with the repair, I returned to the little island, but she was gone. Month after month, back and forth over the roads we went, but I never saw her again.

During the summer of 1763 I had been sent on to Fort Pitt with Colonel Bouquet's relief column and had taken part in the fight on August 5th. Now known as the Battle of Bushy Run. Fort Pitt had been under siege since late June by mostly Delaware Indians. Colonel Bouquet's column was to relieve the Fort which was housing over five hundred soldiers and local inhabitants that had gone into the

Fort for protection during what would come to be known as Pontiac's Rebellion. Just now, when things seemed to be well in hand, this accident had happened. Surgeon Boyd seemed to be correct and my sight had not come back. My life seemed as if it was over. I would have to return home to Philadelphia and try to make a new life.

While lying in the hospital, there had been much time to think. My thoughts often turned to a young friend back in Philadelphia named Will Davies. Will had lost his sight at age seven when he had been kicked in the head by a horse. When he woke up, he could not see. Perhaps I now understood how he had felt.

Will had been born and raised on his parents' farm out in the Welsh Tract. The Welsh Tract was a large area of land that William Penn had offered to Welsh Quakers who wished to come to his new land called Pennsylvania. Will was the youngest of three children. In 1754, his eldest sister Gwynne had married an innkeeper named Ephraim Snyder who had a small run-down looking tavern called the Jug & Mug Tavern. It was located on Pewter-platter Alley. The rest of Will's family moved west to new land beyond Harris's Fairy in the Juniata Valley and had settled near what became known as Fort Shirley. He lived there with his parents and his brother David who was about two years older. In 1756 when Will was about sixteen, their farm had been attacked by Indians. Both of his parents had been killed and their home had been burned. His brother David had been taken west and adopted into a Shawnee tribe. When they learned that Will could not see they had spared his life feeling that he may have had some mystical powers. They took him to the edge of a nearby village and left him there. These neighbors had been kind to him, but when they learned that he had a sister in Philadelphia, he was sent there to live with her in the attic above her inn. Will helped around the inn and did whatever odd jobs he could find around the city.

Jacob Snyder, who was a cousin to Gwynne's husband Ephraim, owned a small tannery located along Dock Creek. One of the things Will liked to do was make powder horns for gunpowder from the cow horns that Jacob gave him.

That is how I had first met Will. A few months before I left to go west with the army, Will had come into the shop with five or six powder horns that he had made wishing to sell them. We often had requests for powder horns to go with rifles and fowling-pieces that we had made or repaired in the shop.

Dad took the horns in his hands, one by one. Turning them over and over and looking critically at each. He let out a long sigh that I was very familiar with when he examined my own work. Next he removed the little stopper pegs and blew into each horn. Several leaked air around the area where the horn was fitted with the large base plug. This brought forth a grunt of dissatisfaction along with some head shaking. Again all signs I was very accustomed to observing.

Sensing some displeasure on Dad's part Will held out his hands and said, "Alright, just give me my horns and I will be on my way."

"Who taught you to make powder horns like that?" Dad asked him. Will just started gathering up the horns from the bench and replacing them in his haversack. He said, "I just taught myself. How else would a blind fellow like me learn anything?"

He turned toward the door and started moving away. "Stop!" Dad said. "Don't you want us to teach you to make these better? What are you using for tools? Let's have a look at them."

Will reluctantly dug back into his haversack and pulled out a rusted file, a scrap of what looked like a piece of iron wagon wheel tire, which he used as a scraper, a pointed rod with a rough area that he must have used as a drill and finally a broken folding pocket knife which appeared to be his prize possession. These brought out more of Dad's very expressive sounds of disappointment.

Turning to me, he said, "Andrew, find him a better file and some other things. I will forge a drill-bit for him. Help him pull those base plugs and show him how to refit them so they do not leak. If they are going to be sold out of this shop they will have to be better than that!" Will stood there, stunned and frowning. Placing my hand on Will's arm, I said, "Smile! If he did not like what you are trying to do, he simply would not bother with you. Now sit here at my bench while I get a few better tools for you and we will see what we can do with these horns." This was the beginning of a friendship between Will and me. He learned quickly and soon Will had a small trade going with Dad. Somehow I guessed I would get to know him a lot better after I returned to Philadelphia.

One day, Barent the post cooper stopped by to visit with me. Barent was a very kindly but quiet man. I had forged a few small things in iron for him that he had been very pleased with. Now he handed me a very smooth staff that he had fashioned for me. "Thought you could use this as you start finding your way about the fort," he said as he placed his gift in my hands. After he left, I felt angry as the staff simply reminded me that I could not see to even walk about. However, as I sat there holding it I realized that it actually was a fine gift. I also realized that it was time for me to start to get about and learn to use this new tool. Remembering that Will had used a staff he had carved from a tree branch to help him find his way about the streets, I decided that Barent had just opened a door for me, and by giving me this simple staff he was inviting me to walk through it into my new world. Soon thereafter, surgeon Boyd told me there was nothing more that could be done for me. It was time to pick up my new staff and try to find my way in a big new world. Stepping through the door of the post hospital, I suddenly felt puzzled. Trying to remember just where my small quarters were I headed off. After a few steps I decided to return to the safety of the hospital. Turning and retracing my steps, I was surprised to find that the door was not where I had just left it. Suddenly a friendly Scottish voice came from my left.

"Good day Master Andrew! And what would ye be looken for?"

"Is that you Ian?" I asked. Ian Duncan was a sergeant with the 42$^{nd}$ Highlanders. Only a few days before the explosion, I had replaced the frizzen spring on one of his strange looking all iron Scottish pistols.

"Aye, lad. And who else do ye think it would be?" he replied. Not wanting to admit that I was already lost, I tried to smile and said, "Just out for a walk."

"Well, if ye be walking much further in the way ye be going, ye'll be drinking out of the horse trough. I could be offering ye something better to drink than horse slobbered water. Why don't ye come with me back to my quarters and we will have a nip to remember the lads ye left in the shed?" Clapping his big hand on my shoulder, he spun me about and propelled me toward his quarters. What else to do? Having already lost the hospital, not having a clue where my own quarters were, and not wishing to fall into the horse trough, well, Ian's quarters did not sound so bad.

"Maybe you could just point me at my own quarters."

"As you wish!" Ian said. "Have ye heard Colonel Bouquet's forward scouts have been spotted? He will be back very shortly." I had lost track of what day it was while in the hospital.

"Why it is the 16$^{th}$ of November? Here's ye quarters. By the way, my pistol has been working well as new."

"Glad to hear it Ian. Thank you for keeping me out of the horse trough." Stepping through the door of my quarters, I tried to remember where everything was. As the door latch clicked closed, I was glad to be in a safe place where no one was watching. After standing there for a minute, I began to slowly explore this tiny room. Leaning my staff against the wall by the door, I slowly began to move along the wall feeling for the candle that was there. Suddenly I froze, realizing that there was no point lighting the candle any longer. I wanted to scream or smash something. Instead I just stood there shaking and filled with rage. There was my chest filled with my tools, books, and clothing. Wondering how many of these items I would be able to use again, I moved beyond the chest to the bed. A chair and a simple writing table completed the furnishings of this small room. Straightening from leaning over the bed, I winced as I rammed my head into a shelf above the bed that I had forgotten about. Sinking down onto the bed, suddenly I felt very tired. On the bed, neatly folded was a pile of my clothing. Phoebe Mills did laundry for some of the officers and others of us in the Fort. She was, or had been the wife of Martin Mills, one of the lads who had been in the shed that night when the powder exploded. She had stopped to talk with me in the hospital several times as she occasionally helped Surgeon Boyd cleaning about the post hospital. Her life had also changed the moment the powder went up. Her husband was gone and she would have to make her own way here in this wilderness fort. There had been some talk already that she might marry Ned Winter who was a sutler at the fort. Feeling suddenly very tired, I collapsed onto the bed and lay there feeling very sad. There was nothing here for me at the fort and I must find my way back to Philadelphia. Captain Simeon Ecuyer, the fort

Commander, had visited me a few days earlier at the hospital. He had told me how sorry he had been to learn of my injury and that he would arrange for me to ride back to Philadelphia with one of the fort supply wagons if that is what I wished to do. He had also had his clerk stop by and write a short note for me to my parents telling them of the accident.

Time passed and I must have drifted off to sleep, only to be awakened by a gentle tapping on my quarter's door. It was Phoebe and she had very thoughtfully brought me a plate with some dinner. Placing the plate on my small table and lighting the candle, she sat on the edge of the bed beside me.

"I brought you some dinner fixin's as I thought you might be getting a mite starved." She sounded cheery and did not seem to be pining for her lost husband. When I said that, she laughed and said, "Poor Martin, he was always in the wrong place at the wrong time. Father made him marry me when I was to have a baby."

"I did not know you had any children," I said.

"I lost it before it was born, but by that time we were married and Martin had brought me out to this miserable wilderness."

Remembering some of the tales I had heard from some of the fort officers concerning Phoebe, I asked, "Was the baby Martin's?"

Laughing again, she said, "It might have been. Will you be going back to Philadelphia now?"

"Yes, there is nothing here for me any longer."

"You are looking so sad."

I did not answer but just raised my hands to cover my still tender face. She placed her hand on my shoulder and we just sat there for some time. She leaned down and kissed me. I thought she was getting up to leave, but suddenly she was there stretched out beside me with her arm sliding around my neck. She was warm and inviting and we both needed the warmth and caring of another human being. Later, much later, as she slid from under the blanket and started pulling her clothing back on, she said, "You mustn't say anything to Ned. He has asked me to marry him and I guess I will be doing that soon."

"Ned is a good man. He will be kind to you," I said.

"Don't forget your dinner," she said as she leaned down to kiss me a last time. I heard the rattle and click of the door latch and she was gone.

The next day, Johnson, Captain Ecuyer's man came to me and told me that the Captain had invited me to dine with him. Johnson said he would stop back and walk over there with me in an hour or so when things were ready. I thanked him and said I would look forward to dining with the Captain. I knew Simeon Ecuyer to be a fellow Free Mason and thought that might be why he was showing me this extra bit of courtesy. Captain Ecuyer was a good officer. He was hard, but when he gave an order he always had a good reason for it and he brooked no nonsense about having his orders carried out. The meal did not start well as I knocked over a glass of wine that Johnson had set beside my plate. Johnson fumed.

"That was from the Captain's own personal stores," Johnson mumbled.

"Tut-tut," said the Captain, "we do have a bit more if you promise not to have the second glass follow the first." Captain Ecuyer told me he was heartily sorry to have learned of the accident. He said the Corporal in charge of the cartridge making group would have been severely punished had he not died in the blast. "Shocking that such lax carelessness should have taken place. Five men killed and a good armorer blinded, to say nothing of cartridges costing three pence apiece. It was a costly bit of foolishness." He asked if my plans were still to return to Philadelphia. Telling him that I wished to return to my family and former home in Philadelphia and try to make a life there, he promised to help. Thanking him for the dinner, I left to make my way back to my quarters. The Captain ordered Johnson to walk me back to my quarters. Telling Johnson I did not need his help, I left the Headquarters building. I felt I wanted to try getting there on my own. Besides, I did not want to hear from Johnson again how I had spilled the Captain's own wine. When my hand closed on the latch of my quarters, I felt rather proud that I had actually found it on my own. At least, I felt good until I heard Johnson say, "Yes, that's the place." He had followed me to be sure that I had not gotten lost after I turned down his offer to help. Turning on him, I said that I had not wanted him to follow me. He replied that it had been the Captain's orders. Knowing that when Captain Ecuyer gave an order, it was to be followed and that Johnson had been right to do so, I shrugged and entered my small room.

The following day, Colonel Bouquet's column returned. They brought with them some of the people who had earlier been taken captive although many did not wish to return to their former lives. This was the case with Will Davies brother David. When I inquired about David, I was told that he had been turned over to the Colonel's expedition, but that he had escaped during the first night and had not again been seen. There was a lot of coming and going about headquarters and many shouted orders. Late in the day, Captain Ecuyer sent me a message that he had arranged for me to travel back in stages along the military road to Philadelphia. Some nearly empty supply wagons were going back as far as Carlisle. From there it would not be difficult to find other wagons that would be making trips back to Philadelphia. The wagons would be leaving in three days, so I should ready my things.

Several sutlers, as well as a few officers stopped by to inquire as to whether or not I wished to sell any of my own personal firearms or tools. I had a nice Pennsylvania rifle that I had made for myself during my apprenticeship as well as a very lovely English London made fowling-piece that someone had brought into the shop as a part payment toward one of Dad's Pennsylvania rifles. It was stocked in walnut and lightly engraved. It had a good balance and felt very nice in one's hands. Dad had given it to me as a gift when I left to go west with the army. It had often been admired when I had taken it afield hunting. There was also a brass barreled saddle pistol. At one time it must have been one of a pair, but now was on its own. I had acquired it some time ago in a trade for my work and had kept it with me. It was a large sixty-two caliber brass barreled, smoothbore weapon. It had been made a few years before by a smith in Ireland. The thought had already come to me that loaded with shot it would be a serviceable weapon for a blind person. I declined all of their offers, feeling as if they were vultures circling over my corpse. They did not actually say it, but the feeling was, now that my useful life was over, I would not be needing my guns, tools, or self-respect. I quickly decided that my things were going back to Philadelphia with me whether I ever used them again or not.

During that time Phoebe came to me twice more. Her gifts of food were very welcome, but her tenderness toward me as a man made a great deal of difference to me in how I felt while facing the unknown of my new life. She encouraged me to believe that I had not turned into a "blind-man." I would not become a common beggar. I was a skilled gunsmith who no longer could see. I had some trouble believing it myself as I knew of no way that I could work with red hot iron at the forge. However, as I thought about it, I believed perhaps I could still do some of the wood work on gun stocks. I had much to think about and at the moment, lots of time to do just that. Surgeon Boyd had done all he could to heal my wounds, but Phoebe had done more to help me heal as a man.

On my last evening in the fort, Hans Myers, who was one of the German wagon drivers, and one of his helpers came to my quarters to carry my tool chest and things to the wagon. I had known Hans for several years as he hauled supplies back and forth over the mountains. He was a kindly older man with a very thick German accent. I was very pleased to be traveling with him. I had done odds and ends of smith work for most of the wagon drivers at one time or another. Hans said the wagons were going back almost empty this time and I would have plenty of room. He had put down a good layer of new straw in the bottom of his wagon where they were going to put my things. With a few blankets, I should be riding like a king. Thanking Hans, I promised to be at his wagon in the morning.

The following day dawned clear but cold. As soon as I heard the morning call, I was up and quickly dressed. Feeling my way about the room I tried to be certain that I was not leaving anything behind. Taking my old coat down from the wall peg by the door, I kept touching the thick heavy wool. I remembered it to be a dark brown color. Running my fingers back and forth over it, I tried to tell myself that I could feel the brown color, but alas, I knew I was only feeling a visual memory: a memory of brown because I had seen it and knew it to be my same old coat. Clapping my tricorn on my head, scooping up my roll of blankets and grasping the staff that Barent had so kindly made for me, I stepped out into the cold morning air. As I left the safety of this little room, I wondered what lay before me in more ways than one.

Following the wall of the quarters building, I moved in the direction of the sounds that the Wagoner's were making as they hitched up the ox teams.

"Out of the way there blind man" yelled a gruff voice. Pressing myself back against the wall of the building, I thought how differently these men had spoken to me when they thought of me as a smith who could be of real help to them. Now they simply thought of me as a blind man who was in their way. Feelings of anger and rage flooded through me. After wandering about for a bit, I heard Hans's voice calling me and soon had found his wagon.

"Don't mind Otto. One of his oxen has gone lame." Hans said while placing my hand on the tailgate of the wagon. "Your things are all inside." Crawling up inside the wagon I found it just as Hans had told me. The bottom of the wagon was covered with straw and there was my chest.

Arranging the blankets that I had carried over from my quarters, I soon made a comfortable spot propped up in a corner. I wondered if Phoebe would come around to say goodbye before we left, but I never saw her again. Years later, I learned that at Christmas time that year, she had married Ned Winter, but had died in childbirth less than a year after. And so, that was how I left Fort Pitt to begin my journey East to Philadelphia.

# 3

# The Journey Home

Over the last several years, I had traveled this same road back and forth many times, stopping at the major forts to repair broken or worn weapons. However, everything now felt strange and confusing. The first night we camped about half way to Fort Ligonier in a place many groups had stopped before. There was a good spring and a level meadow to set-up in.

I felt as if I was not really a part of this group. In the past, everyone simply took on jobs. Some unhitching the oxen, some gathering wood and making a fire and others hauling water. Most of the drivers and several soldiers accompanying the wagons were kind to me, but I simply felt as if I was in the way.

During the afternoon, one of the soldiers had shot a deer. Soon the good smell of cooking drifted over the area near the fire. Hans had helped me settle near the fire and the warmth felt very good indeed. It had been a cold November day and the night promised to be even colder.

After dinner, I found the wagon and started to crawl back into it. Suddenly I realized it was not the same wagon that I had ridden in. Standing there not wanting to ask were my wagon was I suddenly felt Hans's big hand on my shoulder.

"Maybe we should sleep in our own wagon," he said. I simply nodded and let him steer me to the next wagon over. Feeling miserable, I crawled up into our wagon and found my place. Although it seemed cold here away from the fire, with my coat and the blankets, it would be warm enough. It seemed like only a few minutes later and the camp was up and facing the morning chores. The wagon drivers were tending to their teams, checking harnesses and yoke straps as they spoke encouragingly to their animals. I wandered over toward where I could hear the fire crackling and found a small boulder to sit on. One of the soldiers handed me a plate with some warm corn bread that had been brought from the Fort and deer meat from last night. Another handed me a mug of steaming coffee. I had known all of these men in the past and had done work for most of them. They had always spoken to me in a friendly open manner. Now, although they were not unkind, they seemed as if they did not know what to say to me any longer. Someone had brought a bucket of water up from the spring and had been heating it over the fire. Hearing one of the men set it down near my boulder, I offered to wash up the few plates and mugs. This did not require much moving about the camp, and let me feel as if I was helping.

The morning talk around the fire was how it looked as if it would snow today. The hope was that the snow would not prevent us from reaching Fort Ligonier before night. I was glad that I would be in the wagon and out of a storm if it did come. About an hour after we had gotten underway, the snow did begin. Although it slowed the pace, the road felt a bit softer as it was blanketed with the ever falling snow. We did reach Fort Ligonier by nightfall and everyone was glad of it. We stayed an extra day at Ligonier as the storm raged on through the night. Two more days and we had reached Fort Bedford. There we stayed for almost a week while minor repairs were made to the wagons as well as waiting for some military items to be ready that we were to carry on down to Carlisle.

After Hans had his team settled and I had learned that we were to be there for a few days I asked him to show me up to Pendergast's Tavern. Garret Pendergast ran a kind of tavern, inn, and general store that was the hub of the Rays Town community. The village of Rays Town was immediately next to Fort Bedford. As we walked from the Fort, the strong smell of wood smoke from cooking and heating fires seemed to me to be the sign of civilization in the midst of this Pennsylvania wilderness.

Pendergast's was an inviting place. Somehow one always felt that life had just improved whenever one stepped through the wide front door of the great room. At one end there was the low counter where trading and selling was done. At the other was one of the largest fireplaces that I had ever seen. During my many times passing through Fort

Bedford, I had often stayed, or at very least, taken a hearty meal in this great room.

Garret's booming voice greeted us as we stepped through the door.

"Welcome! Come in and sit yourselves down. What can we get for you two? How about some nice warm apple-jack?" he asked. We were glad of Garret's reception as it was bitterly cold outside. "I hear the wagons will be here a few days. will you be wanting a room? I can offer you Captain Ecuyer's favorite one as it is unlikely he will be visiting here for a bit." Garret went on. He always seemed to know just what was going on. The Captain had been making trips back and forth over the mountains from Fort Pitt to Fort Bedford for the last year. Whenever at Fort Bedford he managed to stay a few days at Pendergast's.

I told him I was looking forward to spending a few days at his fine inn and to use the Captain's room would be an honor.

"While you are here, I have a few fire-locks that I would be appreciative if you would look over for me and put in good working order."

"You want me to work on your guns?" I asked.

"Of course! You are a gunsmith aren't you?"

"Well, yes, I used to be."

Garret placed his hand on my arm and said, "Lad, I have heard all about the accident. You may have lost your sight, but your hands look alright. All the knowledge you ever had must still be in that head of yours and I want you to go over all my guns for me and clean, oil and put them in the best working order. I believe it is going to snow again, so you may be here even longer than you think."

We talked for some time then, and over the next several days. I took all of his weapons apart, cleaned and oiled everything and reassembled them. Garret's guns had already been in good condition. I began to realize that as a brother Free Mason, he was giving me a chance to work in my trade again. He was encouraging me to use my hands and my knowledge and continue to be the person that I always had been. Garret was one of the wisest and most kindly men I had ever known. Of course we had an ever stronger bond as we were brother Masons. The Pennsylvania frontier was fortunate indeed to have men who were Masons such as Garret Prendergast. Before leaving, Garret told me the names of several Free Masons who lived along the route that I would be traveling back to Philadelphia. Hans Myers would only be taking his wagon as far as Carlisle. He would take me to Michael Graham in Carlisle. Michael was an attorney, well known to me as a friend of many years. This friendship had begun in Philadelphia but had grown during the time we had shared in Carlisle. He was now living there and working as an attorney dealing with land grants and transfers of title, as well as being a very active Mason. Garrett had told me that Michael wanted to petition to obtain a Warrant to establish a Masonic Lodge in the Carlisle area. We had joined Lodge 2 together in Philadelphia when it had been formed in 1758. There was no question that he would help me.

The time at Garret's passed quickly and soon one evening, Hans told me that we were likely to be leaving on the following day. Although there was still room for my things in his wagon, he told me that he had been told by Lieutenant Lewis that I could ride one of the soldiers' extra horses. I must have looked puzzled for a moment as I next heard Garret's booming laugh.

"Don't worry lad, the horse can see and he is not going to want to stray from the others."

The following morning after a hearty breakfast, Garret walked with me down to where Hans was hitching his oxen to the wagon. Thanking Garret profusely for all his many kindnesses to me, I shook his hand and swung up onto the back of the horse's saddle that Garret had placed my hand on. It was much later in the day that I learned from Lieutenant Lewis that there had been plenty of room in Hans's wagon, but that Garret had come to him and arranged for me to ride one of the horses as he thought it would make me feel more a part of the group rather then just a piece of baggage. As I said, Garret was a very wise man. The following day when we finally reached Carlisle, Hans showed me to Michael Graham's law office. Like Garret, Hans had been very kind to me and I thanked him for all he had done to make this trip not only possible, but more comfortable for me in every way he had been able to do. Although I did not know it at the time, when Michael opened his door, Hans handed him a letter from Captain Ecuyer. The Captain's note told Michael of the accident at the Fort as well as my desire to reach Philadelphia.

Michael and I were old friends as well as Masonic Brothers. We sat long into the evening in front of his fire enjoying several glasses of Madeira and speaking of old times. We both agreed that it was a fortunate thing that I had become a Mason when I had. For if I was now to attempt to petition for Masonic membership, I would not, as a blind person, have been accepted into the craft. However, once a Brother Master Mason, there was no bar to my remaining as a Brother Mason, enjoying all of the rites and privileges of a brother in the craft. Dad had been much opposed to my becoming a Mason. He said there was no need for it and did not understand why I wished to do such a thing. By then I had reached the age of twenty-one and insisted. Now I was very glad that I had done so. Although I believe people would have helped me in life, Masonic Membership certainly opened many doors for me that might have remained closed.

Michael had read law with Benjamin Chew in his law office on Front Street. Michael had a passion for fine weapons and had spent much time in our shop. He had moved to Carlisle to establish himself in a place where he could handle the legal work concerning the numerous land purchases now taking place along the Forbes Road. Michael had the ability to accept my blindness after only a moments shock. He accepted it, readjusted his thoughts and picked up our friendship as if the accident had never happened. He said he had been planning a visit to Lancaster within the next few weeks, but that there was no real reason that he could not move the trip forward. We could leave as soon as we could arrange for the use of a wagon to transport my things. Michael did not own a wagon as he usually traveled about on horseback.

Laughing, he said, "Legal papers do not take up so much room that I need a wagon to haul them about. However, I know of a fellow named Jed Brown, who has settled near here on a fine piece of land. He plans to farm it as well as setting up a saw mill on a pretty little stream which runs through his property. He still owes me for preparing and filing his land claim. I believe he will be able to assist us with the transport that we find ourselves in need of. In the morning we will ride over and see what can be arranged."

The following morning dawned clear and cold. Michael owned two saddle horses and in less than an hour's ride, we reached Jed's place. Michael laughed as he read the new sign that Jed had nailed to a tree at the side of the road. It read, "Brown's Mill." Jed was splitting shingles in his yard.

"Jed, do you think the sign is a bit premature? We did not pass a single person on the last road to your place, and looking about, I do not see a mill," Michael said.

Jed put down his splitting fro and said, "I am looking to the future. Why, did you have some lumber to be milled?"

"No, but I believe you might be able to be of assistance to a fellow Brother Mason of ours."

Quickly, Michael outlined my need to transport my chest of tools and other items back to Philadelphia. Jed immediately agreed. We had left my things at Michael's, so Jed said he would be by in the morning with his wagon and would be glad to drive me as far as Lancaster. Then he insisted that we come in and enjoy a good warm meal that his wife Elisa had simmering on the hearth. We enjoyed both the meal as well as the talk describing his plans for the mill and other projects that he had in mind. The ride back was uneventful, but seemed long as the temperature seemed to be dropping.

In the morning, Jed arrived as promised and soon we were on our way. I rode on the wagon seat with Jed while Michael ranged ahead on his horse. He was planning to stay a few days in Lancaster and would need the horse to return.

Jed was a quiet man and had little to say during our ride. The roads this far east were in better condition and I found myself nodding off as we rumbled along. The sound of a penny whistle cut through my daydreaming.

"What is that?" I asked Jed as we came up on the sound.

"It appears to be a man like yourself."

"Like myself? You mean a gunsmith?"

"No, I mean a blind-man playing a whistle. Michael has ridden past him, but perhaps we should stop and give him a ride."

"Greetings friend! Are you in need of a ride?" Jed called down.

"Oh, I surely am. My feet are so sore and my old bones so tired. It would be a great kindness of you to give a poor blind-man a ride. I am walking all of the way to Lancaster."

Jed stopped the wagon and said, "This is your lucky day. We are on our way to Lancaster ourselves. What is your name?" Jed slid closer to me on the wagon seat as he reached a hand down to the traveler. Pulling him up beside himself.

"Are you settled?" Jed asked.

"Oh yes, but I am so very tired. My name is Calvin Climber. What are you carrying in your wagon?"

"Just my friend's chest of tools and clothing. He is, — ah, — was, — ah, — a gunsmith who has been in an explosion and is blind like you."

"Well, if you have room in back, maybe I could just stretch out back there and have a nap? You don't have any food with you do you? I am so hungry and I don't have a single coin to buy a scrap of bread. I am walking to Lancaster hoping I can play my whistle at a fair and earn enough to eat."

Jed helped him into the back and gave him some food that his wife had packed. Michael rode back.

"What are you doing Jed?" he asked.

"Oh, this is my day to help the blind. We are giving this poor man a ride and some food." Michael's horse was only an arms-length from the front wheel on my side of the wagon. Michael quietly said to me that he wished Jed had not stopped as Michael did not like the look of the man. Jed slid back onto the seat beside me and picked up the reins.

"Jed, take a care now. This road bears some watching!" Michael said. I learned later that as he said these words, he was gesturing and pointing at the new traveler.

We drove on quietly for some time and then I heard the lid of my chest creek in the very familiar way it always did. I had meant to oil the hinges a hundred times, but well, had just never gotten around to doing so. I turned uneasily in my seat listening hard. Next I heard the clink of coins.

"What are you doing back there Climber?" I shouted. "Jed stop the wagon!" The lid of my chest thumped as it rapidly closed.

"He is in my things." Jed pulled the two horses to a stop and suddenly Michael was there.

"Get your person out of that wagon mister!" ordered Michael. Calvin Climber dropped to the ground.

"I was just taking a nap," he said.

"I am thinking it was more than a nap you were taking," I commented.

Michael grabbed Climber roughly by the collar and shook him.

"What did you take?" he asked.

"Nothing, nothing at all!" I heard Climber scream as Michael swung him about and drove him face first into the large rear wheel of the wagon. Noticing a bulge in a coat pocket, Michael ripped the pocket open.

"Andrew does this look as if it is something of yours?" He said as he tossed my leather pouch of coins onto my lap. It was indeed my pouch.

"Those are my coins earned by playing my whistle. Would you steal them from a poor blind man?" Climber whimpered. Jed had gotten down from the wagon and walked around to face Mr. Climber.

"You said you did not have a single coin," he said as he slapped Climber in the face. A quick search of Calvin Climber also recovered a knife and a small silver snuff box that I had taken in trade for a minor repair when I replaced a ramrod of a pistol that an Officer had lost. I searched through my chest, but could not find anything else that seemed to be missing.

Michael threw Mister Climber away from him so hard the man staggered and fell. "Get away from us you miserable disgusting creature."

As Climber got to his feet, he said, "If you were a good Christian man, you would have let me keep the coins. I am a poor blind man and you tore my coat."

"I never said I was a 'good Christian man'. Consider yourself fortunate that I don't break all of your thieving fingers. If I ever come across you thieving again, that is exactly what I will do."

As I climbed back up onto the wagon seat, I felt myself slipping into a deeper state of sorrow than I had experienced since the explosion. Would I slip down into a wretched state like this blind traveler? For now, I had a home and knowledge of a trade, but what did the future hold for me. Would people just assume I was like this beggar? Did dishonesty and poverty have to accompany blindness? I pledged to myself that I would never let it be so.

The hours dragged on, but finally Jed said, "Lancaster is just over the next rise. We will be there very shortly. I believe Michael said you wished to go to Fortney the wheelwright?"

Only minutes later, the iron tires of Jed's wagon were crunching over the gravel of the yard outside of Carter Fortney's Lancaster shop.

Carter Fortney was a well known wheelwright in the Lancaster community. He would certainly be able to help me to another Free Mason along the way, as the closer one got to Philadelphia, the more Free Masons one would find.

I knew Carter slightly from the many trips I had made back and forth over these roads with the 60th Royal Americans. Carter put down his tools and welcomed us warmly. When I told him of my need to find a wagon headed to Philadelphia that I might ride in with my things, he said I was in luck as he was at that very time, repairing two broken fellies and a spoke in a wheel for William Fall. William was also a brother Mason and owned and operated a stable in Philadelphia. The wheel would be finished soon and he thought William would be leaving on the morrow.

After Jed took his leave with my thanks, we stood about chatting with Carter. I had tried to pay Jed for his help, but he had refused and shook my hand with the Masonic sign. He had promised to stop at Dad's gun shop on North Third Street should he need to visit Philadelphia in the future. Wishing me well, he was gone.

Soon William Fall returned and after learning of my need, warmly agreed to let me ride along with him. It would be a two day trip as we would likely stop overnight in Paoli at the Broad Axe Tavern. Michael went off about his business and William and I enjoyed a meal at a local inn before turning in to sleep in Carter's loft. Leaving early the next morning, we chatted easily as the wagon rolled eastward. William Fall ran a livery stable on Locust Street. He had been out in the

Lancaster area buying grain and straw, which he was bringing back in his wagon. While there he had also been looking at a few new horses to purchase for his stable. I had not known William during the time I had lived in Philadelphia. Although he was a Brother in Lodge 2, which was my same Masonic Lodge, he had been made a Mason while I had been on the western frontier. It did not matter. He was a Masonic Brother and helped me as easily and warmly as if I had known him all of my life. During our trip, he had said that the next meeting of our Lodge was to be held in early January. He planned to be in the city then and would stop by the shop if I wished to accompany him to the meeting. It was to be held in the Masonic Lodge building located on what had been Videll's Alley, but was now known as Lodge Alley. This had been the very same lodge building in which I had received my first three degrees and had thereby been made a Mason. Lodge Alley ran west from Second Street between Walnut and Chestnut Streets. It was only a few squares away from the shop. We had spoken of how helpful he and the other Masonic Brothers had been to me while making my return to Philadelphia. I told him that I would very much appreciate accompanying him to the meeting.

The weather had turned slightly colder during the afternoon, and a cold rain and sleet storm made us very glad to stop at the Broad Axe Tavern. As we made our arrangements with the landlord for dinner. I heard fiddle music coming from the main room.

"That is old blind Ezra Zeek. He is in by the fire playing his fiddle. Do you know him?" asked the landlord of the Tavern.

William said he had seen him many times, but I did not remember ever taking notice of him if we had ever met at all. Remembering Mr. Climber, I did not feel so anxious to meet another blind musician.

"Come, I will introduce you. I am sure you will have much to speak of." The landlord continued, "Ezra, stop a moment so I can introduce you to another blind man."

Hearing this, I shuddered. Was I now only to be thought of as just another "blind man?" I felt that same gloom settling over me that I had experienced after meeting Calvin Climber.

Suddenly a small dog began barking.

"Quiet there Snivels!" Ezra said.

"Ezra, this is Mr. Andrew Annaler who has just lost his sight in a gunpowder explosion out at Fort Pitt," said the landlord.

Ezra said, "Gracious. Sit here and enjoy this fine fire."

William caught my elbow and aimed my hand toward the hand that Ezra was waving about in front of us.

The landlord said, "Ezra, I promised you a dinner for playing your fiddle. Why don't you join these gentlemen as they are cold and wish to have their dinner now."

Before I could think of a reason why this would not be what I wished, Ezra jumped up and said, "I would be delighted."

Within minutes, we found ourselves all seated together at a small corner table. I learned that Snivels was Ezra's dog which he said was a great help to him. Ezra Zeek wandered about the countryside looking for places to play his fiddle for food and lodging. He would stay in one place until he wore out his welcome and then move on. He had something of a harness for Snivels that looked like a stick that hooked into Snivels collar. Ezra also used a staff in his other hand and between the two kept from falling into or over obstacles. He said he had trained Snivels himself and hoped he would never have to be without this dog as he was a great aid and comfort.

He asked me if I played an instrument. When I told him that I did not, he went on to tell me that I should find one as soon as I could as it would be a big help in having people give me money. I began to feel ill. I explained to him that I had a family and hoped to return to my trade. He laughed at that and said I was lucky if I had a family to take care of me, but they would most likely tire of that, and sooner or later would put me out. He went on to say that the country folks were more likely to help a poor blind man than the hardhearted city folks. Needless to say, it was a terrible dinner. I was so upset by the conversation that I did not even remember what we had to eat. William, sensing my displeasure, said as soon after dinner as possible, that we had a long journey in the morning and that we were off to get some sleep. As we crossed the yard of the inn, I thanked him for getting me away from old Ezra Zeek.

"Oh, he's not so bad. He has no one to help him so he does what he can to live." As we spread our blankets for the night on the straw in William's wagon, I told him of our encounter with Calvin Climber. In the morning I was glad to leave as soon as we could before having another encounter with another blind beggar.

It was December 22$^{nd}$ and this was to be the last day of my journey home. Late in the afternoon, we rolled to a stop in front of Dad's shop on North Third Street. William helped me lift my chest out of his wagon, shook my hand and I was home.

# 4

# Home Again

Leaving my things next to the front step of the shop, I pushed open the old and very familiar door. I could hear the slow dull tapping of Dad's hammer striking the hot metal at his forge. It was located in a shed which ran across the back of the building. Moving slowly through the shop I reached out to find each bench and other well remembered items of the shop. They were all familiar, yet strange to my touch. Stepping into the shed, I just stood there. After a few minutes, the hammering stopped. Dad walked over and stood there just looking at me.

"I told you not to go," he said. Then he hugged me and said, "Go next door and see your mother. She has been waiting every day for you to come home since we received your letter. This is Ernie my shop apprentice. He is worth about as much as you were at the beginning of your apprenticeship. He will help you with your things. You can share the loft above the shop with him. You liked living up there when you were still an apprentice."

Going next door, I found Mom baking Christmas sweetmeats, pies, and biscuits. The house smelled wonderful. Her loving hug was a great restorative. I was home and it was time to really start my new life. My sister Sarah, who had still been home when I left, had already started her new life. Two years after I had left home, she married Daniel Mason who was a potter. They lived over on Elfreth's Alley and already had one son named Seth who had appeared a few months after they had been married. Now there was another child on the way. Mom said Sarah was due any day now. Mom was so pleased that Sarah had stayed near-by as all of her other children had moved far away. Susan was in Allentown, Pennsylvania and Henry in Elizabeth Town, New Jersey. She rarely heard from either of them. Hugging me again, I could tell that she was crying. She said, "At least you are home again. Now let me look at you. You are so thin. Your clothing looks dreadful. You should put something better on and certainly something cleaner."

"Mom, these are the best clothes that I have left."

Hugging me again, she said, "They will never do. I have only just finished making some things for Ernie for Christmas. I shall start making you new shirts at once. In the meantime, we will send Ernie to get you some leather breeches to wear from Isaac Smallwood's shop. He has been advertising in the Gazette that he has a good quantity of them on hand in his shop on Market Street. He is well known for making the best leather breeches in the City. You will also need a new coat. What you have on looks as if it should be used as rags. You are home with people again, not out in that

God forsaken wilderness with the animals and injins." I knew the coat had a few holes burned in it from the explosion, but it was all I had.

"We must also get you to a doctor as soon as we can. I have been reading in the Gazette about wonderful cures that a Doctor Stork has been performing. He has been able to restore sight to many blind people," she said.

"Mom, I don't think the sight is coming back. I am as I am and must learn to deal with it."

She continued, as she searched through some papers on her sideboard, "I have it here. Listen to what these people have said.

"Doctor STORK acquaints the public THAT he is to continue in Philadelphia till the latter end of February next: Such as stand in Need of his Assistance, may apply to him, at his Lodgings, at Mrs. Child, near the New Meeting house, in Arch Street. We the Subscribers are induced, not only in Gratitude to Dr. Stork, but likewise for the Benefit of our Fellow Sufferers, to communicate to the Public the Recovery of our Sights from Blindness. I John Conrad, of Upper Dublin, Philadelphia County, do certify that having lost my Sight seven Years ago was restored to it again by Dr. Stork, although I am in my 81$^{st}$ Year; also my Wife, aged 78, recovered her Sight, by the Doctor Assistance. I Martin Forster, at Point-no-Point, near Philadelphia, do certify, that my Daughter was born blind, and continued in that State for eleven Years, till lately restored to Sight by Dr. Stork. I Nicholas Bollinger certify, that my Wife, after 16 Years Blindness, recovered her Sight by Dr. Stork Assistance, so than she can read and write; as also my Son Christian, being born blind, in his 18th Year was brought to Sight by the same Gentleman. Dunmeson Township, Northampton County, December 15, 1761. This is to certify, that I Thomas Roberts, of Hopewell, near Trenton, being deprived of Sight these two Years, was restored to it again by Dr. Stork. I Hyam Bon, of Lancaster, think myself in Duty bound, for the Benefit of the Public, and in Gratitude to Dr. Stork, to declare, in this public Manner, that after seven Years Blindness, I was restored to Sight again by Dr. Stork, being able to read and write. Witness my Hand, HYAM BON. Doctor STORK, SURGEON and Oculist to her Royal Highness the Princess of Wales, acquaints the Public that he is to continue in Philadelphia. Such as have lost their Sight, or are afflicted with any other Disorder of the Eyes, may apply to him at his Lodging at Mrs. Child, near the New Meeting House, in Arch Street."

"Mom, do you really believe everything they print in the Gazette? Doctor Boyd out at Fort Pitt told me the sight would not be coming back. He is a good surgeon."

"If he were such a good surgeon, he would not be out in the woods with the savages. I will try to arrange for Doctor Stork to see you. He is only a few steps away on Arch Street."

I did not think Doctor Stork could do anything for me, but I was simply glad to be home and did not wish to argue.

Mom had been baking all day and the house smelled wonderfully; as only baking Christmas cookies and plum hooding can make it. It felt good to be home, and my desire to explore the western wilderness seemed to have vanished. I had been away for five years with only a few short visits home during trips to Philadelphia for supplies. Although both Mom and Dad were very glad to have me home, it struck me how much my parents had aged in these last few years. Weeks later, Sarah told me that news of my accident had seemed to have aged them both overnight.

The following day I went back to the shop. Dad said, "Your bench is where you left it. I had Ernie put your tool-chest at the end of it. I always hoped you would come back where you belong." That was just the point; did I belong? Could I do meaningful work in the shop?

The new apprentice was named Ernie Schmidt. He was from a village in Switzerland near where Dad's family had lived. In fact, he was a distant cousin. Peter and Elizabeth Schmidt, along with their two children, Ernie and Lisa, had decided to make their way in a new land. They had heard that Dad and his family were doing very well in Philadelphia. In 1756 Peter had written to us enquiring about life in Pennsylvania. Mom and Dad had written encouragingly and had promised to help them establish themselves in this wonderful city of Philadelphia. Ernie's father, Peter had been a carpenter and it seemed very likely that he would not have much difficulty finding work here.

In June of 1758 the Schmidt Family sold everything they had in Switzerland, except for Peter's carpenter's tools and the clothing on their backs. They had traveled to Rotterdam where they had taken passage for Philadelphia. While waiting for the ship to board, Peter had taken sick. When the ship was ready, he was still very ill, but the passage had been paid for and there was no turning back. During a very difficult and stormy voyage, Ernie's father Peter had suddenly died at sea leaving his young wife with two young children, ages twelve and eight, to make her own way in an exciting, but frightening, new land.

The Schmidts lived with Mom and Dad. Mom took on the role of a benevolent Aunt and saw to it that both Ernie and Lisa attended the same Friends school that her own children had gone too. Before marrying Dad, Mom had been trained as a seamstress. Elizabeth Schmidt had some knowledge of this craft so Mom set about teaching Elizabeth more and helping her to obtain some work from local shops. Although Ernie was young, he certainly could be a help to Dad in the shop. If he showed interest in gun-making, in a few years he could be formally apprenticed to Dad. That is exactly what happened. In June of 1760 when Ernie had reached age 14, he and Dad signed his apprenticeship papers and Ernie was launched on a career as a gunsmith. In addition, as part of his apprenticeship, Dad insisted that Ernie attend the evening classes that Anthony Lamb offered. These classes helped apprentices understand the principles behind the trades as well as the actual work techniques themselves.

About the same time that Ernie was apprenticed to Dad, Elizabeth, Ernie's mother, had married a German Lutheran Minister named Hans Frim. Elizabeth had met Hans at church. He had recently moved from Germany and planned to take up his call in the Lancaster area. Hans and

Elizabeth were married and, with Elizabeth's daughter Lisa, then almost eleven, left for a church in Lancaster.

Ernie was a pleasant and likeable young fellow. He seemed to get along well with Dad and seemed eager to be helpful as he learned all about making guns.

My first day back in the shop did not go well. Moving about the shop I managed to walk into several boards that were sticking out into the aisles between the benches. Then, while rough shaping a stock blank, I cut myself fairly badly with a chisel.

On the afternoon of the 24th, a lad appeared bringing a message from Sarah's husband Daniel that Sarah needed Mom. It seemed that by Christmas Eve we would have a new addition to the family. I don't think I had ever seen Mom happier.

Late Christmas Eve it began to snow. I stood out in front of our shop feeling the flakes touching my face. It felt as if the Christmas snow was healing me. Christmas always seemed to me to be a good time. A time of caring and sharing. It was very good to be home again. Every church-bell in the city was ringing. Standing there simply glad to be alive, I listened to several teams of horses passing with their harness bells all jingling. A few of the drivers called a Christmas greeting to me. I called back and waved, but recognized very few of the voices. Suddenly I heard footsteps approaching. The snow had so muffled the sound that the person was almost upon me before I knew anyone was there.

"Merry Christmas there Andrew!" It was Sarah's husband Daniel. "The women made me leave, but I came by to tell you and Master Frederick that we have a wonderful new daughter! We are naming her Dorothy after Sarah's mother."

"Daniel, that is truly good news. Are Sarah and the baby both alright?"

"Yes, they are wonderful! I guess that is why all of the bells are ringing." We both laughed as I reached out to shake his hand.

"I do not know what your plans are for the future, but if you would like to stop by my pottery, I could show you how to throw a few pots on the wheel. You might like it and I think working as a potter could be a good trade for a blind person."

"Well, thank you Daniel. That is very kind of you. I think for now I want to see how much I can do here in the shop, but I will keep your kind offer in mind. I might enjoy learning how to work in clay even if I never make it my trade."

"Whatever you wish, but come often and see, I mean visit, Sarah and me. The entire time you have been away, she was always speaking of her favorite brother Andrew. Now let's go inside and tell Master Frederick the good news."

Christmas that year was wonderful. Mom had a new healthy little granddaughter, I had come home, and things were looking brighter than they had looked for some time. Mom made her usual Christmas feast. She saved a piece of the plum pudding to send over to Sarah. It was an old family tradition that Mom would bake into the plum pudding a silver shilling. The person who found it would have good luck for the coming year. As no one had yet found it, it seemed very likely that Sarah would find it in her piece. It turned out to be just so. Mom's people had come from England several generations back. They had settled in Elizabeth Town in the neighboring Colony of New Jersey. Her brother, Ebenezer Butler, had a clock shop there where her first son had been apprenticed. Henry had promised to return to Philadelphia, but he had not yet done so. When Mom was very young, she had gone to live with an aunt in Philadelphia who was a seamstress. Soon thereafter, she had met Dad and well, here we are.

Dad's people had been farmers in Switzerland for generations. Early in life he always said that he knew he did not want to dig in dirt and wished only to make things. His father had managed to arrange an apprenticeship with a Swiss Gunsmith. Dad had been very happy there, but the smith had three sons of his own and the Swiss Canton in which they lived did not seem to need yet another gunsmith. So when he had completed his apprenticeship, he decided to set out in the new world.

Arriving in Pennsylvania in 1724, he had found a need in Philadelphia for his skills. Before long he had managed to buy the shop property and a year later the house next door to it. In 1727 he had married Mom and within a year Alice was born. Alice had not been very healthy and had died within a month of her birth. A year later, Susan was born. She had thrived and grown. Henry had been born in

1732 and had also enjoyed making things. He had shown an interest in sciences, particularly astronomy horology and wished to become a clockmaker like his Uncle Ebenezer.

# 5

## Learning New Ways

As the days passed, things began to become easier for me. Ernie was set to cleaning up the shop and trying to arrange things so fewer sharp edges stuck out and replacing all tools back where they were supposed to be. Gradually I got used to looking at things with my hands and returning to much of my old work. Although I did not do any of the work around the forge using red hot iron, I did do a great deal of the wood-work of shaping, and inletting parts into the wooden stock blanks. Filing cold metal parts was also a large part of any gunsmith's work and this I could also do.

A few days after Christmas, Will Davies appeared in the shop. I did not know until he told me months later, that Dad had sent for him and invited him to visit the shop as much and as often as he liked. Dad thought that I could learn some helpful things from Will. As usual, he was right. The first thing Will suggested was that I never walk about the city without boots. He said that there is so much mud, slop, animal droppings as well as just plain trash that a blind person is always stepping in or on something. Low buckle shoes were alright about the shop, but outdoors was another story. However, he said, mostly that blind folks just had to get used to things on their own. He did tell me to listen as hard as I could to everything around me and always try to pay attention to all the clues that I could hear, smell, or touch.

"Listen for horses splashing through deep puddles. Or wagons coming toward you, so you can avoid them. Know what you are standing on so you know if you are in the street on stones, or in the yard of a house. Pay attention to the smells around you, they will tell you a lot. Pay attention to the sounds of the church and city bells as they all have their own sound. Learn which are which. They will help to get you heading in the right direction when you are lost. Pay attention to everything because you must. It will be easier after the snow melts. It muffles everything and covers all of the landmarks."

Will was a young very likeable lad now in his twenties. He had learned a lot about living without sight. Having come from tough resilient Welsh stock, he made the very best of life every day. In general, life was a hard lot for a blind person in the 18th Century. Many blind people having few skills simply slid down the social ladder to a state of poverty and beggary. Those who had families to help them or trades to rely on were very fortunate indeed. I had both and was determined to make the best of it. Will had his sister and although he did not really have much of a trade, he had found a niche for himself making powder-horns and was not unhappy. In many cases people who had been born blind, or had been so from childhood were never really accepted in the apprenticeship system in which most people learned trades. Why should a master of a shop take on a person who was going to need all kinds of extra help teaching, and who for the most part would never be able to fully perform the trade at the masters level?

Infection, disease, or accidents were all causes of blindness. In most cases the various doctors or surgeons could do little or nothing to improve or restore sight. Blindness often is not an all or nothing business. There were individuals such as Will and myself who were not able to see a thing. There were others who only had one eye. Of this group, there were those who might have had an accident which destroyed one eye, leaving the other seemingly alright, only to find after a period of time the other eye stopped seeing. Many folks said this was a judgment of God. There were folks who did not see very well, but could get by without to much difficulty. There were older folks who had seen well, but as life went on, or they strained their eyes to much with fine needle-work or such had more and more difficulty. Folks often said this was also a judgment of God. Actually anytime anything went badly, there were folks who declared it a judgment of God. With over twenty varieties of religion being practiced in Philadelphia at that time, God seemed to be everywhere, and his judgments seemed to abound. Some doctors were sympathetic, but simply did not know enough to be of much help. Within a few days of my arriving home, Mom did arrange for me to visit the Doctor Stork whom she had read about. I was not surprised to learn that he could do nothing for me. It was sad to hear the change in Mom's voice after she heard Doctor's Stork's words. He could not offer much hope. Mom somehow had wanted to believe so very much that my sight could be restored that when she left the doctor's office; she held my hand very tightly as if I was still a little boy. She said nothing as we walked the two squares back to our home, but I could hear her softly crying. Once we were back in our home, I hugged her and tried to tell her that it would be alright even though I was not sure of this myself.

One interesting thing began to happen as the months went by. Gradually I began to hear things that I never knew I could hear before. Sounds echoed back off buildings, trees, and even some smaller solid objects. This gave me great hope. It was not hope that I would see again, but that I could learn to get about and live as a real person. After a while, people began to ask me if I could see a little bit as they observed that I might avoid a tree, or a carriage which had been left blocking a path.

Soon I began to recognize voices and be able to put names to them. Quickly I relearned the areas surrounding Mom and Dad's home and the shop. The corner pump where we drew our water was but a few steps away. Frequently I met others there and tried to recognize their voices as they drew their water.

One day a pleasant voice of a young woman said, "I have not seen you around here until recently. Have you come to live here?"

I was not certain she was speaking to me as there were several others about the pump. At first I said nothing. Then she touched my arm and said, "My name is Lydia, and I am bound to the Allen's who are the upholsterers here on Arch Street." After she touched my arm, I was sure she was speaking to me. Smiling I introduced myself and said I had lived here all of my life, but I had been away on the frontier for several years and had only recently returned home.

Suddenly the voice of Sadie Campbell, a cranky sounding older neighbor who lived a few doors further north on Third Street, broke in. "He is the blind one who blew himself up out on the frontier. Now he has been brought back to have his family take care of him."

Lydia dropped her hand from my arm and stepped back to pick up her now filled bucket.

I tried to explain that I had been in an accident, but it was not the way Sadie had said it.

Pushing forward, Sadie said, "Out of the way blind man, some of us have more important things to do than stand about in the cold telling stories." As Sadie was one of the biggest busybodies who were always gossiping about the pump, I decided her comments were simply meant to be hurtful and mean.

Returning to the shop, I heard her say to Lydia, "Don't be setting your cap for a blind man. With your looks, you can do better!" Back at my bench in the safety of the shop, I wondered if that is the way most people in the neighborhood felt about me? From time to time I would meet Lydia in this way by the water pump, but it was a cold winter and one did not dally about the pump. However, as the weather turned warmer that spring, I would meet Lydia more and more often.

Occasionally when walking on Arch Street on my way over to Daniel's pottery, I would hear Lydia's cheery greeting as we passed on the street. She frequently seemed to be out and about on errands. I was sad that such errands for an upholsterer's girl would not be likely to bring her to the gun-shop.

In the shop it seemed as if I was not cutting myself as often as at first. In those early days of adjusting, I saw a great deal of Will as Dad had cleared a corner just past my bench and invited Will to keep his horn-making things there. He came and went as he pleased. I was always glad to hear his cheery voice when he entered the shop as he always seemed to know what was going on in the city and often brought with him amusing stories, or tales of adventures that he had that I had not thought I was even up to trying. There was the day he brought me a still warm piece of apple pie. When I asked him who had given it to him, he laughed and said that actually no one had given it to him, but that while walking past widow Summer's kitchen window, he smelled it cooling on her windowsill.

"You just helped yourself to her pie?"

"Sure, she would not have made it if she did not mean for someone to enjoy eating it. So eat it quickly before anyone knows where it went." Most of all, Will seemed to know how I felt when I walked into something, or had something happen to me that I might have avoided had I seen. When talking with him about these things, he would say, "You can not keep thinking about what you might have done had you still been able to see, just do what you need to and do it the best you can." Suddenly Dad was standing at the end of my bench saying, "That does not include learning to steal apple pies off window-sills, no matter how well it is done." Chagrinned, I went back to my stock carving work and Will went off on another errand.

A few days after Will's pie caper, Dad and Ernie were out in the forge. While Dad was straightening an octagonal Pennsylvania Rifle barrel before scraping the rifling grooves into it, Ernie pumped the bellows. Will and I were alone in the shop. I thought it a good time to tell him what I had learned concerning his elder brother David. I told him of Colonel Bouquet's expedition down the Ohio deep into Indian Country to liberate and retrieve the over two-hundred white captives. I described how many had been adopted into whatever tribe was holding them and how many did not wish to return. Before I could finish, he said, "That would be David. The native life fascinated him. That was why the family moved west from the Welsh Tract. David kept pestering Dad to move to a wilder land. He said he was going to go with or without the family. Finally Mom and Dad agreed and look what happened."

"Yes," I told him, "The Colonel did free David and was bringing him back, but David ran away."

"Well, it isn't as if he had much to come back to. I will tell Gwynne."

With that he seemed to close the door on his brother David and rarely ever spoke of him after that.

One evening early in January, William Fall arrived at the door of our shop as we were cleaning up at closing time. He said that he was stopping as promised on his way to dinner and a Masonic Lodge meeting and would be glad if I were to accompany him. I hurried up to the loft above the shop where Ernie and I lived and quickly changed into some of the new clothing that Mom had made for me and soon joined him. I was pleased that he wished to include me.

The Lodge meeting was very reassuring. Although I had not been to a formal meeting in quite some time, I had been to many in the past and the formal ritual was so exactly structured that I felt as if I was SEEING the Business of the Lodge being conducted. Many Brothers who I had not seen in several years came up to me and welcomed me home. The then Worshipful Master of the Lodge, Joseph Stilwell who was a judge in the Pennsylvania Assembly, even suggested that if I now planned to remain in Philadelphia for some time, I might consider taking an office in the Lodge and advancing through the chairs. I felt very accepted. The talk that Michael Graham and I had came back to me. Why would it be that having joined the Masons when I could see, I was now accepted and encouraged to pursue an office in the Lodge. Had I lost my vision first and now tried to join the Brotherhood, I would not be accepted at all. Perhaps it came down to the fact that if accepted, then no matter what, one was still a Brother. But if one were deemed not worthy to join, even though there might be a feeling of compassionate understanding toward those less fortunate, one could not become a Brother of the craft. I wondered if this would change in time. I certainly hoped so. After all, was I not the same person? Maybe: maybe not. It would depend on me to continue a meaningful life rather than to allow myself to slide down to being a lesser person. I left the Lodge meeting filled with determination and hope for my future.

At first I stayed very close to the shop, but as the weeks passed, I began to venture farther out into a city that had once been so familiar to me. One day when we were not very busy in the shop, I decided that I would try to find Daniel Mason's pottery and take him up on learning a bit about throwing a pot on his wheel. Since I had been home, Mom and I had walked over to Sarah and Daniel's many times. This time I wanted to find it on my own.

Much like our home, Daniel and Sarah lived but a few steps from the shed where Daniel worked. It was built along the back of their house and had a small yard behind it that adjoined the area where the water pump was located for their street. In this yard Daniel stored several mounds of clay. The shed itself had a large oven built into the back wall of the house that Daniel used as his kiln. There were several work tables and in the middle of the floor was a large potter's wheel.

Daniel was a cheery man who filled his pottery with warmth and joy. He stopped preparing the clay he was working on and welcomed me to his little shop.

"Sarah will be so glad that you came to visit us."

"Yes, that too. We are not very busy just now at the gun shop and I thought I would take you up on your offer to learn something about making pottery."

"Wonderful! Let me show you about my pottery and introduce you to my wheel."

The wheel was actually two wheels. It felt for all the world like a pair of wagon wheels mounted on an axle. Except they were turned on their side and rotated in a base socket. The upper wheel was covered with wooden boards in order to make a solid work surface. While seated on a high stool, one worked on the upper wheel and kicked the bottom wheel to keep the entire thing spinning.

Daniel plopped a large ball of clay in the middle of the wheel and began to show me how to hold my hands to center the clay as I moved the wheel.

Several hours raced by as he very patiently showed me again and again how to get the clay centered on the wheel.

"That is the big trick Andrew. One must have the clay centered or it will not become a round pot." As the wheel spun I was amazed to feel a shape magically rising into my hands almost as if the clay was alive. Just as I began to think that this was really easy, the shape became more of an oval and then suddenly collapsed under my hands.

"Daniel, why did it do that?"

He laughed. "Because you made it do so. Try again."

While I was working away, the door of the shed swung open and the pottery was filled with a loud booming voice.

"Ah, there you are my good friends! Andrew, it is so good to see you again. I thought the western woods had swallowed you up forever." Turning on the potter's stool I smiled and held my hand out.

"Abraham, Abraham Kiessel! I am so very glad to hear your voice again. I guess the western woods did not like the taste, as they spat me out again."

Abraham put his arm across my shoulders and said, "I am not shaking that hand covered with clay. I am not that glad to see you." He laughed.

Abraham Kiessel was an old friend who was a very successful merchant. He imported many various items that he sold in his Chestnut Street shop under the sign of the Key & Crown. He had come by the pottery to pick up some items that Daniel had made to be sold in Abraham's shop. The next little while was filled with good talk and that warmth that exists between friends and is instantly rekindled even if they have not seen each other in a very long time. As he left, he clapped me on the shoulder and urged me to stop in his shop any time.

"Always fair prices for the finest goods available, under the sign of the Key & Crown," he boomed as the door closed behind him.

After a few hours I had several items which Daniel said he would fire for me in a few days when they dried. "You can not fire them too soon or the water in the clay will make them explode and that could ruin other things in the kiln as well as your own work. Come again and try whenever you wish."

I thanked Daniel and said I had to be getting back home.

"You had best stop and give your greetings to Sarah and the children, or she will not forgive me."

By the next morning, my back, neck and shoulders all hurt from the unfamiliar work. I had enjoyed it but I was especially glad that Daniel had accepted me again as a real person. I had only known him slightly before I had left on my adventure into western Pennsylvania.

I left Daniel's pottery with a whole new respect for the potter's trade.

Daniel had been a member of the Society of Friends. Sarah had met him while attending a Friends school. We had all gone to Friends schools. Our parents could both read and write. Mom had come from a learned family. Her brother Ebenezer was something of a scientist. He was the uncle who my oldest brother Henry was apprenticed to in Elizabeth Town, New Jersey. Mom had insisted that we all attend a Friends school. There was one only a square away on Second Street. The schools, run by the Society of Friends and commonly known as Quaker schools, were thought to be the best in the Colony. Boys and girls both attended these schools, although the studies were a bit different. Sarah had met Daniel and, in fact, had decided to become a member of the Friends Meeting in order for them to marry. However, the clearance committee had rejected her and read Daniel out of Meeting when they learned that Sarah was pregnant.

It had been no surprise to me when I learned in a letter from Mom that Sarah and Daniel were to be married. I had been at Fort Pitt at the time when I received Mom's letter. Although Sarah and I had been very close, given the great distance, there was no thought of going home for the wedding. Besides, from the tone of Mom's letter, the wedding was to take place quite soon. After looking at the date of the letter, I realized that it had taken over a month to reach me and the wedding had already taken place. Mom thought they would be very happy. Daniel had finished his apprenticeship as a potter and had just set up his shop on Elfreth's Alley off Second Street. They would be living in a small house just in front of Daniel's pottery. Mom had said in her letter that she was looking forward to having grandchildren so nearby.

Henry had the best formal education of any of us. Since the stage coach line running from Philadelphia to New York had been established in 1738, Uncle Ebenezer had visited us several times. He had made the trip to Philadelphia to meet with such men as Benjamin Franklin and David Rittenhouse. Both were very learned men of their time. Henry had always gotten on very well with his Uncle, and in 1748 when he was fourteen, he had been apprenticed to Uncle Ebenezer. Henry had so impressed his Uncle that by 1752, Uncle Ebenezer had written to Mom and Dad offering to allow Henry to stop his apprenticeship and begin studying at the College of New Jersey. It had been founded a few years earlier in 1747. Uncle Ebenezer was a bachelor and had no children of his own. He and Henry had become very close during Henry's apprenticeship. Uncle Ebenezer felt so strongly that attending the College of New Jersey would be a good step for Henry that he even offered to pay his tuition. Henry had done very well at the College and had been graduated in 1758. This had been just about the time that I had headed west.

# 6

# Will Davies

"You mean they signaled the ships onto the rocks and then stole the cargo?"

"Andrew, you make everything sound so bad. You wouldn't want the cargo to be ruined would you?"

"Will, they call that being a ship-wrecker!"

"Yeah,—that is what the revenue men said too. After this one large ship struck the rocks, there was a lot of trouble and my Dad thought he might find a new area of Wales to live in. He wandered about for a while but finally thought it might be even better to leave Wales as a sailor on a ship from Cardiff. The ship was bound for Philadelphia so here he came. He wanted to get away from the sea and went inland to some of the small villages in the Welsh Tract. There he met and married Mom and had first Gwynne and later David and then me. David always wanted to be in the woods and not doing the farm work. Mom and Dad were only farming land that belonged to Mom's people. They always wanted their own piece of land. After Gwynne married Ephraim, David said he was going to go west with or without the rest of us.

Mom and Dad decided to go west and you know the rest. I don't think Gwynne loved Ephraim, but she knew the family wanted to go west and she was terrified of the wilderness. She had always enjoyed visiting Philadelphia, so when she had a chance to marry Ephraim and move into the city, well, she made her choice."

"Sure, but that does not mean you should be involved in smuggling now."

"No, it doesn't. What it does mean is that as a blind man in Philadelphia in 1765, I must find a way to earn my own way. Yes, I make powder-horns, but if my sister did not let me live in the attic of her inn, I would be starving on the streets the way Jim Rotten-teeth has to."

Jim Rotten-teeth was a blind beggar. No one knew or cared what his real name was. Everyone simply called him "Jim Rotten-teeth." I had often seen him down on Water Street near the wharves before I had gone west with the army. He was a ragged, filthy specimen of humanity.

"Is he still alive? Jim Rotten-teeth doesn't even try to help himself," I said.

"So what do you want him to do?" Will asked. "He has no family that I ever heard of. No one wants him and if I did not have my sister, or you, or your family, we could be out there sharing the streets with Jim Rotten-teeth or any of the others who are not much better off than him. You come home from the western forest after the army doesn't want you and you have a home to live in. You have family to care about you and take care of you. Your Mom starts making you new clothing as soon as you walk through the door, your Dad sets your bench up and lays out your tools. I bet he even sharpens your chisels and knife blade edges."

I knew Will had always had trouble putting a good edge on his knife blade.

"Don't be so self righteous. You are the lucky one."

As Will said that, I remembered Surgeon Boyd saying, "Lad, you are the fortunate one. The others are gone."

"So should I be taking my smuggled coffee which was a gift to you and the shop here and be on my way?"

"No Will, thank you for the coffee. We will all enjoy it. Let us get some water from the street pump and brew up some over the shop fire."

"I will get the water," Will said. In a few minutes the shop began to smell like coffee. The door swung open and Ernie appeared having just returned from an errand that Dad had sent him on, stamped the snow off his feet and shrugged out of his coat.

He said, "That smells great! Are we having coffee?" Dad came in from the forge and said, "Have your coffee, but there is work to be done. Four people working in this shop with plenty to do, but only one is actually working!" He clamped a stock blank in the vise and began to plane it. Soon the good smell of the wood shavings, mixed with the aromatic smell of the freshly brewing coffee filled the shop. It made me realize what a truly pleasant and inviting place to be this shop was. Tapping Will on the shoulder, I asked him if he had noticed that Dad had described the shop as having four people working in it.

"You are one of us Will. You don't have to ever be like Jim Rotten-teeth."

"Neither do you," he replied. The days and weeks passed and life fell back into a familiar pattern. I became more comfortable with all of the shop tools again. The wood-working part of the trade was the most pleasant for me. However, we not only made and repaired guns, we also sold guns that people had brought in. Often when someone wanted to upgrade to one of Dad's fine Pennsylvania rifles, they would bring in an old fowling-piece and ask if we would take it in trade as a part of the payment. We would then go over these guns and make them as good as possible. Soon I took over the buying, selling and trading of imported or used weapons. One wall of the shop was covered with these and it soon became part of my job to keep track of these orphan weapons and sell them to folks who could not afford a fine new rifle, but wished to have a serviceable flintlock arm for hunting. My own personal weapons now hung on that same wall. I still did not wish to sell them, but it seemed a good place to keep them. On pegs in among these weapons, I hung the powder horns that Will had for sale. Over the last several years, he had become quite good at making really fine horns. Ernie was something of an artist. When things were slow in the shop, he scratched a few figures of animals, maps or ships on the horns for Will. When a customer came in looking for a firearm, he often left with a powder horn as part of the deal.

Dad had always seemed friendly to Will. While I had been away, Dad had helped him with many of his horn projects and taught him many little tricks. One of the reasons that Will had been having trouble with his first horns being water tight was that he had tried shaping the plug as close as he could to the open end of the horn and then tried hammering it in. Early on he had cracked a few horns before someone had told him to boil the horns to make them soft. This does work, but most horns require being boiled in oil rather than water and brought up to a much higher temperature before they become soft enough to force into a new shape. Dad took a horn that Will was ready to start a plug for and showed him a different way.

After having Will saw the end off so it would be square, Dad took the small scrap ring and placed it on a piece of wood large enough for the plug. Next he told Will to hammer small nails around the ring to keep it from moving about. When it was secure, he handed Will a sharp scriber and had him make a deep line around the inside of the ring. When they removed both the nails and the ring, Will had a deep line that he could feel that was the pattern of the plug to be fitted into the horn. From this point, Will was able to chisel down about an inch all around the line. This formed something like an upside down mushroom. This worked very well for him and his horns became much better.

Will showed me how Dad had taught him to do this on the same day that he told me Dad had asked him to spend more time in the shop so that I could learn from him other lessons about being blind. Now Will was in and out of the shop quite often. During the summer months, he would sit out of doors and scrape horns, but when I came home it was

Christmas. That winter and spring he spent a lot of time with us in the shop. I had always liked Will, but now we became close friends. Ernie was often with us and we became a little group of our own.  Often I went to the Coffee & Crown coffee house which was but a stones throw away from our shop, on 3rd Street just across Arch Street. Sometimes, when the three of us were together, I was outvoted by the other two and we would go to other places. Ernie and Will both seemed to know the best taverns and such places that young men of the city might enjoy. The Running Horse Tavern on Blackhorse Alley was just such a place. It was not far away. We would often walk over there for a mug or two after the shop was closed. We did this much against Master Frederick's advice or approval. The Running Horse was known to accommodate some low and disreputable women. When I pointed this out to Will, he wondered aloud if that was not just the reason to go there. Ernie had a fancy for a serving maid named Jane who worked there.

One evening while there, Ernie said he was going to leave us for a bit as he thought Jane might be able to get a bit of time away. Will laughed and wished him good fortune.

When Ernie had gone, Will asked me if I was interested in getting to know any of the women who worked here. He said he knew most of them and would be glad to help me find one. I gently declined his offer. We sat there in silence for a bit. I realized that I had offended him when he burst out, "Who do you think you are now? The women here are the only kind of women who will ever be interested in a blind man. You think the ladies of good character will want to bother with you now? Those days are over for you my friend! What do you think you could ever offer them? Before you went away you were a skilled gunsmith. You made a good living and were respected in the community. Now you are nothing, like me."

"Will, I am not nothing. I am trying to pick up my old life and do the best that I can."

"Yes, you are, but without your family and their shop to return to you would be nothing. What other shop would even take you in as a journeyman? Besides making a living, I asked you what woman better than the ones here would ever go to bed with a blind man?"

I did not answer him, but sat there thinking about the several women I had known in my life. During the time I had been an apprentice, there had been an experimental time with a woman in the neighborhood not much better than the company Will was offering to help me find. When I had gone west, there had been the daughter of a sutler in Carlisle. I had even thought about marrying her, but now I could not think why. There had been that wild night with the daughter of an Indian chief who offered his daughter to me when I had cut down a broken musket for him. Those had been wild and exciting times. Then there had been Phoebe. She had come to me when I really needed help and encouragement. I sat there wondering how, and where, she was now. My thoughts also frequently turned to the young woman who had placed her hand on my arm at the water pump and had said, "My name is Lydia." I had only seen her briefly since. She had always seemed very friendly.

I had been glad that Sadie Campbell had not been there on those occasions.

Will slapped my arm in a friendly manner. "You will do what you want when you are ready. If you change your mind let me know." After ordering another mug, Will's mood lightened and he told me how dangerous women could be. He said that while I had been away, for many months, Jacob Snyder at the tannery had refused to give him any more horns. Jacob believed that Will and his daughter Martha had been all too friendly. Will said it all blew over when Martha married a stone mason and moved to Reading. He laughed and said that he had given her husband a very nice horn that he had made as a wedding gift. I commented that I thought that was a nice thing for him to have done. Laughing even harder, he said that he thought it was only right as he had already given Martha his very best horn several times before the wedding.

# 7

## Michael Graham

As spring turned to summer, we began to hear talk of a new tax called the Stamp Act that would be a tax on many legal papers and other items such as cards and dice. Neither cards nor dice were of any interest to me, but it seemed to be a major topic of discussion in the taverns and coffee houses. It had been passed by Parliament in March, and was to go into effect the following November. The point was to raise and recoup some of the funds that had been spent by the Crown during the Seven Years War. Here in the Colonies we had called it the French & Indian War. It had been followed by Pontiac's rebellion which had generated even more cost for the Crown to defend the frontier. During October of 1763 a proclamation had been made to prevent Colonists from moving over the mountains. This had been largely ignored by folks hungry for land. Until recently, I had been a part of the British Army's effort to enforce this proclamation. I could easily understand the costs involved and was not surprised that the Crown would have had Parliament pass such an act. Nor did I feel it was unjust. In the evenings, either Mom or Dad would read articles aloud from *The Pennsylvania Gazette*. There seemed to be a great deal of public hard feeling against this tax. I wondered how my old friend Michael Graham, who was an attorney, felt about this new tax. I did not have long to wonder.

One day not long after, the door of the shop swung open and Michael strolled in.

"And a hearty and gracious good day to all," he boomed. After greeting him warmly, I suggested that we step across Arch Street and enjoy a bowl of coffee at the Crown & Coffee. I knew we would be able to talk there.

Michael told me that he did not mind the taxes on the legal paper and such. "After all, I am an attorney. I can simply pass those costs and fees on to my clients. It is the fact that they wish to tax the cards and dice."

"I did not know you had taken to gambling Michael," I said.

"I have not! However, to place a tax on items that the poorer element of society uses to amuse themselves and can ill afford to pay seems, well it seems niggling and harsh."

Over a bowl of coffee, we had a fine chat about many topics. He had many questions concerning my new life and how I had been adjusting to it since my return. His questions probed deeply as a clever attorney's questions can do. Answering his questions with as much honesty as I could, I knew I would think hard and long about them later. I kept hearing in my mind Will's comments, but struggled against them. Michael had accepted me as a person. Daniel Mason had accepted me. Abraham Kiessel had accepted me. However, there were all the voices that

I met every day that did not conceal their feelings of pity or contempt. Michael's questions forced me to realize how far I had come in a relatively short time, but how far society had not.

While I sipped my coffee and turned these ideas over in my mind, Michael picked up a copy of the newspaper *The Gazette*. It was several weeks old, but he commented that he needed a good new pair of boots and the following advertisement just caught his eye.

# The Pennsylvania Gazette

March 14, 1765
ALEXANDER RUTHERFORD, */Shoemaker /*, TAKES this Method to inform Gentlemen, Ladies and others, he is removed from next Door to the Sign of the Tun, in Water street, to the Sign of the Boot and Spatterdash, in front street, opposite Mr. Anthony Morrisold Brew house, and two Doors below Benjamin Chew, Esq.; where he makes all Manner of Boots, Spatterdashes, Shoes and Pumps; also Women's Silk, Stuff and Leather, as good and neat as any imported from Europe, either by Wholesale or Retail. He is greatly obligated to his former Customers, and those who are pleased to favour him with their Commands, may depend on the utmost Care and Dispatch of their very humble Servant, ALEXANDER RUTHERFORD.

"Do you know this fellow Rutherford?" he asked me. "He seems to have moved his shop near Benjamin Chew's law office where I read law."

"Oh yes, he made these very boots that I have on now. He has just moved his shop to Front Street, and is trying hard to please in his new location."

Michael slid the paper away and said, "I believe I shall pay that gentleman a visit after we have concluded our business. I had best get some boots before Parliament decides to tax them." After our coffee, we strolled back over to the shop where I helped Michael choose three fowling-pieces and several of Will's horns. Michael planned to take these back with him for individuals, who, knowing Michael was going to be in the city had asked him to do so. Admiring the artwork on the horns, he asked Ernie to add a Masonic square and compass to one of the ones that he had selected. Ernie was glad to do this for my old friend. Ernie had shown a great deal of interest in the mystery of the Masons but was not old enough yet to join. I was sure that when he finished his apprenticeship and was twenty-one years of age, he would most likely ask me to be his recommender and help him petition the Lodge for membership. I had come to think very well of Ernie and already thought of him as a little brother of my own; so I would be very pleased to have him be made a Brother of the Craft. I had noticed that Dad had become very lax with the rules for apprentices. In my day, we were not allowed to run the streets at night, or frequent the taverns the way Ernie did. When I had said this to Ernie I wondered out loud whether Dad was getting soft, or the next generation was going to hell.

Ernie replied that he thought I was just getting old.

Michael also spent a bit of time with Dad discussing the details of a Pennsylvania rifle that he wished Dad to make for him. Leaving the shop he said he was lodging at the Royal Standard on Market Street and that he had legal business in town that would take a few days, but would stop in again before heading west. Placing his hand on my shoulder, he left without another word. That small touch had said it all.

# 8

# My Dog Spark

During this time a very important event occurred in my life. Whenever I had time, I had visited Daniel Mason's pottery. I enjoyed feeling the clay rise through my hands as the wheel spun. Sarah had a very friendly female dog named Brindle. It was not of any particular breed, but a wonderful devoted dog that followed her everywhere. Most folks kept their dogs outside, but Sarah had made a pet of this dog and allowed her in their house. In June, 1765, this dog had a litter of several pups. In late July, Sarah presented me with the one she said was the best and smartest of the litter. This pup had come to me during several visits to Sarah or to Daniel's pottery. Of course one of my pottery projects was to make this pup water and food bowls. Making a collar and leash from rope, I walked back to the shop along Arch Street.

"Good day Andrew. You have a new pup." It was Lydia who had stopped me to admire my new pup.

"Yes, my Sister Sarah just gave her to me."

"She is beautiful! What is her name?"

"I have not yet decided. Do you have a suggestion?"

"Hummm, — I don't know, but one will come to you. I must be off. Good bye now." And she was gone.

Releasing the pup when we reached the shop, she bounded about both the shop and forge. Dad said, "She is as lively as a spark."

Smiling, I said, "What a great name. I declare this pup will now be known as Spark." The next time we saw Lydia while out walking, I told her that my new pup was named Spark. She thought it a wonderful choice and rubbed Spark's ears and told her that she was a beautiful girl. I said nothing, but I thought the same comment could apply to Lydia.

Spark turned out to be a great friend. She stayed near my bench and quickly learned to always move out of my way as soon as I rose from the bench. As she did not move for either Dad or Ernie, I concluded that somehow, she knew that I was blind. So often when moving about the shop, Spark would jump up from a nap and put herself in-between me and something that I was about to walk into. Using the rope collar and leash, I tried to see if she would keep me from walking into things outside. Until now I had been using the staff that Barent had given me back in Fort Pitt. It seemed amazing to me but Spark quickly learned to lead me around things. My thoughts drifted back to meeting Ezra Zeek and his dog Snivels. Could Spark grow into a dog that would really be a help to me traveling about the city? Mom told me that she had heard in Europe sometimes dogs helped blind men find their way about. After watching us for a bit, Mom suggested that I take Spark over to William Bedford, whose shop was on Chestnut Street.

"He makes all sorts of bridles, harnesses, saddles and saddle-bags, portmanteaus, and does excellent workmanship. See if he would make some kind of a harness for Spark that would be an improvement on that rope," Mom said.

This seemed a great idea and soon I was walking down to Chestnut Street with Spark.

Although I had visited William Bedford's shop many times in earlier years, I was not exactly certain which door was the correct entrance to his shop. Pulling one open, I immediately realized that it was in fact the harness shop. The good smell of new leather greeted us at once. Thinking about it, I began to realize that Will's point had been well taken about being aware of everything around me. The smell was very important. A harness shop had the good smell of new leather. A bakery had a very wonderful warm smell of things baking. A book or stationery store had a very strong smell of paper and ink. An apothecary's shop smelled like freshly ground herbs or chemicals.

"Greetings Andrew! How can I be of help to you?" William's voice boomed out in welcome.

"William, I want you to meet Spark, my new friend. We are hoping you can make Spark a harness that might help her lead me about."

William was a bit surprised at my request and did not take me seriously at first. When he realized that I was quite serious indeed, he looked Spark over very carefully. We discussed ideas that we thought might work. We spoke for quite some time about what might be helpful. After measuring Spark he told us to come back in three days and he would have something that I could try. I did not know it then, but he followed us back to the shop trying to see if Spark actually was of any help to me. He was impressed enough that on the afternoon of the second day, he appeared in our shop and said he wanted to try the new harness on the dog. He showed me how to buckle it on and we walked around outside for a few minutes. Taking it back with him, he said there were one or two things he yet wanted to do, but that it would be ready in the morning. Good as his word, when we walked into his shop the following morning, there it was completely finished. A new leather collar, leash, and harness. The harness had two long thin poles. These thin poles ran loosely through small loops on each side of the strap that went around Spark's body. They were then connected to the chest strap next to her shoulders. The collar was a separate piece to which the leash was clipped. The ends of the poles were connected together with a crossbar that I would hold. Will had supplied several poles in different lengths in order that I could try them to determine what might work best. It would take some practice for Spark and I to get used to this, but it seemed as if it might be really a big help.

The next time Will Davies came in the shop I showed him the harness, thinking he might be interested. He wished me well, but said that he was doing fine with a staff and did not want to have to take care of a dog. He said he had enough to take care of himself.

# 9

# Lydia

A few days later, we met Lydia again out on Arch Street.

"What is this Spark is wearing?" Lydia asked.

I explained to her how much help Spark had been and that I was trying to make it easier for her to show me around things by using this new harness. Lydia hugged Spark and told her what a good girl she was to be helping me so. During my Sunday afternoons, I started making it a habit to take Spark for a long walk on the streets about the shop. At first we only walked on the very familiar ones that I already knew, but as the weeks passed, we kept expanding the range of our walks. Several times Lydia just seemed to be coming out of her house at the same time and would walk a bit with us. Soon we were agreeing to meet and our walks together became a regular weekly event. Lydia helped us learn streets that we had never ventured down. As we would walk a given street she would say the names of and often describe the businesses that we passed.

Lydia was one of eight children. Her father had died during the French & Indian War. Her mother had remarried a year or so later, but Lydia did not get along with her step-father. At age sixteen she had been bound to the Allens to learn the trade of upholsterer. When we first met, she had just turned eighteen. She was to serve with the Allens until her twenty-first birthday.

All three of us came to truly enjoy and look forward to these outings.

On one of our Sunday afternoon walks, Spark, Lydia and I had wandered quite a distance from Third and Arch Streets. We had walked north along Second Street toward the German Town Road. We were actually out of the city when a sudden storm moved in and it began to rain very hard. Lydia spotted an open shed that would offer us some protection. We ran to it and ducked under the roof. We huddled against the back wall of the shed and tried to stay dry.

Along with the rain, the wind had come up. I pulled my warm woolen cloak about us both and held her very close. It had been almost a year since I had been with Phoebe and it felt very nice to have Lydia pressed against me. She was about nineteen at that time and was living at the shop of Joseph and Marie Allen who were Upholsterers. Her family lived on a farm a bit north of the city in Germantown.

Feeling the warmth of her body under our cloaks, I wanted her very much. However, this young woman was no gift from an Indian chief. She was not an experienced woman as Phoebe had been. She was no tavern wench as

Will had offered to find for me. Huddled there together, I came to realize how much this young woman meant to me.

The rain showed no signs of stopping. The time was getting late and the daylight fading. We agreed that we would simply have to walk home in the rain. In that last second before moving apart, I leaned down and kissed her. I meant it to simply be a kiss, but it turned into several. Those kisses silently promised that there would be more. I pulled the hood of her cloak up over her beautiful long hair, which she had told me was chestnut brown. Catching Spark's harness handle, we moved out into the rain as she slid her hand into mine and squeezed it firmly.

There were not all that many places one could invite a young woman to on a Sunday afternoon. However, every Sunday afternoon, Mom always had tea on and usually something that smelled good had just come out of the oven. So the following Sunday afternoon, after a short walk, I suggested that we stop at Mom's for tea. Lydia protested that she had only dressed to come out for a walk and I should have told her I wanted to do that before. Why could we not stop for tea the following week? I agreed and looked forward to it all through that next week.

The tea went very well and everyone seemed surprisingly at ease. I had not known it before, but Mom knew quite a bit about Lydia as she was friendly with the Allens. From then on, stopping at Mom's for tea after one of our walks became a frequent occurrence. This was especially so as we were getting into colder and colder weather and so our walks became shorter.

# 10

## The Stamp Act

My twenty-ninth birthday came and went quietly. It no longer seemed as such a wonderful date to commemorate since the accident had taken place on that very day. The date itself was overshadowed by the constant talk concerning the Stamp Act. The hated stamps had by early October arrived in the city. Although I did not wish to become involved in the political discussions that raged in the coffeehouses and taverns, it seemed as if there was no other topic of interest. I still felt strongly that the Crown needed to recover some of the costs involved in making the Colonies safe from the French, and mostly safe from the various Indian tribes that always were such a threat to the western frontier. Having been a part of the British Military system, I felt some loyalty to the Crown's Military efforts. If these needed to be supported by a small stamp tax, I did not see the harm. I often wondered if the French had not been chased out of Canada and had remained a threat, if the Colony groups would be as loud with their protests. They certainly had been loud enough demanding military protection from the Crown during the French & Indian War period. But this was not a popular position to take.

On the 10th of October, Ernie returned from one of the coffeehouses with a copy of the *Gazette* for that day.

"Let me read to you what the latest news is concerning the stamps." he said.

**PHILADELPHIA, October 10.**

On Saturday, the 5th Instant, the Ship Royal Charlotte, Capt. Holland, came up to this City, attended by His Majesty Ship Sardine, James Hawker, Esq.; Commander. Capt. Holland having brought from London the Stamped Papers for Maryland, New Jersey and this Province, had remained some Time at New Castle, on Delaware, under Protection of the Man of War; and on the first Appearance of these Ships round Gloucester Point, all the Vessels in the Harbour hoisted their Colours half Mast high, the Bells began to ring, being first muffled, and continued so until the Evening, and every Countenance added to the Appearance of sincere Mourning, for approaching Loss of Liberty. At Four o'clock in the Afternoon several Thousand Citizens met at the State house, to consider the proper Ways and Means for preventing that unconstitutional Act of parliament (the Stamp Act) being carried into Execution: The first Measure was, to send seven of their Number to Mr. Hughes, Stamp Distributor for this Province, to request he would resign that Office. He assured them; no Act of his should tend to carry that Law into Execution here, until it was generally complied with in the other colonies, but refused to sign any Resignation at that Time, for various Reasons, which he assigned. On the Gentlemen's Return to the State House, and reporting this Answer, the Company were instantly transported with

Resentment, and it is impossible to say what Lengths their Rage might have carried them, had not the Gentlemen who waited on Mr. Hughes represented him in the Light he appeared to them, at the Point of Death; his Situation raised their Compassion, and they happily communicated their Feelings to all the People assembled: and instead of the Multitude repairing instantly to his House for a positive Answer, they agreed to make their Requisition in Writing, and gave Mr. Hughes until Monday Morning to make a Reply. In Consequence of this Determination, a short Paper was instantly drawn up, and sent to him; and on Monday Morning the Deputies received from him a Writing, which was brought to the Court House, and there read aloud to a vast Concourse of People, as follows.

Pausing in his reading, Ernie said, "Yes, it was quite a gathering. I was there at the State-House with a number of other apprentices."

"You were there? I did not know apprentices were worried about paying Stamp Taxes," I commented.

"We are not, but there was a lot of excitement and it was fun to be there."

"I never knew that being part of a mob was fun," I replied.

"Oh Andrew, were you more fun when you could see?" Ernie asked.

"I do not know, but I am not in favor of mobs and public disorder."

After a long pause, Ernie continued to read aloud.

Philadelphia,
Monday Morning, October 7, */1765 /*.

WHEREAS about Six o'clock on Saturday Evening last, a Paper was sent to me, expressing, that great Number of Citizens of Philadelphia, assembled at the State House, do demand of Mr. John Hughes, Distributor of Stamps for Pennsylvania, that he will give them Assurance, under his Hand, that he will not execute that Office; and expect that he will give them a fair, candid and direct Answer by Monday next, at Ten o'clock, when he will be waited on for that purpose."

Saturday, October 5, */1765 /*.

I DO therefore return for Answer to those Gentlemen, and all their Associates, That I have not hitherto taken any Step, tending to put the late Act of Parliament into Execution in this Province; and that I will not, either by myself or my Deputies, do any Act or Thing that shall have the least Tendency to put the said Act into Execution in this Province, until the said Act shall be put into Execution generally in the neighbouring Colonies, and this I am determined to abide by.

And WHEREAS my Commission includes the three Counties of New Castle, Kent and Sussex, upon Delaware, I do, therefore, hereby voluntarily inform the good People of those Counties, that no Act of mine shall, either directly or indirectly, involve them into any Difficulties with respect to the said Stamp Act, before the same shall take Place generally in the neighbouring Colonies.

JOHN HUGHES.

This Paper from Mr. Hughes at first gained the Approbation of three Huzza; but we find many People much dissatisfied with it since, as they think he ought to have resigned his Office without Reservation; and, from the Spirit which discovers itself amongst all Ranks of People, we have Reason to think this Declaration would not have quieted the Inhabitants, had Mr. Hughes been in better Health. Captain Hawker, having taken the Stamp Papers on board His Majesty Ship, prevents them from being exposed to the Resentment of an injured and enraged People. Thus have we, in some Degree, followed the Example of our */ Fellow /**/Sufferers /* in the neighbouring Colonies; and the cool thinking People among us, congratulate themselves, and their Country, on finding Spirit enough exerted, to put us on the same Footing with the rest of the Continent; and that this was done by Men who had Moderation not to proceed to any unnecessary Acts of Violence. — It may not be amiss to inform the Public, that Mr. Hughes did declare, upon his Honour, he would not receive, or take any Charge of the stamped Papers; and, as we have no Reason to doubt his firm Adherence to any Resolution he makes, we think there is no Danger of their being distributed in this Province." I hoped that things would quiet down, but the lines seemed drawn and the feeling continued to run very high.

I kept thinking about Ernie's question. Was I less fun because I could not see? Was it just that I was older now? I thought back over some of the adventures that I and other apprentices had out on the streets of this exciting city. I decided that my so called lack of fun was just growing up and had nothing to do with my losing my sight.

# 11

# Steven

During late November, Mom received a letter from my elder brother Henry. He informed us that he had been corresponding with a prominent Philadelphia astronomer and clock-maker named David Rittenhouse. Henry was planning a visit to Philadelphia in the near future and depending on that meeting, he might remain in Philadelphia for an extended period of time. Mom was glowing. Slowly her children were returning to the roost.

Mom was so filled with joy after reading Henry's note that she said she was going to walk over to Sarah's and tell her the good news. I decided that Spark and I would accompany her.

Sarah was very glad for Mom, but as Henry was a lot older than she was and had been away so long, she was not glowing the way Mom sounded. She put on a pot of tea and urged us to stay a while.

"Andrew, step out to Daniel's shed. He has a new lad working with him who he is considering as a possible apprentice. I know Daniel wants you to meet him."

As Spark and I entered the pottery, Daniel's cheery greeting filled the air. It was a warm day, but the heat from the kiln made it feel as if we had just stepped into an oven. I guess in a way we had.

"Come in Andrew and meet Steven. He is a new lad who I may have as an apprentice in a year or so if he takes to pottery."

"Greetings Steven," I said holding out my hand. I was surprised when no hand came to take mine. As I was about to withdraw it, Daniel's hand caught my elbow in a firm grip and turned me slightly as he propelled me across the floor. Suddenly a smaller hand was in mine. I was completely surprised when Daniel said, "Steven doesn't see very much better than you do, so I thought I would help you find each other's hands."

"You are considering Steven for an apprenticeship?" I asked. "Why Daniel that is wonderful."

"Yes," he replied. "I have watched how you have worked in my shop and seen the enjoyment in your face when you are working the clay in your hands. I know you wish to stay in the gun trade, but seeing you at my wheel, well, it put me to thinking that, well, pottery might be a good trade for a blind person. Steven's father works over at the Pass & Stow Foundry. A foundry is no place for a blind person, but pottery might be just the thing. Steven is a bit young, but his mother has recently died and he needs a place. I thought he might see if he takes to pottery."

"Daniel, I think that is wonderful!"

Steven was a bit shy and said very little to me on that first visit, but he seemed to be enjoying making a bowl and I wished him well and went back to speak with Sarah and Mom.

Sarah explained how Daniel had thought and thought about it. Although he had never thought of employing a blind person, after seeing me in his shop he had decided he wanted to find a young lad who could not see and give him a chance. He had gone to the Friends Meeting and spoke of it and learned about Steven. Sarah told us that not only had Steven's mother died, but recently his father had been badly hurt in an accident at the foundry. Steven desperately needed a place to be. I was so pleased to learn of Daniel's thoughtfulness as it was almost unheard of for a master of a shop to offer an apprenticeship to a blind lad. When we left Sarah's I stopped again in Daniel's pottery and shook his hand.

"Daniel, you are a good man."

When I reentered the pottery, Daniel had been reading from the *Gazette*. He now said, "Andrew, I have just been reading about the Stamp act in the *Gazette*. Let me share this news with you."

# The Pennsylvania Gazette

**PHILADELPHIA,** November 14.

THE Merchants and Traders of the City of Philadelphia, taking into their Consideration the melancholy State of the North American Commerce in general, and the distressed Situation of the Province of

Pennsylvania in particular, do unanimously agree, THAT the many difficulties they now labour under as a Trading People, are owing to the Restrictions, Prohibitions, and ill advised Regulations, made in the several Acts of the Parliament of Great Britain, lately passed, to regulate the Colonies; which have limited the Exportation of some Part of our Country Produce, increased the Cost and Expense of many Articles of our Importation, and cut off from us all Means of supplying ourselves with Specie enough even to pay the Duties imposed on us, much less to serve as a Medium of our Trade. THAT this Province is heavily in Debt to Great Britain for the Manufacturers, and other Importations, from thence, which the Produce of our Lands have been found unequal to pay for, when a free Exportation of it to the best Markets was allowed of, and such Trades open as supplied us with Cash, and other Articles, of immediate Remittance to Great Britain. THAT the late unconstitutional Law (the Stamp Act) is carried into Execution in this Province, will further tend to prevent our making those Remittances to Great Britain, for Payment of old Debts, or Purchase of more Goods, which the Faith subsisting between the Individuals trading with each other requires; and therefore, in Justice to ourselves, to the Traders of Great Britain, who usually give us Credit, and to the Consumers of British Manufactures in this Province, the Subscribers hereto, have voluntarily and unanimously come into the following Resolutions and Agreements, in Hopes that their Example will stimulate the good People of this Province to be frugal in the Use and Consumption of all Manufactures, excepting those of America, and lawful Goods coming directly from Ireland, manufactured there, whilst the Necessities of our Country are such as to require it; and in Hopes that their Brethren, the Merchants and Manufacturers of Great Britain, will find their own

Interest so intimately connected with ours, that they will be spurred on to befriend us from that Motive, if no other should take Place.    FIRST. It is unanimously Resolved and Agreed, that in all Orders, any of the Subscribers to this Paper may send to Great Britain for Goods, they shall and will direct their Correspondents not to ship them until the STAMP ACT is repealed.    SECONDLY. That all those amongst the Subscribers that have already sent Orders to Great Britain for Goods, shall and will immediately countermand the same, until the STAMP ACT is repealed. Except such Merchants as are Owners of Vessels already gone, or now cleared out for Great Britain, who are at Liberty to bring back in them, on their own Accounts, Coals, Casks of Earthen Ware, Grindstones, Pipes, Iron Pots, Empty Bottles, and such other bulky Articles, as Owners usually fill up their Ships with, but no Dry Goods of any Kind, except such kind of Dye Stuffs and Utensils necessary for carrying on Manufactures, that may be ordered by any Person. THIRDLY. That none of the Subscribers hereto, shall or will vend any Goods or Merchandizes whatever, that shall be shipped them on Commission from Great Britain, after the First of January next, unless the STAMP ACT be repealed. FOURTHLY. That these Resolves and Agreements shall be binding on all and each of us the Subscribers, who do hereby, each and every Person for himself, upon his Word of Honour, agree, that he will strictly and firmly adhere to, and abide by, every Article from this Time, until the First Day of May next, when a Meeting of the Subscribers shall be called, to consider whether the further Continuance of this Obligation be then necessary. FIFTHLY. It is agreed, that if Goods of any Kind to arrive from Great Britain at such Time, or under such Circumstances, as to render any Signer of this Agreement suspected of having broke his Promises, the Committee now appointed shall enquire into the Premises, and if such suspected Person refuses, or cannot give them Satisfaction, the Subscribers hereto will unanimously take all prudent Measures to discountenance and prevent the Sale of such Goods, until they are released from this Agreement by mutual and general Consent. LASTLY. As it may be necessary that a Committee of the Subscribers be appointed to wait on the Traders of this City, to get this present Agreement generally subscribed, the following Gentlemen are appointed for that Purpose, viz. Thomas Willing, and Samuel Mifflin, Esquires; Thomas Montgomery, Samuel Howell, Samuel Wharton, John Rhea, William Fisher, Joshua Fisher, Peter Chevalier, Benjamin Fuller, and Abel James. (The above is signed by above 400 Traders.)

Waving the paper excitedly in the air, his voice filled with emotion, Daniel continued reading.

WE the Retailers of the City of Philadelphia, at a General Meeting, taking into Consideration the melancholy State of the North American Commerce in general, and the distressed Situation of the Province of Pennsylvania in particular, occasioned by the late unconstitutional Law (the STAMP ACT) if carried into Execution, do hereby voluntarily and unanimously promise and oblige all and each of us, upon our Word of Honour, not to buy any Goods, Wares or Merchandizes, of any Vendue master, or other Person or Persons whatsoever, that shall be shipped from Great Britain after the First Day of January next, unless that unconstitutional Law (the STAMP ACT) shall be repealed; excepting such Goods and Merchandizes as shall be approved and allowed of by the Committee of Merchants nominated and appointed for that Purpose, and all lawful Goods coming directly from Ireland, manufactured there.   The above to be binding on us till the First Day of May next, at which Time we purpose another General Meeting, to consider whether the further Continuance of this Obligation be necessary. As Witness our Hands, &c.   The following Gentlemen are appointed to wait on the Retailers of this City, to get the above Agreement generally subscribed to, viz. John Ord, Francis Wade, Joseph Deane, David Dashler, George Bartram, Andrew Doz, George Schlosser, James Hunter, Thomas Paschall, Thomas West, and Valentine Charles."

"Daniel, that is a little difficult to follow, but do you think too much is being made about this stamp act?" I asked him.

"Oh no Andrew. This is a very serious issue. This tax must not be allowed to stand," he replied.

I had never enjoyed the political discussions that took place in the coffee-houses and did not wish to get into such a discussion with Daniel, especially as I had stopped to tell him what a great thing he was doing for Steven. Taking my leave I returned to our shop and continued filing some brass trigger-guards that I was cleaning up from the sand-cast mold. We obtained all of our brass cast parts such as trigger-guards and butt-plates from James Smith BRASS FOUNDER, who had lately moved from Front street, and now carries on his Business at the North End of Fourth street, at the Sign of the Bell. He makes and sells all Sorts of Brass Work, large and small.

# 12

## The Map

One day in late November, the door of the shop opened and Nick the tinker walked in.

"Greetings my friend! I thought I might find you here working at your bench," he called as he entered.

Nick was an old friend who I had first met while I had been in Carlisle. Working as a Tinker and peddler, he worked independently, but often traveled with the army. We had been together during Forbes' campaign back in 1758 and again with Colonel Bouquet when he led a column to relieve Fort Pitt during Pontiac's rebellion. We had both taken part in the battle of Bushy Run in August of 1763. As a tinker, Nick was a very handy fellow. He seemed to be able to repair most things as well as having a rapacious store of goods for sale that he produced from time to time out of his enormous pack. During the next year, I had seen him off and on although he had not been at Fort Pitt during the autumn of 1764 when the explosion had taken place. He approached my bench and shook my hand warmly.

"It is so very good to see you again," he said.

"What brings you to Philadelphia at this time old friend?" I asked.

He explained that he had returned to restock many of the small items that he carried and had just been over to William Shewards and bought a new stock of his fine sewing needles. "Can never have too many sewing needles. They love them on the frontier. Also got some of his fine fish hooks. They are better than any I have ever come across. While in town I also wish to get a good supply of brass buttons. I understand that Caspar Wistar sells the very finest brass buttons in Philadelphia. There is also a fellow named John Balthus who has very fine shoe buckles. One can usually find a shoemaker on the frontier, but a good pair of brass shoe buckles, well, they are few and far between. I stopped in here as I thought you might have some good English gun flints. I was so saddened to learn of the explosion. Damn careless it was! I am so very pleased to see you doing so well."

Thanking him for his interest and concern, I asked him if he had been over to deal with Abraham Kiessel. I had just understood that the Ship Margarete Anne had recently arrived from London and Abraham had many new things to offer that Nick might wish to consider adding to his stock of trade items.

"Don't believe I know merchant Kiessel," he replied.

"Then we must see that you meet him," I said, removing my leather apron and hanging it on a peg at the end of my bench. "Let us get you those flints and then we will walk over to the sign of the Key & crown and I shall introduce you. Abraham is an honest man with fair prices." Smiling, I said, "He will be the first to tell you so."

Moving over to a cabinet that ran along one wall of the shop, I pulled out a wide shallow drawer where we kept the gun flints. It was divided into compartments by thin wooden slats which acted like partitions. The flints were neatly sorted by sizes. Beginning at the left end of the drawer were the smallest flints which were used in small pocket pistols. The next compartment held flints used in either large saddle pistols, rifles or fouling-pieces. The compartment all of the way to the right held the largest musket flints.

"Take your pick old friend," I offered. We spent a little time sorting through the flints to find the ones with the best shape and having good edges on them. Nick chose several dozen and I put them into small sacks that Mom sewed for just such purchases.

Reaching for my coat, I called to Spark to join us. She had been sleeping under my bench, but as soon as I lifted her harness from its peg, she bounded over.

"What is this?" Nick asked.

"Nick, meet Spark! She is the smartest and best dog in the world. She is a big help to me in getting about the city," I commented. Nick said that he had known animals that were smarter than many folks he knew and was glad to learn that I had found one that would help me. I told him Spark's story. How Sarah had given Spark to me and how much help she had come to be.

Walking down 3rd Street, crossing Arch, Market and Chestnut Streets, Nick hung back to watch Spark work.

As we reached Church Alley, I stopped and asked if he were planning to take back any tools as we were passing Samuel Caruther's shop. Samuel was a tool maker who was an old friend of Dad's.

"Why yes, of course if I can get a good deal on some."

"You will find none better than right here at the sign of the plane and saw."

As I was telling him this, he had just seen and began to read aloud from an advertisement cut from the *Pennsylvania Gazette* which was pasted in the window of Samuel's shop. It listed many of the tools and other items that were carried within.

SAMUEL CARUTHERS, PLANE MAKER, At the Sign of the */Carpenter /* Plane and Hand Saw, the third door above Church Alley, in Third street, Continued to make all sorts of planes, his work having recommended itself these twenty years in this city. He has on hand the following articles, viz. mill, pitt, cross cut, steel plate, hand, pannel, tennat, sash, dovetail, compass and key hole saws, turning ditto, iron plate hand ditto, steel plate wood cutters ditto, with or without frames, iron plate ditto, at a low price, both whet and set, and by the dozen for exportation, carpenters axes, adzes, iron squares, socket chizels and gouges, and all other sorts and sizes of chizels, firmers and gouges, different sizes of hatchets, shingling ditto, different sizes of kentish and common claw hammers, all sorts of gimblets, best box brass joint two feet rules, with or without sliders, common ditto, four fold box yards, different sizes of steel point compasses, pinchers, nippers, bench plane irons, all sizes of soft moulding plane irons, tough ditto, Turkey oil stones, (the SCOTCH STONE, so often asked for by carpenters, joiners, scriveners, &c. is now come to hand,) best Barlow penknives, steel muzzles brace stocks, with a number of polished bits sorted, common low priced brace stocks, woth pods, English glue, all sorts of bright and common augers saw sets, saw handles and screws, an assortment of wood screws, bed screws, center, pinning, doweling, spinning wheel and chair makers bitts, a general assortment (by retail) of nails, springs and tacks, turning chizels and gouges, London brick trowels, plastering ditto, lathing hammers, coopers double and single mouthjointers, block planes, croze stocks, brace stocks, axes, adzes, howels, drawing knives, vizes, bung and tap borers, bow compasses, from 9 to 13 inches, &c. smith anvils, vizes, beak irons, pinchers, rubbers, a variety of files, rests &c. shoemakers knives, hammers, pinchers, nippers, size sticks dotted, awl blades, stitching, common, and pegging awl ditto, &c. gun locks, a few guns, pushing files, silvered and common coffin handle, letters and figures, a neat assortment of brass mounting for chests of drawers and desks, desk setts, brass H hinges, brass knockers and cocks, brass wire, brass balled candlesticks and snuffers, brass curtain rings, brass dividers, brass screws for sashes, pullies and sash lines, 3 bolt brass chamber door locks, from 5 to 8 inches, 2 bolt ditto, from 5 to 7 inches, iron rimmed locks, from 4 to 7 inches, ditto draw back, double bolt padlocks, several sizes of hanging locks, and splinter padlocks, portmantua ditto, different sorts and sizes of chest, trunk, box and till locks, too tedious to mention, egg knob and thumb latches, different sizes of flat and round bolts, also a bolt that commands the chamber door, without rising from the bed or chair, and answers a call for servants, HL hinges from 4 to 12 inches, H ditto from 3 to 8 inches, different sizes of T hinges, strap, chest and box hinges, small hooks and hinges, ivory, red ebony and common table knives and forks, brass and iron headed fire shovels and tongs, chamber and common bellows, pistol tinder boxes, flat irons, coffee mills, English, straw cutting knives, a few iron pots, from 9 to 16 gallons, roasting jacks, frying pans, iron plating, iron traces for sleighs, carts and wagons, a small assortment of cutlery, &c.

"I must stop back here and acquire some of these tools to take back with me," Nick said.

"Then let us step inside now and I shall introduce you to Samuel Caruther. As I told you he is an old friend of Dad's and I have known him these many years. I am certain you will like him."

Entering the shop, Nick continued to gaze about at the vast array of inventory that Samuel carried and offered for sale. Samuel had begun many years ago here in Philadelphia making tools. Dad said that Samuel's tools were very well made and any artisan should be proud to have and use them.

Over the years, Samuel made fewer and fewer of the tools himself, but had several apprentices working in the back room. He had expanded into carrying and offering for sale the wide variety that was now in the shop. Many of these items were imported from England or Holland, but increasingly, Samuel liked to carry items made here in this country. As Nick peered about, I listened to Samuel's gruff voice as he finished up with another customer.

Finally he quietly walked up to us.

"Good day Andrew. What brings you out to my shop this day? Has my old friend Master Frederick sent you for some item that I might have?"

"Good day Samuel. I would like you to meet my friend Nick the Tinker. He is in town getting together some items to take west with him. I wanted you to meet him as I am sure that he will find many interesting items of quality here."

"Indeed he will. I have just this day received a shipment of Barlow knives from England. They are a wonderfully made folding pocket knife. Perfect to take with you to the western frontier. I have been importing them for over a dozen years now and never a complaint."

He handed us each one of the well made Barlow knives. They felt good in the hand and appeared strongly made. I decided to purchase several myself there and then. I thought they would make fine Christmas gifts to give to both Will and Ernie. An hour rapidly slipped away as Nick and Samuel looked at items and examined their fine points. Nick was a craftsman in his own right and appreciated finely made tools and good materials. Leaving a list of items that he wanted, Nick promised to return the following day. we then continued on to Abraham Kiessel's shop. Approaching the sign of the key & crown, Nick declared how impressed he was with Spark.

As we entered the shop, a man in a rush pushed past and quickly disappeared down Chestnut Street. Nick bent down and picked up a torn piece of paper saying. "That rude son of a bitch dropped something."

Abraham came forward and greeted us warmly.

"Don't mind him. That was Jack Stoner. He is in a great hurry," said Abraham.

"Abraham, are you dealing with Mr. Stoner? I understand he is a smuggler," I said.

"A smuggler?" replied Abraham. "I would rather think of him as a man of business," he continued.

"Call him what you wish, he's still a rude son of a bitch," said Nick as he smoothed out the paper that he had just picked up. Quickly glancing at it, he frowned and slid it into his pocket.

After introducing Nick to Abraham and explaining his mission, I left them together. As I left Abraham's shop, I heard him enthusiastically explaining that he had just received a shipment of candles from Providence Rhode Island.

"Everyone knows that the finest candles in the Colonies are made in Providence Rhode Island," boomed Abraham as the door closed behind me.

Nick had promised that he would stop back to the gun shop when he had completed his business and we would stroll over to the Indian Queen Tavern on Water Street where he was lodging and enjoy a dinner together while catching up on news from the frontier.

Returning to the gun shop I found Will examining a large brass barreled blunderbuss that we had taken into the shop a few weeks earlier. It was a lovely, well made Dutch weapon, having a bell mouthed brass barrel of about 18 inches in length. The breech was octagonal. After a few wedding-ring turnings, the barrel continued round. Although it was only 69 caliber, the bell mouth made it appear as if it were a cannon. The purpose of a bell mouth muzzle on such a weapon was for ease of loading, but it also served to have an intimidating effect upon anyone unfortunate enough to be looking down it. It was stocked in walnut with the pinched look about the comb so reminiscent of a Brown Bess musket. It was the type of weapon used by mail-coach guards because of its short handy length brass barrel and deadly effect, popular with boarding parties aboard ship at sea. When it had come into the shop, I had commented laughingly that it was the perfect weapon for a blind person, as one could hardly miss one's target with it.

"I might be wishing to borrow this little canon this evening," Will commented.

"Why would you be needing a blunderbuss such as that this evening?" I asked him.

"Well, one never knows what might happen on these city streets late at night," he replied. Often when I stepped out in the evening, I took with me under my coat or cloak, the single brass barreled saddle pistol that I had brought home with me from Fort Pitt. I kept it loaded with shot and thought of it as a very good weapon for my own self protection. My brush with Jack Stoner a few minutes earlier reminded me of Will's acquaintance with that individual.

"I just ran into your friend Jack Stoner. Well, actually, he ran into me as I was entering Abraham's shop. Could he have anything to do with your need of such a weapon?" I asked him. Will laughed and said Jack is always in a hurry. "He is most likely trying to get Abraham to commit to taking part of the deal Jack is currently arranging. Actually, you may be interested in a little part of it yourself."

"I somehow do not think I want to be involved in any dealings with Mr. Stoner."

"Well, this one you might, as it has to do with a substantial amount of coffee beans from South America. Jack can arrange these things, but he has no warehouse and needs to move things along and out of his hands quickly. If a Captain reports the loss of a part or all of his cargo, it does not look good to drive about the city with a wagonload of the same kind of cargo. Abraham has lots of storage and might be able to help Jack out." Will explained quietly. He spoke in a soft voice and there was no longer a trace of laughter in his voice. I urged Will to stay clear of such a questionable venture.

Several customers wandered into the shop at that moment and nothing more was spoken of concerning Mr. Stoner, and his business interests.

Later Nick reappeared as promised and we set off for the Indian Queen Tavern.

"Thank you old friend for introducing me to both of those fellows. However, now you have cost me a bit more money as I have agreed to buy so many items that I will have to purchase a pack horse or two to carry everything back."

"Well, if you need horses, try William Fall down on Locust Street. He is an honest man and I am sure he will be fair to deal with."

Before taking up the tinker's trade, Nick had spent several years at sea. He was very comfortable about the docks. He could switch from backwoods man to sailor in the blink of an eye. The Indian Queen Tavern was on Water Street near the docks and was a favorite of sailors and watermen of all types. Nick was an old friend who I had shared many adventures with during my days with the British Army. Although we had not spoken in over a year, we fell into conversation as if we had only spoken weeks earlier. The Indian Queen Tavern was only a few squares away and we reached it quickly. During our walk Nick commented with great praise on Sparks' ability to guide me around piles of nasty things in the streets as well as over broken or rough areas.

It was November and the evening air was cold and the wind had come up sharply. Nick commented that he thought we might have a heavy storm soon. We would both be glad when we stepped into the warmth of the front room of this old tavern. It had a large painted sign of an Indian princess above the walkway in front of the tavern. The wind was making the sign creak and groan as it swung on its rusted chains. As we pushed the door open, we were greeted with a mixture of warm air laden with pipe smoke, cooking smells, and laughter. I did not often come here as it was a bit of a rough tavern, but Nick assured me the food was good and the tavern wenches were both comely and friendly. This proved to be the case. After we settled into a corner table out of the way and where it might be a bit quieter, Nick introduced me to a serving wench named Rebecca. Nick's description of the wenches here as friendly certainly was correct. When Rebecca leaned over my shoulder to take my dinner order, she made sure I could tell what a nice shape she had, as well as a pleasant voice. As she walked away from the table, Nick assured me that she was as fine to look upon as I may have come to think from her introduction while taking my order.

The evening passed very pleasantly. The dinner was very good and we followed it up with several glasses of rum. Frequently Rebecca returned to see if we needed anything. She repeatedly assured us that she was there to serve us.

Our conversation ranged over many topics. These included people we had both known, places we had been to, and, the about to be enforced stamp taxes. Nick was not too concerned with the stamp taxes as he traded so far out on the frontier that it was unlikely that anyone would actually take much notice of them. After Rebecca had left the table, having delivered a final round of rum, Nick drew from his pocket the paper that Jack Stoner had dropped in the doorway of Abraham Kiessel's shop. Smoothing it on the table, he said that although it was crudely drawn, it appeared to him to be a kind of map. It showed Delaware Bay and River as well as several coves along the Jersey coast. The map showed small waterways crossing the lower part of that Colony with Cape May at the far edge of the map. Names written in next to some of the lines gave understanding to what was a less than artistic rendering.

I explained that I believed from what I had heard that Mr. Stoner might be involved in a smuggling venture having to do with coffee beans from South America.

I also thought that, if in fact, that map showed some of the smuggling routes across South Jersey, it might not even be healthy to keep it.

After settling our account with Rebecca and receiving a last invitation to stay, Nick insisted on walking back to the shop with Spark and me. He said he had a bit more business to complete in the city, but would stop by before heading west again. Climbing the steep stairway to our loft, I heard Ernie stirring.

"Will was in earlier this evening. He left with that Dutch Brass-barreled blunderbuss. The one that he spoke with you about. If all went well, he said he would pay for it in a few days."

"Oh, no! Yes, he was in this afternoon and said he wanted to borrow it, but I was not sure he meant it. I hope he stays out of trouble. I do not mind him having the blunderbuss, but if he uses it, someone is going to get hurt or killed." Little did I know that both would actually happen.

Will did not come by the shop the next day, nor the day after. I was becoming increasingly worried about him. There had not been any rumor of anyone getting shot or hurt, so I hoped for the best and tried to focus on a stocking project that I was working on. I was making up a pair of dueling pistols. All of the metal parts were finished. I was trying to make a pair of stocks in cherry wood. The trick was to get them the same so that they would look like a pair when they were finished. This is trickier than it sounds, and took all my concentration. On the third day, Nick reentered the shop and said he was on his way out of the city headed west again. He wished me all of the best and said he might not be back this way for a year or more. We shook hands warmly and he was on his way.

As he reached the door, I asked, "Nick, by the way, did you get rid of that map?"

"Map? Oh, that map that Stoner fellow dropped? Yeah, the strangest thing. When I returned to the Indian Queen after walking you back here, an old waterman with only one hand and a large scar on the left side of his face, looked like an old sword or cutlass wound, came up to me and told me that Rebecca had seen us looking at a map; and wondered if I would sell it to him? Well, I had been about to throw it away, so I wondered what he would offer. He said he owned a share in the tavern and that he knew I had a bill at the tavern for several nights and he would take care of it for me if I gave him the map. We called the innkeeper over and when he agreed to the arrangement, I gave scar face the map and that was the last that I have heard of it. Did you want the map?"

"No, I just wondered. Be safe my friend." The door closed and he was on his way. Will did not reappear for another two weeks. Spark and I had walked over to his sister's tavern to inquire if he was well. His sister Gwynne could only tell me that he had told her he might be away for a few days, but she knew, or would say, nothing more.

Finally one day the shop door swung open and there stood Will. He came in carrying a large bag of coffee beans which he said was a gift for allowing him to borrow the blunderbuss. He also said that he now wished to buy the blunderbuss and had silver with him to do so. He said it had saved his life. It seemed that Jack had arranged to receive a load of coffee in Cape May. He had a good size canoe and would bring the coffee across South Jersey by that fashion, making several trips. If Will helped him paddle he would pay him in silver as soon as he sold the cargo. All had gone well until two people ambushed them as they were almost to the Delaware River. Jack had been shot in the side and could not paddle. Will had sat there waiting until the two came up to him. Thinking that he was blind and was no threat, they were surprised when Will raised the blunderbuss and blew one in half. The other who had been standing nearby had also been wounded but managed to limp away. Jack could not paddle, but could direct Will and they had been able to reach the Pennsylvania shore after a long time. Jack said it had been dark, so he did not get a good look at either of them. He did know that the one who shot him only had one hand and that he thought he looked like someone he had seen down at the docks. The other was dead for sure as he took most of the blast from Will's blunderbuss in the body from only a few feet away. The one handed man had certainly been hit, but had limped off into the darkness after dropping his pistol. Jack planned to paddle back over there when he was better, to see if he could learn anything more. In the meantime, Abraham had taken in the coffee bags from the canoe and would keep things quiet. Will said, "So you can see how the blunderbuss saved me. I only wished I had killed both of them."

Inviting Ernie to accompany Spark and myself, we left to take our dinner at the Indian Queen Tavern that night. If Rebecca was there, I thought I might find out whom the gentleman was who bought Nick's map.

The tavern was just as busy as it had been when I had been there with Nick. Fortunately we were not there long before Rebecca appeared and lightly rubbing against my arm, said, "Thought you might be back. Where is your other friend?"

"He has gone back to western parts. I am wondering if you could tell me who the fellow was who you told about Nick's map."

"Oh you must mean Timothy Leamy. He has just died of a gunshot wound. The poor man has had the worst luck. He had that awful scar on his face from a fight on a ship. Then he lost a hand unloading some cargo. A few nights ago, he said that he was attacked by some thieves down near the docks and when he had nothing to give them, they just shot him! He managed to crawl here, but died a few hours later. It is terrible dangerous out there near the docks at night."

We finished our dinners and left. Ernie had wanted to stay as he said Rebecca was very good to look at. I assured him she was trouble and that we had to go. He wondered why I wanted to know about some old waterman, but I told him it was a long story. The next time that I saw Will, I told him that I was fairly certain that he had gotten his wish. When he asked me what I was talking about, I reminded him that when telling me of his shooting one of the thieves with the blunderbuss, he had said that he wished he had killed both of them.

Relating to him the whole story, I said that I had thought he had wounded Leamy badly enough with the blast that he had died not long after. Will asked me how I had learned all of this, and I told him of Nick's finding the map, our visit to the Indian Queen Tavern and my belief that a young woman named Rebecca had known a great deal of what was going on there. I also told him of the visit Ernie and I had made to the Indian Queen to learn more from Rebecca. He asked me if I would introduce him to Rebecca. I told him that I would not, but thought he would find her on his own if he really wished to do so. I learned later that Jack had acquired much too much coffee to bring over in one canoe load. Jack was not well enough to paddle, but had hired John Cooper, who with Will, was going to make several more trips.

John Cooper was a very likeable, quiet spoken laborer from the docks. He had one eye as a result of a tavern brawl years earlier. He lived in a boarding house down on Spruce Street. John had no certain trade, but was always willing to put his hand to anything that he could earn a shilling doing. He had grown up in England and had been convicted of horse stealing in Liverpool. He had told me once that it was all a big mistake as anyone who knew his old horse Dobbin would agree that one he found looked exactly like him. Thinking that old Dobbin had come back to life, John had taken him with him to care for his old horse. Having been convicted of horse stealing, John had been transported to Georgia, which was a penal Colony.

Somehow as the ship arrived at the dock in Georgia John said he had fallen overboard and when finally reaching shore, was not certain where he was supposed to go. He had walked all of the way to Philadelphia and now worked off and on at the docks.

John had little interest in our weapons, but often visited our shop on an errand for other tradesmen. He was now in the shop as Jack Stoner had asked him to find out if he could hire Ernie to make a few trips with John and Will. Dad was out at the time, but I told him that Ernie was not allowed to go.

"We do not hire out our apprentices to take part in smuggling ventures," I said.

The more I learned about this entire plan of Jack Stoner's, the less I liked the sound of it. Wishing that my friends were not involved in it I went back to my work.

The pair of dueling pistol stocks that I had been working on took all of my attention and I took little note when the shop door opened. Ernie was there and he would take care of any customers who might wander in. I paid little notice as Ernie asked, "Can I help you Miss?"

In a few minutes, a small voice spoke to me from across my bench.

"Master Andrew, can you help me?"

Stopping the cuts I had been making with the chisel, I tried to remember where I had heard that voice.

"Master Andrew, do you remember me?"

"I am not the master of this shop," I replied setting down my chisel.

"That is what we called you at Fort Pitt. Don't you remember me from Fort Pitt? Don't you remember Freddy Baker the drummer boy for the 60th?"

Now the voice registered.

"Is that you Freddy?" I asked.

"Yes sir and I need your help. I have run away and am trying to get over the river to my mother's home in the Jerseys. I tried to stay with my brother Bartholomew. He is an inn-keeper on Market Street, but he will have nothing to do with me. He does not like how I have dressed to hide here in the city."   I did remember the lad. He had always been getting picked on by the soldiers as he was a frail little creature. In fact several of the soldiers had referred to him as their little girl. I Remembered Ernie addressing him as "Miss" when he had entered the shop. Apparently he had run away and was hiding here in Philadelphia dressed as a young woman. Weeks ago I remembered Mom reading an article to me from the *Gazette* that concerned this very person. She had wondered if I knew the person since he had been in the 60th Royal Americans.

Philadelphia, May 20, 1765
EIGHT   DOLLARS   Reward.   DESERTED   the 4th Inst. from His Majesty First Battalion, 60th or Royal American Regiment, Frederick Baker, a Lad about 15 Years of Age, of a fair Complexion, and pretty well set; had on, when he deserted, his Regimentals for a fifer, having listed some Time ago for that Purpose at Lancaster; he has a Brother, named Bartholomew Baker, a */Tavern /* Keeper, that lives in Market street, Philadelphia, and his Mother lives a little Way over in the Jerseys; one of which

Places it is supposed he is concealed at. Whoever will give Information where said Deserter is concealed, or have him secured in any of His MajestyGoals, and will give Notice to Captain PROVOST, in New York, or Mr. FRANCIS WADE, in Philadelphia, shall receive the above Reward, exclusive of His Majesty Bounty for taking up Deserters.

"Freddy, I am sorry; I can not be helping deserters from the 60$^{th}$. This is not a good place for you to be as Officers of the Crown are in and out of here every day. I will not turn you in, but really, you should leave.

John Cooper, who was still speaking with Will, now stepped over to my bench.

"Perhaps I can help you. But Andrew is right; this is not a good place for you to be seen. Why don't you come with me?"

They left together and I had a feeling that John had just found a third person to help with the canoe paddling.

The next time John came into the shop, I inquired if he had been able to help the runaway. After a moment, he replied that he had no knowledge of any runaways, but if I was referring to a young lady who had not long ago been in the shop seeking aid crossing the Delaware, he believed she had been successful in reaching the Jerseys. Smiling, I said that it had been very gentlemanly of him to help her.

"You are wrong on both counts. I am no gentleman and I did not say that I helped her," John said as he left the shop.

# 13

# Fire Aboard the Three Friends

December was very cold that year, but the shop was a pleasant and cheerful place to work. Ernie kept the fire well stoked as Dad always seemed to be cold these days. Life had settled into a kind of peaceful rhythm. The pair of pistol stocks that I had been working on were turning out well. I was so pleased one day when Dad looked at them and said that they were not too bad. This was high praise from him indeed.

Henry's visit had been postponed as he had written that Uncle Ebenezer was not well. He had developed a terrible cough and spent most of his time in bed. Henry did not feel he should leave until his dear Uncle was better. Then in mid December, Mom received a letter from Henry saying that Uncle Ebenezer had taken a turn for the worse and after having a high fever and being mostly unconscious for two days had slipped away and died in his sleep. There was a great deal for Henry to do in Elizabeth, but in a few months, after he had taken care of things, he still planned to come to Philadelphia. In fact, now more than ever, he thought he might move back and establish himself nearby. Mom was very saddened about the passing of her only older brother, but was somewhat cheered by the fact that another of her sons might be returning home. Before long it was almost Christmas. I suddenly realized that I had been back home an entire year. I felt I had made great progress in adjusting to not seeing. Spark continued to be a wonderful help and a good companion as well.

For days before Christmas, Mom was busy planning and preparing her usual Christmas feast. Little Dorothy was one year old and Seth five. Sarah and the children were often over visiting. Sarah had been helping Dad keep the shop books and Seth acted as if he was running the shop. I marveled at the tolerance Dad showed toward him. When Seth handled the tools roughly Dad asked him to stop and put them down as what he was doing was not good for the tools. I smiled to myself thinking that when Henry and I had been smaller and had not handled the tools carefully, a swift clout followed by a sharp command to "stop!" was the general rule. I pointed this out to Ernie as yet another sign of Dad's aging. Ernie simply laughed and went on with his work.

The Christmas feast was a great success. This year Ernie bit into Mom's plum pudding and found the Silver shilling. Seth was delighted with a small wagon that Dad had made for him. Ernie was very pleased with his new Barlow knife. Several days before Christmas, Will had stopped by and told me quietly that he might be away for a few days helping Jack Stoner with another project. I asked if he and John were to be paddling across New Jersey again. He told me that this was much closer to home, but that he could not say more. He did not want us to be concerned if he did not come by on Christmas day. I gave him the Barlow knife then and thought he was very touched. He said it was the best knife he had ever had. I cautioned him to be careful and wished him well.

The day after Christmas, Mom read an article to me from the *Gazette* concerning a ship fire. Somehow I had a very bad feeling that Will and possibly John were involved.

**PHILADELPHIA**, December 26.
On Thursday Morning last the Schooner Three Friends, William Smith Master, lying in one of our Docks, was discovered to be on */Fire /*, when a Number of the Inhabitants immediately assembled, and got it extinguished, without any Noise being then made about the Affair. But, in the Evening of that Day, the same Vessel was hauled off into the Stream, and about Three o'clock the next Morning, was seen to be on */Fire /* again from the Shore; upon which the Alarm was given, and some Boats were immediately manned with Ship Carpenters, who went to her Assistance, and on going aboard, found only one Man (Smith) in the Vessel, who seemed a good Deal confused, and appeared to be in Liquor, the Vessel burning very violently, with the Hatches shut, which were immediately opened; they then cut away her Foremast, scuttled her, cut the Cable, and towed her ashore on the Bar, by which the */Fire /* was suppressed —- The People staid by her till Daylight, when some of her Cargoes was brought ashore, in very strong Boxes, well nailed up, which, on being opened, the Contents proved to be nothing else but Pieces of Rozin, Rozin Staves, some Pewter, a few Silk Handkerchiefs, and Straw, packed up together. Of these Sort

of Boxes, there were several on board, all filled with the same Sort of Cargoes; and no other kind of Goods found in the Vessel —- This occasioning some Suspicions that all was not right, but that something base was intended by somebody, the Person that passed for the Owner of the Vessel; a Foreigner, who was also concerned; and the Captain, were all taken up, and carried before the Chief Justice, who, after Examination, ordered them to Goal, where they now remain —- The Vessel was got off the Bar, but much damaged.

Will did not visit the shop for almost two weeks. Each day my suspicions that he and possibly John Cooper may have been involved deepened. Then one day, there he was.

"Will, where have you been?" I asked.

"Sometimes it is not the best to ask of a person's recent activities, or their place of lodging."

"Were you involved with the burning of the ship the Three Friends?"

"As I said, some things are best forgotten."

Later, he commented to me that in fact he had been out for a walk that morning with Jack Stoner. They had gone aboard the vessel to visit with the Master when the ship caught fire. Jack had recently owned the ship. Jack was very concerned about the fire and had gone ashore, leaving Will aboard with the Master. He just happened to be aboard when the second fire broke out.

"Will, why would you have wanted to be a part of such a venture?" I asked.

"Andrew, we have discussed these matters before. You have a family and a living here. I do live in my sister's tavern, but I must make my way in the world the best that I can. Gwynne's husband does not really like me being there and makes it hard for Gwynne. Stoner is not a good person, but he makes it possible for me to put a bit aside so that someday I may be able to escape. Besides, having friends such as Mr. Stoner keeps Ephraim worried enough that he may not harm Gwynne any more."

"Has he harmed her?" I asked.

"She will only say that she fell on the stairs of the tavern, but I believe Ephraim has done things to her I would rather not think about. When he is drinking with some of his fellows at the tavern bar, he forgets that he is the landlord and joins the customers. While I was away, he was on one of his benders. Gwynne says he thinks I had something to do with the fire on the Three Friends."

"Well, didn't you?"

"Oh Andrew, I have told you it did not work out quite as well as I had hoped," Will commented.

"What were you trying to accomplish?"

"Jack had a big financial interest in the Vessel. He had taken it in payment for a debt. Just before Christmas, he had sold it to Don Carlo. Jack had received a very good price for the ship and did not want Don Carlo to learn that her bottom was badly rotted and that she could never make another voyage."

"You mean he cheated Don Carlo and was afraid he would get caught?" I asked.

"Andrew, I have told you before, you have a dark way of looking at situations that make things look bad. The magistrate locked Don Carlo up suspecting that he had tried to burn his ship for the insurance money."

"It was heavily insured?" I asked.

"No, that is the problem. Don Carlo was still trying to arrange for the insurance inspection and when it burned, well, the poor man had no insurance. Jack knew the ship would never pass a real inspection. Now he hopes the ship is so badly burned it will be hard to prove anything, we hope."

"Why or how were you involved?" I asked.

"Jack got Smith the ship's Master drunk and left me aboard so Jack could be seen ashore when the fires broke out. He and John Cooper came out with the carpenters and we disappeared over into the Jerseys. Don Carlo has been in jail, but soon he may be out."

"Does Don Carlo know you and Jack were involved?" I asked.

"Andrew, let us hope not!" Will said.

Don Carlo was released when he was able to prove that he had no insurance and nothing to gain. The Master Smith took the blame for being careless and not taking care of the ship. He left the city soon thereafter. Jack disappeared into the Jerseys. I think over to Cape May, and Will returned to his normal activities. He had received a goodly some of cash in gold from Stoner for his part in the "Three Friends" burning, but did not want to have it appear as if he had suddenly come into gold at the time of the fire. John Cooper told me that I should not be concerned about how

Jack obtained Don Carlo's gold and had then shared it with Will and John. It was not as if Jack had really cheated Don Carlo. Jack had said that Don Carlo was an evil man who had made the gold in some dishonest and nefarious way. It was simple Justice to help Don Carlo to give up his ill-gotten gains. Telling him that this sounded a bit like his old Dobbin story, he laughed and agreed, but said it had a much better ending.

# 14

## Ephraim Meets His Just Dessert

As the weeks passed, Will seemed to be in a dark mood. I thought he was worried about Don Carlo returning to make some mischief. When I asked him about this, he said that was not the problem. He told me that he was increasingly worried about his sister. Ephraim was continuing to hurt her and Will was getting more and more angry.

One day early in February, he came into the shop bleeding and badly hurt. He told us that he had had a fight with Ephraim over the way he was treating his sister and Ephraim had punched and kicked him repeatedly and told him never to return to his tavern. Will had continued to try to fight, but as a blind person fighting against a large angry Landlord who had been drinking he had little chance. Finally he had been knocked out and awakened in the gutter where Ephraim had thrown his unconscious body.

Ernie and I took Will next door where Mom helped clean up his cuts and bruises. I had Ernie make up another bed in our loft above the gun-shop where we slept and when Mom had done what she could, Ernie and I carried Will to the loft.

I had been disturbed to learn that Will's sister was being abused by her husband Ephraim, but did not know what could be done about it. Mom sent good soups and meals over for Will and in about a week, he was able to come back downstairs. During the time he had been laid up in our loft, his sister Gwynne had come to ask us if we knew where he was. Ernie said Gwynne did not look to well herself with many bruises. She would not say that Ephraim had beaten her, but she was very worried about her brother. Mom took her next door and they had a long woman-to-woman chat. She urged us not to let Will come back to the tavern as Ephraim had said the next time that blind son of a bitch put his face in the tavern, he would kill him.

Will's friend John Cooper came by almost every day. I had the feeling that they were hatching up something between them. Little did I know how right I was. One day while Dad was out, I heard Ernie grinding something on the big grindstone out in the forge. When I asked him what he was working on, he showed me a large heavy knife that John had given Will as a present. Will had never been good at putting a good edge on a knife and had asked Ernie to sharpen it for him. John said he had found it down near the docks. It had been very rusty. The blade had been badly chipped from breaking open barrels and crates on the docks. When Ernie was finished with it the blade had two new cleanly ground edges. He had hafted it with a good maple handle made in a tapered octagonal shape. The pommel was made from a brass disk filed to the shape of the haft. The guard was made from another piece of heavy brass.

"Very nicely done Ernie," I said handing it back to him.

Ernie said quietly, that if anything should happen with this knife, maybe it would be best if I would say that I had never seen it. I told him with a smile, that in fact I HAD never seen it. By the first week in March, Will was up and around again. One night he left quietly late in the evening saying he had something that he had to take care of. I did not know it then, but within a day the following story unfolded. Will and John Cooper met up and went to Will's sister's tavern. It was the eleventh of March and near the time that Ephraim closed up. The tavern had gone into a decline in the last year. This was mostly due to Ephraim's frequent drinking and general unpleasantness. Very few folks stayed there in rooms, but if they did go there, they used it more as a drinking house. Consequently, it was attracting a lower and lower element.

John went inside and had a drink, which he nursed along as long as he could. Will hid out behind the privy. When the last customer left and Ephraim told John to finish up and get out, John went out and along the side of the tavern where he could see the back door and the path to the privy. When Ephraim went into the privy, he gave a particular whistle that he and Will had agreed upon. That alerted Will to be ready. When Ephraim stepped out of the privy, Will came around the corner and drove his large heavy bladed new knife into Ephraim's back. Ephraim staggered and fell. Will jumped on him and stabbed him over and over again telling him this was for all the misery he had caused his sister. As a final blow, he rolled Ephraim over and stomped his face into a pulp before making absolutely sure of Ephraim's death by slitting his throat. Wiping his knife on Ephraim's coat, he stood and walked into the shadows. He returned to our loft and started to clean up. I woke up and asked him what happened and he said he had just been in a fight. The next day a young boy arrived at the shop asking for Will. He said he had a message from Will's sister Gwynne and that she needed him at the tavern right away as Ephraim had been killed. As the morning went on, we learned of the attack and the killing of Ephraim Snyder.

There was some talk and speculation as to who could have done this deed, but most folks agreed that he had it coming. Not well liked, he was not considered to be a loss to the city. The constable did ask Will where he had been, and if he knew anything of the killing. Will denied any knowledge, and Ernie said Will had never left the loft that evening. The constable said a blind man Will's size most likely could not have killed a large strong man such as Ephraim Snyder anyway. Ephraim's killer was never identified or apprehended.

# 15

# The Cooperage

Gwynne closed the tavern and Will moved back in to help her clean it and fix it up. Whatever gold Will had obtained from his adventures with Jack Stoner must have come in very handy as there was a great deal of work to be done on the old building.

It was an old three story brick structure with a low ceilinged attic above. The roofline had five small dormers (three in front and two in the rear), allowing for plenty of light and air. This attic was where Will had lived. The building itself was constructed of brick. There were two large rooms on the first floor divided by a central hall. The room on the left was a dining room. The one on the right was used as a coffee room and bar. Across the back, a large almost square room was used as a kitchen as it had an enormous fireplace. The kitchen itself was flanked, one on each side, by two small rooms. They had been used as storage rooms, but were now to have a better use. The one became a pantry, but the one behind the dining-room would become a small bedroom known as the cook's room. The kitchen addition had no rooms above it. Rising from the central hallway, was a nice stairway. The second floor was divided into four rooms with the front end of the hallway being made into an additional small room adjoining one of the front rooms. These rooms were all used as sleeping accommodations for the public as the tavern , once again, served more as an inn than simply a drinking house as it had become under Ephraim's direction. It would now become a much happier establishment. The third floor had an identical floor plan as the second and, along with the attic, was reserved for the family.

Carpenters replaced some of the rotted eave boards as well as the back steps from the kitchen. A new privy was built and the brick yard around the pump was reset. Will chose a nice sunny spot and had a bench placed so he could sit there and scrape his cow-horns. The floors inside were scraped and everything was repainted or varnished.

This new inn was to prosper. In future years, it became widely known throughout the city that a poor blind person coming to this bench by the kitchen door and asking for food would never be turned away hungry. During this same period, Gwynne had invited her Mother's sister Bronwyn Evans to come and live with them. Bronwyn was about sixty years of age and had never married. She and Gwynne had been very close when Gwynne was small, but once Gwynne had married Ephraim they had drifted apart. Bronwyn did not approve of Ephraim and had strongly told her niece not to marry him as he was a bad man. Gwynne had wanted to stay in what she called civilization and not move west with her family. Instead, against everyone's advice, she had married Ephraim. Now that he was gone, Gwynne had written to her

Aunt Bronwyn and it was very quickly arranged that Bronwyn would move to Philadelphia and help with the cooking in the new inn. William Fall made frequent trips with his wagon to the many small towns located along Lancaster Pike to purchase hay and grain for his stable. When he learned of the plan to have Gwynne's aunt travel to Philadelphia, he offered to collect her and her things on his next trip.

The Evans family had been Welsh Quakers who had taken advantage of William Penn's offer to take up land on what was called the Welsh Tract. Bronwyn had been born in Wales back during Queen Anne's reign. She was the eldest of seven children. All of the others had been born in this new land out on what became the family holdings. As is sometimes the case with eldest daughters, much of the work raising the youngest children fell to her. She had become an excellent cook and housekeeper, skilled in clothing and feeding many mouths.

Her prize possession was an ancient harp that had been her grandmother's. Bronwyn played it beautifully. It seemed to be her escape from the day-to-day cares of life. Often on a summers evening, one could hear the ethereal sound of the harp floating on the air in Pewter-Platter Alley.

Bronwyn was a stern sounding no nonsense woman who was of the greatest help to Gwynne in getting the inn going again. As soon as she moved into the cook's room, there was no doubt that she was in charge of the kitchen area of the inn. Her stern, no nonsense exterior hid the fact that she had a heart of gold. We saw little of Will during this time of cleaning and repair. We did not see much of Will's friend John Cooper either. He was helping with the cleaning and repainting. I thought he was simply doing so because he was a friend of Will's, but I would come to learn that John had always admired Gwynne. He had never taken any action in her direction because she was a married woman. Most folks had not wanted to bring the displeasure of Ephraim Snyder down about their shoulders, but Ephraim was gone. And John was making himself as helpful as possible. Soon he left the boardinghouse on Spruce Street where he had been staying and moved into Gwynne's tavern.

There was a lot of discussion as to what the name of the new tavern was to be. After Gwynne and John announced that they were to be married, the question of a name for the tavern suddenly resolved itself. John's last name was Cooper. Soon it became known as "The Cooperage." John made a sign from the head of a barrel with two barrel staves nailed across it like an X. Ernie painted a board mounted at the top of the staves that simply read "Cooperage."  Gwynne and John were married at Christ Church on June 1st. On June 4th, on King George III's birthday, John hung his new sign above the freshly painted door and declared "welcome to the Cooperage!" He was heard to be telling passers-by all day that he believed even King George III was celebrating all day in London. "Most likely in honor of the opening of this fine new tavern."

# 16

## The Repeal of
## the Stamp Act

Earlier in May another party had taken place that swept the entire city. It was a grand party celebrating the repeal of the hated Stamp Act. One day late in May, Sarah's husband Daniel burst into the shop and shouted, "Have you heard the good news?" Reading from a paper that he held in his hands, he said, "Made by His Majesty, at the Repealing of that Law, He was most graciously pleased to declare, 'That could He have conceived the Act would have been so injurious and disagreeable to His Subjects, He never would have given his Assent to it,' therefore most cheerfully repealed."

"Let me read it to you Andrew. I have the *Gazette* right here."

# The Pennsylvania Gazette

*Date: *May 22, 1766
*Title: *PHILADELPHIA, May 22.

PHILADELPHIA, May 22. On Monday Morning last arrived here the Brig Minerva, Captain WISE, from Poole, in Eight Weeks and brought with him what we have been long impatiently waiting for, An ACT OF PARLIAMENT, repealing the */STAMP /**/ACT /*. We had before an Account, that this Bill had been supported by a Majority in the House of COMMONS, and was sent up to the House of LORDS, where, it seems, long and warm Debates arose; but, on the Eleventh of March last, upon the Question being put, it was carried in Favour of the Bill by a Majority of THIRTY FOUR LORDS; and on the 18th, this Law received the ROYAL ASSENT——— An Event that has caused almost universal Joy in England, especially amongst those People who value their Liberty, and have Sense enough to know the Blessings it annexes to their Existence. No Wonder then, if the Transports of our Joy, on this Side the Atlantic, should lead us into Modes of Expression not quite consistent with the Moderation our Friends in England advice. However, notwithstanding the GREAT and GLORIOUS CAUSE of our present Rejoicings, not one single Instance of that Kind of Triumph, so much dreaded by our Friends, and wished for by our Enemies in England, has escaped the warmest Son of Liberty in this City, as will appear by the following Account of our Proceedings. The Minerva came to an Anchor opposite the Town, before it was known from whence she came, or the News she brought; but one of the Inhabitants having immediately gone on board, he received the Glorious Tidings, and instantly proclaimed

the News, brought the Law on Shore, as published by
BASKET, the KING Printer, read it aloud at the London
Coffee House, and, a Multitude being by this Time
collected three loud Huzzas testified their Approbation; a
Deputation from their Number was directly sent down
to wait on Captain Wise, and having first made the Ship
Company a Present, they conducted him to the Coffee
House with Colours flying, &c. A large Bowl of Punch
was ready, in which he drank Prosperity to America,
and was complimented with a Gold laced Hat, for having
brought the first certain Account of the */Stamp /**/Act
/* being totally repealed. The Inhabitants then appointed
the next Evening to illuminate the City, which was
done to the universal Satisfaction of all Spectators; the
Houses made a most beautiful Appearance, to which
the Regularity of our Streets contributed not a little; the
Scene was, however, variegated, by the different Manner
of placing the Lights, Devices, &c. for which the Public
is indebted to the Ladies, who exercised their Fancies
on the Occasion. It was very remarkable, that the City
was not disturbed by any */Riot /* or Mob, as is common
on such Occasions, but the whole was begun, continued
and ended, to the universal Satisfaction of the Inhabitants.
A large Quantity of Wood was given for a Bonfire, and
many Barrels of Beer to the Populace. And yesterday the
principal Inhabitants gave an elegant Entertainment at
the State House, at which his HONOUR the GOVERNOR,
and the Officers of Government; the Military Gentlemen;
Captain Hawker, of His Majesty Ship Sardine, the other
Gentlemen of the Navy, and the Strangers in the City, were
present. The Honours of the Table were performed by
the Worshipful Mayor of the City, assisted by some of
the Aldermen; and, considering that not less than Three
Hundred Plates were laid, the whole was conducted with the
greatest Elegance and Decorum; so that Detraction

itself must be silent on the Occasion. After Dinner the
following Toasts were drank, in flowing Glasses, viz. 1.
The KING. 2. The QUEEN. 3. PRINCE of WALES,
and ROYAL FAMILY. 4. May the Illustrious House of
HANOVER preside over the United British Empire, to
the End of Time. 5. The House of LORDS. 6. The House
of COMMONS. 7. The present Worthy MINISTRY. 8. The
Glorious and Immortal Mr. PITT. 9. That Lover and
Supporter of Justice, Lord CAMDEN. 10. The LONDON
COMMITTEE of MERCHANTS. 11. American Friends in
Great Britain. 12. The VIRGINIA ASSEMBLY. 13. All
other ASSEMBLIES on the Continent, actuated by the like
Zeal for the Liberties of their Country. 14. Prosperity to
the Spirited Inhabitants of St. CHRISTOPHER'S. 15. The
NAVY and ARMY. 16. DANIEL DULANY, Esquire. 17.
May the Interest of GREAT BRITAIN and her COLONIES
be always United. 18. TRADE and NAVIGATION. 19.
American Friends in Ireland. 20. Prosperity to the
Province of PENNSYLVANIA. 21. The Liberty of the
PRESS in America. With many others, of the same public
Nature. The Cannon belonging to the Province, being
placed in the State House Yard, the Royal Salute was
fired on drinking the King, and Seven Guns after every
succeeding Toast. The whole concluded in the Evening
with Bonfires, Ringing of Bells, and Strong Beer to
the Populace, and gave general Satisfaction to every Person
concerned. The following Resolution was unanimously
agreed to by the Company, viz. That to demonstrate our
Affection to Great Britain, and our Gratitude for the
REPEAL of the */STAMP /**/ACT /*, each of us will, on
the Fourth of June next, being the Birth Day of our most
gracious Sovereign GEORGE, III. dress ourselves in a
new Suit, of the Manufactures of England, and give what

HOME SPUN we have to the POOR. On this Occasion, the Public are much obliged to Captain Hawker, of His Majesty Ship Sardine, as be brought her up before the Town, and dressed her off with a Variety of Colours.

"Andrew, this is a great day! King George III has realized his mistake and we will be troubled no more with these taxes."

Hoping he was correct, but knowing there was still a large expense being created by the British Army on the Western borders, it seemed very unlikely that we had really heard the last of taxation.

# 17

## The Two Irish Girls

We did not see as much of Will for a while as he was very busy helping his sister and John at the Cooperage. However, he did try to stop by when he could. One day while he was visiting, John Cooper burst into the shop looking for Will.

"I have just come from Morris's Wharf where I went to look at the indentured servants that were advertised in The Gazette. John Hart is handling the sale on shore for Captain Price as the Captain is anxious to have some repairs done on his ship The Sally Anne and get off to the islands." It was common for people who wished to immigrate to the Colonies, but did not have the cost of the passage, to go to the Captain of a ship and make a contract called an indenture. In this contract, the Captain would agree to transport the person to the Colonies without charging them. However, these people had agreed that when they had arrived, the Captain had the right to sell that persons service for a given number of years to recover his costs.

John continued, "The indentures were going quite reasonable like. They had a plasterer listed who I thought we might use for a while at the Cooperage, but he had already signed and was committed. His name is Patrick Walsh. When I spoke with him, talking about the tavern we had just opened and he saw I had but one eye, he asked if I might have a place for his two young nieces. He told me that he, along with his sister and her two daughters had come to the new country after a very hard time back in Ireland. During the passage, his sister had taken a fever and had not recovered. His indenture had been picked up, but his nieces were both very hard of seeing. Their mother had concealed that from the Captain, but now that she was gone, Mr. Hart said he could not find anyone who wanted two blind girls. Mr. Hart thought his only chance of getting rid of them would be to sell them to a brothel below South Street. In fact after their mother had died, the Captain offered to help them work off their passage in his cabin. Patrick said Captain Price's hand was still bandaged from the bad bite that Sheila had given him when he tried to rip her blouse open. The good Captain said he had enough of these ungrateful troublesome blind girls and that Mr. Hart should just get rid of them for any offer he might get. Patrick said he knew they would be hard workers cleaning and serving in the tavern."

"So, what is the problem?" Will asked.

"Well, you know you don't see at all, and I only have one eye. I thought these two poor lasses needed a chance and they could be a big help to Gwynne. So, well, I signed their papers for practically nothing. They are outside, but I want you to come with me and help explain to your sister why I am bringing two young women home with me."

We all had a good laugh. Ernie was quick to peek outside the door to see what they looked like. He reported later that they looked a bit disheveled, but maybe they would clean up all right.

Sheila, at sixteen was the elder of the two. She had a small amount of vision. Molly was only thirteen and was almost completely blind. Later, Doctors would tell us that both girls had been born with cataracts. At that time there was little that could be done for them to improve their sight.

I began to think how before I had gone west, I never knew many blind people and hardly ever thought about them. In fact, at that time the only blind person I had actually met was Will. Yes, there were a few others such as Jim Rotten Teeth, but I never really knew them. Now I seemed to be finding, or at least taking notice of, a number of blind people. Beside Will and myself, there was Steven over in Daniel's pottery, John Cooper who only had one eye, to say nothing of the two blind minstrels that I had encountered on my journey back to Philadelphia from Fort Pitt. Now these two young Irish girls who had very little vision. I wondered how they would work out at the Cooperage. I had no doubt that Gwynne would be kind to them because of her brother Will being blind.

Aunt Bronwyn was not only to be the cook; she was in charge of the rapidly growing staff. She quickly embraced this new role, and became a caring mother hen to these new very scared young girls. We learned later, that when John and Will had arrived at the Cooperage with the two young lasses in tow, there had been a big discussion. Bronwyn had been placed in charge of the two girls and had immediately set out to improve their lot. She demanded that John and Will bring firewood and lots of water to the kitchen for baths. There was an old wooden cask in the kitchen that was used for bathing. Bronwyn had the water boiled and the cask filled. After ordering John and Will to leave the kitchen; she commanded both young bound girls to strip out of their filthy rags and get in the tub. After they had been completely bathed and deloused from their long sea voyage, she gave them new clothing that she and Gwynne provided. The clothing did not fit quite correctly, but in the next few days, the girls would receive all clean, new things that fit them better.

John's good hearted, chance acquisition of the indentured girls turned out to be a very fortunate one for all concerned. The girls, who had arrived in a very bedraggled and scared condition, were, as their uncle had promised, very willing workers. Under Bronwyn's direction, both girls blossomed.

Sheila loved learning about so many new foods as well as how to prepare them. Food had been scarce in Ireland. Their small family farm had been worn from many generations of farming and produced little. One night when the thatching of the roof of their home caught afire, their entire home with everything they had in the world had burned. Their father, Thomas, Patrick's brother, had been badly burned and died a few days later.

Their mother begged Patrick who was just leaving for the new world to take them with him.

The girls' mother, whose name was Mary, did her best to conceal the girls' blindness. Even so, Captain Price refused at first. Their mother was in tears and begged him to allow them aboard. With a little smirk, the Captain said that there was one way he might consider it. If Mary traveled in his cabin he might be willing. Their mother seeing no other way out, nodded and holding her daughters firmly by the hands, the three of them went aboard. Mary cried the entire time the ship was getting under way. When they were at sea, and Captain Price told Mary to get below to his cabin, she hugged her daughters and promised them things would be better in the new world. Captain Price got as much as he could from his bargain, but wasted little food or water on his passengers. Within a few weeks, their mother came down with the fever that finally killed her.

By the time they arrived in Philadelphia, Molly would hardly speak to anyone and did not want to let go of her big sister's hand. After all of her experience helping to raise her own brothers and sisters, as well as many of their children, Bronwyn knew how to comfort and reassure these two young spirits that now were in her charge. Keeping them close to her in a warm and cheerful kitchen she saw to it that they had good food to eat. Under her caring guidance, they slowly opened to her spell. They would do whatever she asked and seemed to enjoy learning anything she taught them.

Although she rarely ever let anyone touch her harp, when she saw how interested Molly was in it when she played it, soon she not only let the young girl touch the harp, but started to teach her to play it. It did not take long before everyone realized that a love for these two almost blind young Irish girls was growing stronger by the day in Bronwyn's heart.

Their uncle Patrick had been bound to a man in the three lower counties. The area usually known as Delaware. Their uncle hugged each girl as he pressed into their hands a gold coin, brought from Ireland, that he had torn from his own clothing. Patrick said that he was so very sorry that he could not keep them all together, but that he had done all he could for them. Wiping their tears with his sleeve, he also said that John Cooper looked like a kindly man. Leaving the dock, they all knew that they might never see one another again. None of the three were able to write.

# 18

# Henry's Story

Henry had been writing to Mom every few weeks during the spring of 1766, pushing back his planned visit to Philadelphia again and again. It seemed that he had many things to do to settle Uncle Ebenezer's estate. Ebenezer had left Mom, who was his only sister, a handsome bequest, but the bulk of his estate, including his house and clock shop in Elizabeth New Jersey he had left to Henry. Henry was anxious to come to Philadelphia to work on the clock project he had been corresponding with David Rittenhouse about. Henry had been courting a young lady named Cynthia Caldwell from a small settlement near Elizabeth known as Connecticut Farms. Her father was a Presbyterian minister there and Henry had first met her while he had been attending the college of New Jersey where her father had been teaching. She had been too young then, but had just now turned eighteen. Although he wished to return to Philadelphia, he did not want to leave Cynthia. They discussed this with her father who demanded that they postpone the marriage until Henry was better established. However, when he learned that Henry was the principle heir of Uncle Ebenezer's will, he decided the time was right. Soon thereafter he agreed to conduct their marriage service. Henry had arranged to sell both Uncle Ebenezer's house and clock shop to a journeyman who had been first an apprentice and later a journeyman with Uncle Ebenezer. Although this young man had little capital, they had worked out an agreement and as long as he made his payments, Henry would have a steady income for many years. This, in addition to the considerable sum he had as a direct inheritance from his uncle, left him in a good financial position to support a wife and establish his new business in Philadelphia.

He now planned to be in Philadelphia by early June. Actually his letter arrived only a few days before he and his new wife did.

I had not seen Henry for several years. Growing up together we had many pleasant memories to talk over. They came flooding back as if we had never been apart: the many times that we had climbed over fences to steal an apple, or gone for long hikes through the woods north of the city. The times we climbed the highest trees to see how far we could see, or peeled out of our clothing and swam in various creeks. The times Dad took us with him to a place in the woods where he would proof fire a new barrel that he had just made. Although I never knew one to fail, he always did this. While on these trips, we always took other weapons along and used the day as a way of learning to use and fire them as well as simply enjoying shooting at a target. As we grew older, some of these trips became hunting trips as the game was very plentiful in those days and Mom was always glad of a tasty piece of meat to cook. She did not appreciate it if it still looked like the animal it had been, so Dad usually made us clean it and bring it home in a state that was ready to enter the kitchen. Dad always insisted that we never shoot at an animal that we did not intend to eat, or that we could not kill cleanly with that shot. If we wished to simply shoot to enjoy shooting or hitting a target, there were plenty of other marks to aim at. Henry and I went on long hikes and would camp overnight pretending that we were soldiers of the Crown on some important mission. The actual danger from Indians that close to Philadelphia was, even in those days, very unlikely. The 1730's and 1740's were good times to grow up in South Eastern Pennsylvania. Henry brought a large silver watch as a gift for me. It had a hunter's case so the hands were protected. Once the cover was sprung open, one could lift the crystal and touch the hands. Attached to the end of the chain was a small key. This was used both to set the time and to wind the watch spring once a day. I had never had a watch of my own and thought it a wonderful gift. Most people did not have watches as they were very expensive. A good silver watch like the one Henry brought me cost about twenty guineas. Most people simply relied on the clocks found about the city in churches and bell towers. As a watch and clock maker, Henry felt time was very important. He said that knowing a blind person could not see these steeple clocks he thought I should have a good watch.

Until he had found a place of his own, Henry and his wife Cynthia would live with Mom and Dad in their house on Third Street, next to Dad's gun shop. Henry had arrived with a wagon of tools, clocks, and other items from

Uncle Ebenezer's shop that he wished to keep. He planned to set up his own clock and watch shop here in Philadelphia after first meeting with David Rittenhouse. While seeking out a house and shop of his own, he decided to rent a small place. By early July, he had established himself in a shop on Second Street and was advertising for a lad as an apprentice.

# The Pennsylvania Gazette

**July 31st**
Henry Annaler, Watch and */Clockmaker /*, A little below the Friends Meeting House, in SECOND STREET, PHILADELPHIA, TAKES this Method to inform the Public, that he carries on the Business of WATCH & CLOCK MAKING & MENDING, in all its particular Branches; he therefore flatters himself, that he will give Satisfaction to his Customers as well as to himself, by completing their Work in a careful and correct Manner on reasonable Terms. —- He has for Sale, a Parcel of good new LONDON WATCHES. Also desires to employ a young lad seeking an apprenticeship in the above trade.

Dad brought to Henry's attention a property that had been for sale for some time. It was nearby on Arch Street and might be just what he needed. That house belonged to a Mr. Jervis who was a Whitesmith. Mr. Jervis was older and not well. He had closed his business about a year ago and had gone to live with a daughter in New Brunswick, New Jersey. The house had been offered for sale in September of

1765, but as it was not in good repair, and Mr. Jervis wanted a goodly sum for it, it had remained empty. Mom found a *Gazette* advertisement and brought it to Henry's notice.

# The Pennsylvania Gazette

**May 8, 1766**
**TO BE SOLD, A** House and Lot of Ground, situated and being on the North Side of Arch street, between Second and Front streets, in this City, now in the Tenure of John Jervis, */Whitesmith /*, containing 20 Feet Front on said Street, and 102 Feet in Depth, clear of Ground or Quit rent. For further Particulars enquire of Mr. **VANDERSPIEGEL**, in Philadelphia, or **SAMUEL H. SULLIVAN**, in New Brunswick, by whom an indisputable Title will be given.

Henry liked the property, thinking that it would be ideally suited to his needs, but did not wish to pay the amount that Mr. Jervis was asking, as the house did need a great deal of work. During the time that Mr. Jervis had left it empty, it had received the attention of vandals, and a number of windows had been broken, as well as some other damage. About this time, my friend, attorney Michael Graham, was visiting in the city. He had come to collect the rifle that he had contracted with Dad to make for him as well as file a number of legal papers in the Philadelphia courts regarding the western land sales that he was so involved with. While dining with us at Mom and Dad's home, we spoke of Henry's interest in purchasing a house and shop in the city. Michael offered to handle any negotiations or other legal work that Henry might need to have done concerning the purchase of this property while Michael was still in the City. He was acquainted with Mr. Vanderspiegel who was listed in the *Gazette* as handling the sale for Mr. Jervis.

Within a few weeks Mr. Jervis had accepted Henry's offer and the sale was closed on the 1st of August 1766. It turned out that Mr. Jervis' health had been failing rapidly. He was anxious to conclude the sale of his empty house before any additional damage was done to it.

# 19

# The Duel

During the time of the house purchase, Michael remained in Philadelphia, staying at the Royal Standard on Market Street. One day while he was in the shop chatting with us, the door burst open and a Royal Officer staggered in. It was clear that he had just come from a tavern as not only was he staggering, but his words were slurred. Catching the end of a bench, he steadied himself.

"I have come to observe for myself the blind mendicant who pretends to be a gunsmith," he announced. "It has the ring of a tale that merits a good laugh."

"I am blind, but I am not a mendicant."

"All blind people are mendicants. Are they not?" he said.

"No, we are not all mendicants! I was trained as a gunsmith before I became blind and now continue to carry out that part of the trade that I am able to do. How can I be of service to you?"

"You can not be of service to me or most likely anyone else if you are blind!"

"Then if you have no further business in this shop, you may take your leave at once," I replied.

"You will address me as Sir! You insolent piece of blind rubbish. All of you blind mendicants should be rounded up and put away somewhere so that decent people do not need to look upon you. I am an officer of the Crown. My name is Captain James Eagleby. I have just arrived in this provincial backwater of Philadelphia, on my way to join my Regiment, (the 77th Foot), which I understand is lost somewhere in the woods of Pennsylvania."

"You may not know where it is, but I seriously doubt that the 77th is lost. Perhaps you ought to go look for your regiment and leave this shop now!"

"I told you to show me some respect. You will address me as Sir!"

Dad had been working in the forge. When he heard the tone of the officer's voice, he stopped hammering and walked into the shop. "Leave! You have insulted my son, my trade, my shop, and me. Leave now! Ernie, open the door for this horse's ass."

Captain Eagleby stammered, "I am a King's Officer!"

The moment was frozen in time. Dad stood there slowly swinging his long-handled hammer. Michael Graham slid from the stool at the end of my bench and drew his hunting sword. Advancing on the Captain, he said, "You have been invited to leave. Do so!"

Ernie had pulled the door open and Michael gently, but firmly, with the tip of his sword pressed the officer backwards through it.

"How dare you assault a King's Officer? I will have the lot of you whipped."

He seemed to have forgotten the two stone steps that led up into the shop. In his condition, he tripped on the top one and caught his spur in the hem of his long regimental uniform coat. This further hampered his movements and the next sound I heard was the tearing of cloth, followed by a thud as he fell backwards across the sidewalk and into the gutter. Like an enraged bull he tried to rise, but at that very moment, a heavy carter's dray wagon rumbled passed splashing the Captain's uniform with mud and whatever else might have been in the gutter. Staggering to his feet, he screamed, "I demand satisfaction Sir!"

Michael smiled and replied, "It will be my pleasure. My name is Michael Graham Esq. You or your second will find me at the Royal Standard on Market Street. Good Day." Stepping back inside the shop, he sheathed his sword and closed the door. "He will either sleep it off, or I will hear from him." Later that evening, Michael, Ernie, Will Davies, John Cooper and I were all in the Cooperage enjoying a convivial bowl or two, while discussing Captain Eagleby's visit and comments of the afternoon. I had found them very unsettling.

"Is that how people really feel about us? Is that what they say about the city?" I ask.

My question hung in the air for some moments. Finally, Ernie said, "There are some very rude people in town who might say anything."

Michael commented, "There are those who care not how they hurt others with their tongues. They are very self-centered people who are not worth bothering with."

"Yes, but is that what the world thinks of us?" I ask sadly.

Will slammed his empty mug down on the table top. "What do we care what the world thinks of us? I have explained this all to you several times before. There was a time when you were one of them. You could see then, but now you cannot. People are not going to think you are just as good as you were before the explosion, because you are not just as good. You are blind! Get used to it."

John leaned forward and spoke. "You are not the same person who you were. You do not feel the same way about things as you once did. You do not work the same way. Why should you be thinking that folks are going to feel the same about you?"

Michael placed his hand on my arm. "Andrew, you must realize, many blind people, well, yes, let me say most blind people are not as fortunate as you. Most have no one who cares about them. Many live on the streets in any fashion that they can. They have a very hard life with little prospects of improvement. Perhaps a day will come in time when a kinder, more caring, society will do better by those individuals. That day has not yet arrived, which is all the more reason that you should never forget that you are not one of them. You have a loving family, good friends, ample food and shelter, and the knowledge and skills to carry out a respectable trade. Do not worry what the fools of the world such as Captain James Eagleby say or do."

As I sat there thinking over the words of my good friends, I could hear Surgeon Boyd's words ringing in my ears. "You are the fortunate one." Yes, I had a great deal to be thankful for. I resolved there and then to do what I could to help other blind people in the city to find their way up into a better life. Two days later, Michael ambled into the shop.

"Well, that is over and hopefully behind us," he said in his cheery way.

"Are you referring to that odious British Officer who was in here the other day?" I asked.

"Ah yes, the very one. A young Coronet named Josiah Wingsbeck came around yesterday informing me that he was reluctantly acting as Captain Eagleby's Second. Joshua Morris and I were enjoying a bowl of coffee in the Royal Standard at the time. Joshua, who is a true gentleman, kindly offered to act as my Second, so there you have it. We set it up to meet this morning at dawn in the Northern Libries. Devilish nice pair of London pistols Eagleby brought. In fact, I asked him if I could purchase them as I felt he would have no further need for dueling pistols after this morning. He refused and blustered out a few rather unpleasant comments concerning my lineage. After it was over, I also made the same request to have the right of purchase of the pistols from Wingsbeck his Second. However, that young officer thought it best to have them returned to his family with his other effects."

"Michael, did you kill him?" I asked.

"You know Andrew, sometimes I believe your friend Will Davies is correct in that you do have a dark way of looking at things. Personally, I would rather think of it as a situation where the good Captain stepped into the path of a solid sphere of lead which was moving at a very high rate of speed. When this said sphere of lead entered his body cavity, it caused grievous harm encouraging his mortal soul to leave his earthly body post haste."

"You mean he is dead?" I asked.

"Perhaps that does describe the situation accurately," Michael replied. "Besides that, we know many of the lads in the 77th Foot. They are a decent lot. You would not have wished this bore on them would you? Look what the bugger did to me hat: about ruined it; the old sod." Dropping his hat on the bench in front of me, he guided my finger into a 54 caliber hole; punched neatly through the brim. It was a tricorn hat and the bullet had gone down the left side of the hat passing through both places were the brim was turned up over the left shoulder.

Smiling, I replied, "Let us hope his family understands how dangerous life can be in the woods of Pennsylvania." A few days later, Michael returned to Carlisle. This had taken place in July of 1766. One day, months later, during February of 1767, Coronet Josiah Wingsbeck entered the gun shop. Under his arm he carried a flat polished wooden box containing a beautiful pair of London made flintlock dueling pistols. He asked if I knew a Michael Graham as he believed that Mr. Graham may have some interest in these pistols. He went on to explain that he had been the Second for a Captain James Eagleby in a duel which was fought last July between Captain Eagleby and Mr. Graham Esq. Mr. Graham had indicated that he wished to purchase the pistols from Captain Eagleby's estate after the Captain had departed this world. Josiah had written to the father of the Captain and learned that the Captain's father had no desire to have the pistols that his son had been killed with and that Josiah should simply sell them for whatever he could and send the father the money. Josiah had gone to the Royal Standard seeking the whereabouts of Mr. Graham, but no one knew of his present abode. He had been directed to inquire at this gunsmith's shop. Josiah said he would have tried to locate Mr. Graham and correspond with him concerning the possible purchase, but that Josiah had just been posted to New York and wished to conclude this matter as rapidly as possible.

I offered to purchase them with the assurance that I would see that Mr. Graham ultimately received them. After examining them, I agreed with Michael that they were indeed a lovely pair made in the 1750's by a London maker named John Wilson. We agreed on an amount and that was the last of Coronet Josiah Wingsbeck that I saw. It would be ten years later that our paths would cross again, but I did not know that at that time.

The cover of the box had an oval brass plate with the head of an Eagle engraved upon it. Beneath the head the name James Eagleby was engraved. Removing the plate and using it as a template, I first sawed out, and then filed a new plate until it was the same size and shape. Taking this new plate with me one day, I stopped in to Henry's watch and clock shop and asked him to have a thistle engraved upon it over the Name Graham. When the plate was returned to me, I replaced it on the box and put it aside until Michael's next visit. At that time I would present it to him.

# 20

# Ernie & Sheila

By the time Christmas 1766 came, the necessary repairs had been completed on Henry's house, and he and Cynthia moved into their new home.

During Mom's Christmas feast, Cynthia announced that she was pregnant. Mom was very pleased to learn that 1767 would bring another grandchild into the family. I wondered to myself if it was a chance happening, or if Mom had arranged things so that Cynthia was the one to find the silver shilling in the plum pudding that Christmas?

Ernie believed the silver shilling that he had found in the plum pudding the year before, had brought him good fortune in the form of Sheila. After his first peek out the shop door at the two sisters that John had signed indentured papers for in June, Ernie had decided to get to know them a bit better. I began to notice that he was spending more and more of his free time at the Cooperage. He said he was helping Gwynne and John, as well as visiting with Will. Somehow, I felt he was visiting more than Will. As the months passed, he and Sheila seemed to become good friends. Actually very good friends. Then, one day in early January, while Will was in our shop, he asked if Ernie had any bite marks on his hands. Since he was laughing so hard when he asked this, I was sure he was referring to Sheila's having fought off Captain Price's unwanted advances. Ernie mumbled something about it being hard enough to steal a kiss with Aunt Bronwyn always watching and went out to the forge.

Will laughed and said, "That is certain true. Just the other day while passing through the kitchen at the Cooperage, I just stopped a moment to pat Molly's little buns."

"Will, shame on you, the lass is only a child," I replied.

"Maybe she is, but her shape doesn't feel like a child's."

"Did she object?" I asked.

"No, she did not seem to mind, but Aunt Bronwyn saw me and tried to beat me to death with her wooden spoon. I was lucky to escape with my life. I could hear her screaming at me all of the way down Pewter-Platter Alley."

"Will, you do have a reputation. Maybe you should leave those two Irish girls alone. They are lucky to have found John and your Sister Gwynne to take them in. You don't want to go and ruin it for them."

"Ah, it was just a friendly little pat. Shouldn't a blind guy be allowed?"

"No! No, a blind guy should not be aloud to pat the bottoms of young indentured girls. Besides if it's Sheila's bottom you start patting, Ernie might just have an issue with you."

Ernie always sounded so happy whenever Sheila's name came up that I thought he must certainly be interested in her. Whenever he did mention her, he did not speak much about her blindness. The fact that Sheila could only see a very small amount did not seem to bother him. A few days later, when I spoke with him about it, he said that maybe it would have bothered him, but he had gotten so used to Will and I that he did not think having a wife who could not see well would be that much of a problem. Dad overheard us, and pointed out that Ernie's apprenticeship had a number of months yet to run and whether or not a wife could see or not, a wife was expensive to keep.

Ernie said very little the rest of that day, but that evening in our loft, I assured him that Dad's bark was worse than his bite.

"Well, yes, I know, but he does know how to pour cold water on a pleasant idea," said Ernie as he blew out the candle. In July Henry's wife Cynthia had given birth to a daughter which they named after Cynthia's mother, Elizabeth. Mom was glowing with joy, but she also was aging and often did not feel well. Her joy in having a new granddaughter was clouded by a letter she received in September from Thomas Ward, who was her eldest daughter's husband. Thomas wrote that Susan had grown a large lump in her breast and had, during the month of July, died. Mom had not seen Susan in many years. Susan had married in 1748. Soon thereafter, she and her new husband Thomas had moved to Allentown. Susan had two sons. Timothy was born in 1750 and Thomas in 1753. Timothy had been apprenticed to his father as a cooper. Thomas had been apprenticed to a harness and saddle maker also in the Allentown area. More than that we knew little of them. In fact we had not heard very much from Susan as she did not often write. This letter from Thomas, bringing such sad news weighed heavily upon Mom's spirit.  Earlier, during the spring of 1767, we all began to notice that Dad had slowed down. He did not make as many rifles from scratch as he used too. He relied more and more on the inexpensive factory made locks now available from London and Birmingham makers. He focused more on repairs and reconditioning older or broken weapons. Philadelphia had by then grown to over twenty thousand people and the demand for inexpensive rifles, fowling pieces, and pistols had increased. We developed a steady and growing trade of these less expensive weapons.

When Ernie finished his apprenticeship in June, Dad announced that he would take on no more apprentices. Ernie stayed on as a journeyman and seemed quite happy.

Now that he was twenty one, he asked me to be his recommender for Masonic membership. As it was necessary to have two recommenders to petition for membership, I asked William Fall, who Ernie knew well from William's many visits to our shop, to be his second recommender. Soon a committee of other members, appointed by the Master of the Lodge came to interview Ernie. By September he was given his first Degree. At night in our comfortable loft, I worked with him, and during our lodge meeting early in December 1767; he was made a third degree Master Mason.  One day in October, Ernie announced in the shop that he and Sheila wished to marry as soon as Ernie could find a place for them to live. Gwynne approved and had offered them the attic of the Cooperage if Will could move into our loft where Ernie was then living. Will had stayed with us many times in the past when Gwynne was annoyed with him for one reason or another. We all agreed and Ernie and Sheila began to make their marriage plans.

Sheila, and her younger sister Molly had been brought up in the Catholic Church in Ireland. Once they had left Ireland, they had stopped going to any church at all. Ernie had been brought up in the Lutheran faith, but had not been to any church as long as I had known him. At that time, Philadelphia had a Catholic Church. It was St. Joseph's Church on Wheeling Alley. Sheila insisted they go there and make their marriage plans with the Priest. However, they were both put off by the Priest's attitude. He said he would not marry them until Ernie became a Catholic. But when he learned that Ernie was a FreeMason, he refused to marry them at all, saying that he would not be a part of giving a young woman to the devil.

After some discussion, they attended a few services at Christ Church at the corner of Second and Market Streets and posted their marriage bands. They arranged to be married on the day after Christmas, 1767. Mom had always been something between a Mom and an Aunt to Ernie. She was very proud of Ernie for wanting to marry Sheila. As a young indentured girl who was almost blind and with little or no family, Sheila might well have had a very hard life indeed. However, as a Philadelphia gunsmith, Ernie would certainly be able to give her a good and secure life. Mom was so pleased with Ernie; she offered to make Sheila's wedding dress. By all reports, it was really lovely.

As Mom worked on Sheila's dress, they became closer and closer. I was absolutely certain this year that Mom had decided who should find the silver shilling in her Christmas plum pudding when Sheila found it on her first bite. Everyone agreed it was a good omen for the young couple's life. However, I kept this little suspicion to myself, as some thoughts ought to be kept. After the Church service, there was a grand party held at the Cooperage. As a wedding gift to the young couple, John tore up both girls indenture papers. Sheila would continue helping at the Cooperage, but she was so pleased that she and her sister were not to be indentured girls any longer.

# 21

# Sarah's School

Remembering my desire to help other blind people, every week or two, Spark and I went over to Daniel's pottery. I always enjoyed the opportunity of making things in clay, but also I wanted to see how young Steven was doing. He lived with Sarah and Daniel and seemed to have become part of their family. His father had died from the burns that he had received in the accident at Pass & Stowe Foundry. His mother had died some months before he had come to Sarah and Daniel. Now he was really an orphan. He always seemed a bit withdrawn. Daniel said he was a quiet but willing lad. Sarah treated him like a son. Steven did seem to like the work in clay and by January of 1767, Daniel offered to take him on formally as an apprentice. Seth and Steven got on very well. Steven was enough older that he was not competing with Seth, but could still be fun as a sort of big brother. Steven did not attend the Quaker school, but Sarah spent as much time teaching him what she could. Although he did not see well enough to read, she said he could learn his letters and numbers, as well as listen to the many stories that Sarah read to him. Daniel encouraged her to come out into the pottery and read aloud to everyone at the same time. Daniel's pottery was always a warm and cheery place to be.

That day when Spark and I walked in, Sarah was teaching both Steven and Seth to write. She had directed them to role out flat slabs of clay about a half inch thick. Using a dull knife, she had them square up their clay tablets, until they were the size of a sheet of paper. Next she took a pottery tool with a rounded end and dragged it across the clay tablet. She made lines with this tool about a quarter of an inch deep and a little more than an inch apart. After watching her a time or two, Seth became very good at preparing these clay tablets.

Using another pottery tool shaped much like a quill pen; she carefully drew the letters of the alphabet as well as the first ten numbers. Sarah next showed them each how to hold the tool and start to copy what she had written. Daniel later took the sample tablets that Sarah had made as examples of the letters and fired and glazed them that they might be kept as permanent models for further study. "Sarah, I think what you are doing is wonderful," I said.

Sarah replied, "Just because Steven can not see, there is no reason why he can not learn to write. I can write my name without looking. I will not have my boys grow up and not be able to write."

Of course Seth would go on to the same Friends School that we had gone to, but this way they were both learning together.

"Sarah, have you thought of teaching other blind people to write in this way using clay tablets?"

"No, I have not. Do you need to learn again since you have lost your sight?"

"No, I believe I can still write, but I was thinking of those two young Irish girls who live over at the Cooperage. I do not believe that either of them knows how to write." Daniel was not the only one looking for apprentices that year. In February, now settled into his new shop, Henry ran the following advertisement in the *Pennsylvania Gazette:*

*Date: *February 20, 1767 * WANTED, an Apprentice to a */Watch /**/maker /*; he must be a Lad of Genius, and of creditable Parents; he must serve Seven Years, and notwithstanding he will have an Opportunity (which is not very common in America) of making the Movement, and finishing the same, the Apprentice Fee (if small) provided the Boy suits, will be accepted. Any Person having such a Boy to put as an Apprentice, may send to Henry Annaler, Watchmaker, in Philadelphia, who is the Person that wants the Boy.

He also took on two journeymen and by May, just a bit less than a year after his returning to Philadelphia, his business was a going concern. Soon he ran the following advertisement:

# The Pennsylvania Gazette

May 14th 1767
Henry Annaler, Watch maker, UNDERTAKES to make good, sound, and neat silver watches, for L

12 currency; and as many people have been under the necessity of importing good watches from England or Ireland, he now assures those who would incline to have good watches, that he has, besides himself, two regular bred workmen from England; the one a movement */ maker /*, and the other a motion */maker /*: Therefore any person who wants a */watch /*, he will warrant it for three years, without mending, to the purchaser, and whatever size the purchaser chooses, from the size of a half dollar, to a larger, they may have, and in three months time from bespeaking of it. He also repairs watches after the neatest and best manner, and at a reasonable price. N.B. He also makes wheels, pinions, verges, &c. for watch menders, which he will sell low. Any person wanting a */ watch /* of Twenty Guineas price, may be here supplied as in London.

# 22

# The Townshend Acts

The autumn of 1767 brought us news of what would come to be known as the Townshend Acts. These acts, named for Charles Townshend, the Chancellor of the Exchequer were a continuing attempt by Parliament to make the North American Colonies bear more of the costs of having the military stationed here. These acts also were an attempt to clamp down on the smuggling trade which had been very lucrative for many merchants and ship owners. Additional customs officers were sent to the Colonies and the new taxes on items such as paper, paint, lead, glass and tea all were designed to cover these additional costs of the Crown.

The success that the Colonists had in achieving the repeal of the Stamp Act gave people cause and hope that they could achieve the same result yet again.

My sympathies continued to be with the Crown. I had always believed that the Colonies would one way or another need to be made to pay for the large military presence here. These new taxes would not really bother us too greatly and I felt them to be just. Thinking about it, I also did not feel badly that such shady individuals as Jack Stoner would be brought under control. We had seen nothing of Jack for some time, and that was quite fine. However, there were many folks pursuing the same livelihood and I did not think it a bad thing to have trade benefit the Crown's effort to protect the Colonies rather than enriching the pockets of such as Mr. Stoner.

Listening to the angry talk in the coffeehouses and taverns about the city, I realized that my opinion was certainly a minority one and I rarely made any comments at all. This was not a problem as no one really cared what the opinion of a blind man was in the 1760's in Philadelphia.

Daniel was, of course, very adamant that once again, the Colonists must stand up for their rights and have a strong and unified voice protesting what he and his friends referred to as these latest abuses of Parliament. I feared for him as I thought he was becoming too well known as a leader speaking out against English rule and the Crown's authority to do so. I felt this might lead to no good. I did not try to argue with Daniel, as a man with a cause is not one who is listening to others. However, I had several talks with Sarah. She was very distressed about Daniel's vehement attitude. She also felt his leadership in such protests could only bring problems down upon her family.

# 23

# The Parents

Later, we all agreed that the autumn of 1767 was one in which both parents slowed down. It was almost as if we could observe them becoming older every day. Dad often complained about the cold. When not close to the fire in his forge, he would come into the front room of the shop and sit for a bit by the fire. Ernie took over most of the forge work. Sarah came to the shop a part of every week to help with book-work as well as other writing tasks. Dad said he was letting her do this as she had a beautiful clear hand for writing. The truth was Sarah had been helping in that way for several years, but he now seemed to rely even more heavily upon her. While she was with us, Mom would watch her granddaughter Dorothy and sometimes Seth and the new baby Elizabeth as well. Although Dorothy, then a bit over two years of age, was the apple of her eye, Mom loved watching all her grandchildren, but she often spoke of how tired she now always felt. January 1768 was a very cold month that year. Dad spent more and more time sitting by the fire. He would often say that his insides were being eaten up. He would then rise and go next door to lie down. By the beginning of April, he stopped coming to the shop. We all knew he was dying as he had never missed coming over to work in the past. Mom had Dr. John Redman in to see Dad, but the Doctor said there was nothing that he could do. At the end of the month, Mom told us that Dad had died quietly in his sleep.

The shop was never the same. Ernie worked on as a journeyman and did quite well. I continued the stock work and taking care of the resale of the weapons that we took in and had repaired, or of ones that we were buying directly from London merchants. We both felt as if Master Frederick would walk back into the shop at any moment and take us to task for some minor deviation of his standards. Our hearts would have been filled with joy to even once more receive his rebuke. Although we kept waiting for him to enter, he never reappeared. As long as I continued in the shop, I never stopped thinking of it as his shop.

Mom seemed to lose heart in living and never came over to the shop to visit during the day as she used to do. I worried about her being alone so much of the time. Then one day while inletting a barrel, a great thought came to me.

I stopped work and walked over to Ernie's bench.

"Ernie, are not you and Sheila a bit cramped in the attic of the Cooperage?" I asked.

"Oh yes, but we are getting by," he replied.

"Mom has a house here next door. Mom is now there alone. Would you and Sheila wish to move in and live there? You know Mom has always thought of you as a son and I think she would be glad of Sheila's company. I know Sheila would not be there all of the time as she has work to do at the Cooperage, but I believe she would be a big help to Mom. And you two would have much more room. Would you think about it? If you think you might wish to do so, I will speak with Mom today."

"Why yes, of course. I think that would be wonderful. Let me know soon as I should tell Sheila."

Within a few days it was all arranged and everyone seemed happier. Even Sarah hugged me the next time she was in the shop and said she thought it to be a wonderful idea.

Mom and Dad's house was a small one. Although with the shop directly next door, with its sleeping loft above, it had always been adequate enough for our needs. It had a large front sitting-room on the first floor behind which was Mom's kitchen. The second floor had two bedrooms and above that, under the roof, was an attic that could be used as a sleeping loft. When we had all been at home, Henry and I lived above the shop as well as any apprentices that Dad may have taken on. Mom and Dad used the front room and our sisters all shared the back room. Mom now moved to the back room which had a small stairway that connected directly down to the kitchen where she spent most of her time. Ernie and Sheila had the larger front room and everyone seemed happy. One day in October, Ernie burst into the shop one morning carrying a copy of the *Gazette*.

"Look what your Mom has just brought to my attention," he commented.

"What would that be that has you sounding so interested?" I asked. Ernie unfolded the paper and began to read.

CURIOUS */FIRE /* WORKS, At GEORGE HONEY, the upper end of Arch street, ON Tuesday next, being the 25th instant, for the last time, weather permitting, a more curious set of fireworks than has been performed before in this city, divided into four acts; to be disposed of in the following order, viz.

FIRST FIRING. 1. Eight rockets. 2. A capricious wheel. 3. One illuminated wheel, of a new invention. 4. One torment, of different changes.

SECOND FIRING. 5. Eight rockets. 6. One wheel with maroons. 7. One illuminated wheel, of various colours. 8. Three Chinese fountains, with Italian candles, which will communicate */fire /* to a magnificent tornant, of different changes of */fire /*.

THIRD FIRING. 9. Eight rockets. 10. A new fashioned diamond piece. 11. a large wheel, of different compositions, representing a Chinese looking-glass.

FOURTH FIRING 13. Eight rockets. 14. A pigeon on a line, which will communicate */fire /* to a beautiful piece, representing three triumphal arches, adorned with a curious illumination, Chinese */fire /*, Italian candles, and brilliant */fire /*. 14. A palm tree in the centre, with a moving globe on each side, the whole representing a curious academy of */fire /*. 15. A cistern of water, of a different construction. 16. A tornant, forming the sun and moon, and return to the sun again. 17. A large fixed sun, of two changes, or red, and in brilliant */fire /*. To conclude with several flights of rockets, full of serpents, snakes, stars, and crackers.

Tickets to be had at the London Coffee House; at the Golden fleece tavern, in Second street; and, at Theodore Meminger, in Second street, near Arch street. —— Gallery, 3s. 9d. —- The yard, 2s. —- No tickets to be had at the gate. The music to begin at five o, and the fireworks precisely at six.

"Why is that so exciting?" I asked.

"Oh Andrew, I have never seen anything like what they describe here. I want to take Sheila and tell her about everything that I see. Why don't you and Lydia come with us?"

"Ernie, why would I want to go to something like that which I can not even see? I saw quite enough fireworks while I was with the 60th Royal Americans."

"Andrew, you might not get that much out of it and perhaps Sheila will not either, but I will tell her about everything I see. I am sure Lydia will do the same for you! Don't be such a stick in the mud. I am sure Lydia will enjoy it."

As I continued shaping the stock blank that I was working on I thought a great deal about what Ernie had said.

"Ernie, I think you are correct. I will ask Lydia. If she wishes to go, perhaps we four can all go together. I say four as I think maybe I should leave Spark home with Mom as she might be distressed with all of the sound and noise."

"Wonderful, let me know, and I will walk over and get all of our tickets," Ernie said as he caught up a bar of iron he was planning to turn into a gun barrel and headed out into the forge.

Lydia was very excited about the idea of going and suddenly I found myself looking forward to the outing as well.

Afterwards, I was very glad that we had gone. Both women seemed pleased with the event. I still did not feel that fireworks were the perfect thing for a blind person, but the interest and joy that both Lydia and Ernie seemed to experience made it all worth it. I had no idea that within a few days, an event would take place that would change my life.

# 24

# Marrying Lydia

Month by month, Lydia and I had become closer and closer. Her contract with the Allens was to be completed on Lydia's twenty-first birthday in December of 1768. We had expanded our walks as well as lengthened the time that we spent at Mom's. Many hours were pleasurably passed together in Mom's front room by the large fireplace while Lydia read to me. These were pleasant times. When her contract had a bit less than a year to run, we had begun to speak of a future. I had come to love her and was only hesitant to move ahead as I worried that she would not wish to marry a blind man. I felt the income from the shop would let me support her, but I did not want to ask her and have her turn me down.

One Sunday I observed her to be so very sad. When asking her what was wrong, she began to quietly cry. She told me that she had received a letter from her parents who had just arranged a marriage for her.

I felt my heart turn over feeling that my world was falling apart. We were but a few steps from the door of the

Gun-shop. Taking her hand, I said please come in here. We need to talk privately.

Inside the shop she began to tell me how her parents had just written to her explaining how they had made an agreement with an older friend of her step-father's to marry her. His name was Warren Brickles. His wife had just died. I thought my heart stopped at this news. She went on to say that this man had never been good to his wife as he had wanted her to bear sons for him, and she had never seemed to be able to carry a child to term. He had told Lydia's family that he was glad she had died so he could now marry a young woman who could start making sons as soon as they were married as he was already sixty-six years of age.

Pulling her to me, I asked her if that was what she wanted. I felt her shake her head from side to side as she cried even harder. Leaning down, I kissed her and said, "Lydia, I love you! Would you marry me?"

She slowly stopped crying as she hugged me.

"Why have you never asked me before now?"

"Lydia, I have been afraid that you would not want me because I can no longer see. I know blind people are not well thought of, people seem to think of us all as helpless beggars, but I do love you and I think I can support us here with the shop." She wiped her face against my shirt to clear her tears and stretched up to kiss me.

"You silly man, of course I will marry you. I have been waiting for you to ask, but you have not until now. I did not think you were going to and that you did not really love me because you have never asked." For a long time neither one of us spoke, but soon we found ourselves mounting the stairs to the loft where we spent that afternoon becoming married in body and spirit if not yet in law. That afternoon, Spark did not get a walk. We talked for hours working out the details. She told me the letter had said her step-father was coming with Warren Brickles to take her back to his farm on her birthday. We must find a Magistrate who would marry us on the morning of her birthday so it would all be taken care of by the time they arrived. If not, they would try to prevent it and try to force her to marry this older man. Her contract with the Allens would not let her be free to marry until it was completed and so she was not free to marry until she was twenty-one.

Lydia's twenty-first birthday was the 13th of December. We planned to meet that morning and immediately leave to find a Magistrate. Ernie and John Cooper planned to accompany us. The two weeks that had to pass until that date were filled with dread and anxiety that her father might arrive early or cause some other hitch in our plans. She did not want to write to her parents ahead of time as that would only have tipped our hand and possibly led to more problems.

The morning of the 13th dawned beautifully. While drawing the morning water at the pump, I could feel the sun on my face and knew this would be a wonderful day.

By nine o'clock, the shop door opened and Lydia stepped through it. She hurried to my bench and wrapped her arms about me. We all left quickly to go to the Justice's chambers. By noon we had returned to the shop. Our haste had been none too soon. Early in the afternoon, Mr.

Cope accompanied by Mr. Brickles had arrived to collect Lydia. The Allens had said she had quietly left earlier but they expected her to return at any moment. Mrs. Allen went to the room Lydia had been using to bring some of her things down for her step-father, and found a note that Lydia had left. She had explained that she would not marry Warren Brickles and that she was by the time they would read this note be Mrs. Annaler and would be living above the Gunsmith's shop at the corner.

Mr. Cope was furious and demanded to know how Mrs. Allen could have allowed such a thing to have taken place. He charged into the gun-shop without knocking, closely followed by Mr. Brickles. None of us were working that afternoon. We were all sitting about enjoying a cup of coffee.

Emland Cope burst through the door and said, "There you are you little whore! Get next door. My wagon is waiting to take your willful person home where you are to be married to Warren!"

"Father, I am already happily married! This is Andrew my husband, and this is my home."

Standing, I said, "Mr. Cope I do not believe we have ever met, but my name is Andrew Annaler, and I am your daughter's husband. I will take loving care of her and give her a good home."

"Lydia, do as you are told and get yourself next door. I have already accepted a generous payment from Warren who is waiting to bed you this very evening. I will not let this blind beggar steal you."

Warren Brickles shouldered past Emland Cope and glared at both Lydia and myself. Speaking to Lydia, he said, "A good whipping when I get you home will straighten you out in a hurry."

"You will not speak to my wife that way!" I said to Warren Brickles. Turning to Lydia's step-father I said, "Mr. Cope, I did not steal her. Neither did I try to sell her as you have tried to do. You should be ashamed to attempt to sell your step-daughter."

"Shut your mouth! This has nothing to do with you, blind man!" said Warren Brickles, as he drove his fist into the side of my face. Turning to Lydia, he said, "Get out to my wagon you little bitch."

Drawing the large caliber brass barreled pistol that I had brought home with me from Fort Pitt, I cocked the flint hammer and said, "It has everything to do with me as Lydia is now my wife. If either of you ever strike either my wife or me again, I will kill you! Now leave my shop."

"You can not even see me to shoot me blind man!"

"I can not see you, but this pistol is loaded with shot and at this range I can hardly miss you. Now leave!"

As a reply, he spat full in my face. The sound of the 62 caliber pistol was deafening in the close confines of the shop. His chest had only been inches from the muzzle. The shot bored a terrible hole in him. He crumpled backwards and fell dead on the floor of the shop.

Lydia screamed as she saw her father draw a pistol from under his own coat. He screamed in pain as Ernie clubbed down on his forearm with an iron rifle barrel that he had on his bench. Emland Cope's forearm was shattered just above the wrist. Dropping his pistol, he stumbled back out through the door screaming that we had not heard the last of this.

Lydia handed me a cloth that she had dipped into our water bucket to wash my face. Turning to John Cooper who had stayed with us after the marriage, I said, "John, perhaps you should look for a constable." Lydia went upstairs to lie down. About an hour later, the constable arrived. His name was Jeremiah Williams. He was a man for whom we had often done repair work. He determined that both men had been armed and were attempting to kidnap my wife. It appeared to him that I had been defending my wife, myself, and my shop. No charges were pressed. He arranged to have the body removed.

I set about to cleaning and reloading my old brass barreled pistol. Ernie wiped up places where blood had splattered. John invited us all back to the Cooperage for a wedding dinner that he said Gwynne and Bronwyn had been planning in our honor.

"We need to get things off to a better start with this marriage," John said.

It was a wonderful evening. Everyone was very warm and accepting of Lydia. Mom was especially happy, saying she was now glad to see her children settled with mates. The following day, Mrs. Allen arrived at the door of the shop with the things that Lydia had left. She said that Mr. Cope had been very disagreeable and had yelled at her for letting this happen before he and that Brickles fellow came over to the shop. She hugged Lydia and said she was so very glad that Lydia did not have to marry that awful, mean looking Brickles person. She had not known of the shooting for a while, but did see Lydia's step-father Cope stumbling to his wagon while holding his arm. She said he appeared in pain and was very mean to his horse as he drove off. I hoped we would never have to see him again.

Sadie Campbell was heard to tell Mrs. Allen that she had told Lydia that no good would come of a match with that blind man, and now look what has happened.

Ernie asked me if now that I had married, I would want him and Sheila to move. I told him that we did not. I thought their living with Mom had worked well. Lydia and I would be fine for now living in the Gun-shop loft. We would all share the kitchen at Mom's house. Will had moved back to the Cooperage days earlier when he learned of our wedding plans. That year at Christmas, I was again certain that Mom was fixing who would receive the silver shilling when Lydia found it in her piece of plum pudding. I just hugged Mom and whispered, "Thank you." Over the next several months, Lydia and Sarah became very close. Lydia asked if she could help Sarah with her teaching. For now Sarah had taken on teaching Sheila and Molly as well as Steven and her own children to read. I approved heartily and wondered if they would be the first to establish a school for blind people in Philadelphia.

While Sarah worked with them on writing and reading, she spent even more time on teaching them their sums. Daniel was teaching Steven the art of being a potter. Bronwyn was teaching the girls all about everyday life especially cooking, spinning and related domestic arts. Gwynne had John on a short rein and was making him be much more responsible with the running of their inn. As part of this, she was insisting that he sit in on some of the school lessons as John had admitted that he did not read well. Actually, he did not seem to read at all. Gwynne wanted him to be able to help with the book-keeping. He would sometimes complain to me that life had been easier when he was on his own and did whatever he wanted and did not have to worry about anyone or anything. I would ask him if he had a better life now. He quickly agreed that life had never been better, but a little harmless grumbling was not out of place. All in all, everyone seemed to have a better life than they had been having prior to then. Everyone seemed to be learning new things and enjoying life. Sarah was again pregnant and seemed as if she was looking forward to having a third child. Although Daniel was happy, he was increasingly becoming more involved in Colonial politics. He had become quite friendly with an attorney named John Dickenson. They seemed to always be meeting and they spent hours on writing, rewriting and discussing documents that they called "Letters from a Pennsylvania Farmer." They hoped these letters would show King George III the errors of his and Parliament's ways. I did not have such confidence and tried very hard to stay out of these political discussions. Sarah admitted to me that she thought that Daniel was spending so much time on politics that his work and the pottery were suffering. This would not be a good thing at any time, but now with a third child on the way it was very troubling to her.

# 25

1769, a Year of Changes

The year of 1769 brought another healthy baby girl to
Cynthia and Henry's household. In April of that year, Cynthia
gave birth to a daughter which they named Anne. Although
as the year continued, sadness also visited our family. In July,
Sarah lost the baby she had been carrying.

Mom had not been feeling well and had slowly been
failing since Dad had died. Each family death seemed to
weigh more heavily upon her spirit. Her Brother Ebenezer,
her daughter Susan, her husband Frederick and now the
loss of this unborn grandchild was yet another blow. In early
autumn a new young doctor named Benjamin Rush had just
returned to Philadelphia after receiving medical training in
Edinburgh, Scotland. We had him visit as Mom did not even
wish to get out of bed any longer.

"Bleeding. Bleeding is the thing. It will help to restore
your mother to good health," he said. I took an instant dislike
to this man and really was not in favor of the treatment. Dr.
Boyd out on the frontier military posts had often said, "Other

medical men always seem to want to bleed, but you only have so much blood to lose. You know you boys do not feel better when you have been wounded and are losing blood. Therefore, I never recommend giving up blood when you don't have to."

At first I refused to allow him to go ahead. I spoke of this with Mom, remembering her faith in medical men when I had come home. She said that doctors had not helped her Susan, nor had they helped me, or her husband. Day by day, she became weaker and weaker. Sarah urged her to reconsider and let Doctor Rush do for her what he could. Doctor Rush refused to return unless we agreed to let him perform the bleeding that he was sure would make a wondrous change in her condition. On a Wednesday afternoon, in late November, he returned to the house and bled Mom as he had recommended. Mom seemed to lapse into a sleep. The good Doctor said she was resting and would be quite restored when she awakened. He promised to stop in the morning and speak with her. I sat with her all night. The only sound in the room was the quiet regular sound of her breathing. Then even this stopped. She died quietly in her sleep. A great lady was gone. When Doctor Rush stopped in the morning, he chided us for not having let him bleed her earlier. That Christmas Sarah announced that she would take on Mom's tradition of having a family feast complete with plum pudding. However, as the family had grown so with Ernie being married to Sheila, Sheila's sister Molly, Henry and Cynthia with their growing family, Sarah, Daniel and their children as well as Steven, and now Lydia and I, we decided to use the dining room of the Cooperage and include Will, Gwynne, John and Aunt Bronwyn. This became the new tradition and would last for many years. Sarah personally took over the making and serving of the plum pudding. I think she also took over the right to select the recipient of the shilling. That year I found it in my piece of plum pudding. 1770 brought the repeal of the hated Townshend Act duties. Daniel was joyous. However, it also brought news of an incident in Boston where several people were hurt and killed when the British soldiers fired into a crowd. It quickly became known as the Boston Massacre. As the details came to light, it seemed to me that the soldiers had been being harassed by a mob that was attempting to provoke an incident. In fact, I believed the soldiers had every right to fire into the mob in order to restore peace after the mob had gotten out of control. This opinion I kept to myself as the public feeling ran very high against the soldiers. We learned there was to be a trial in Boston. The soldiers were to be represented by a young lawyer named John Adams. Every time we had news from Boston it seemed to rile up the patrons of the coffee-houses. The discussions became more and more heated.

My old friend Michael Graham was in and out of the city now on a regular basis. He had helped us with the legal work after Mom's passing. The way things settled out, Mom had left Sarah the house that she and Dad had raised us in. Sarah had the largest growing family and could make good use of a larger home. By May, Sarah announced that she was again pregnant. She already had two children of her own and seemed to consider Steven yet another. Ernie and Sheila rented a small house a bit farther north on third Street. Sarah, Daniel and their children moved into Mom and Dad's old house. Their old house in front of Daniel's pottery was only three rooms. Each was piled one atop the other in the style of the houses on that street. Daniel converted the first floor room of their old very small house into a store for the sale of the pottery that he had become so well known for. His wares were in ever increasing demand. Lydia would often help out in this store. The second floor became the school room. The upper room on the third floor became Steven's.

Henry had been left a sum of money that he put to good use in his growing watch and clock shop. They were very comfortable in their house on Arch Street.

I had been left the gun-shop as well as a substantial sum of money. Lydia and I continued to live above the shop and take meals with Sarah and her family as we had done when Mom had still been alive. Ernie and I became partners in the gun business. He was positively glowing the day he finished hand lettering our new sign. "Annaler & Schmidt — Gunsmiths" This was lettered above a drawing of crossed muskets with a powder horn hanging down in- between them. Ernie had always been an easy going, likeable person and we got on quite well. He did all of the work in the forge, and I took care of the sale of items in the front of the shop. We both did the stock shaping and cold filing work. It was a happy shop, although we never stopped commenting to each other that something was or was not the way Master Frederick would have wanted it to be.

# 26

## Nick's Second Visit

Sarah seemed to be trying to take Mom's place and look after all of us.

Two or three weeks before Christmas 1770, my old friend Nick the Tinker arrived in Philadelphia. He planned to spend the rest of the winter here as he had some family business that might take some time to conclude. Nick had brought with him two pack horses loaded with furs from the western frontier. Most of these he wished to turn into hard cash. The rest he would keep and tan during the winter. As he planned to be here for a number of months, he wondered if I could steer him to a clean, honest place to stay. Of course I sent him to the Cooperage. Will was in the shop at the time and offered to walk him over there and help him get acquainted and settle his things in. I was sure William Fall could stable his two pack horses and that Abraham Kiessel would be glad to purchase his furs.

Nick and Will went off together and we all agreed to meet that evening at the Cooperage and catch up on old times over Aunt Bronwyn's good cooking. Ernie usually dined there anyway as Sheila and Molly continued to work there for wages. Their indentures had ended when John had torn up their papers at Sheila and Ernie's wedding.

When Ernie, Lydia and I, accompanied by Spark, arrived at the Cooperage, John greeted us warmly and directed us to the kitchen, where Nick had settled in and was chatting with Aunt Bronwyn as if they had been acquainted for many years. Will told me that Abraham had been glad to purchase the furs, although he had gone on for some time about how bad business was and he did not know if he could pay top dollar. After some prolonged haggling, which Will said they both had seemed to enjoy, Abraham said he guessed he could pay a high figure for Nick's furs as they were first rate and after all, he was a friend of ours. Nick had sold the pack horses to William Fall as he thought that was a better thing to do rather than boarding them since he would be here for so long.

After a great and hearty meal, we sat long into the night speaking of old times and old adventures. Nick had been at the treaty of Fort Stanwix back in the autumn of 1768 and had much to relay. The French & Indian War had been a complicated struggle. The French presence in Canada had long been a bar to westward expansion on the population of the thirteen British Colonies. In fact, that was what the war had really been about. For decades there had been a precarious balance between the tribes loyal to French interests and those loyal to British interests. Unfortunately for the Indian population, no one actually had a care for the interests of the various tribes. Once the French threat was gone, the British settlers, hungry for new and free land, poured westward. This is what the Proclamation line of October 1763 had been all about. This proclamation was supposed to prevent the settlers from moving west into lands that had been set aside for the tribes. Having taken vast tracts of land from every tribe, the Crown was willing to say that some of these tribes could now retain and enjoy some of their own land. The proclamation had drawn a line down the western mountains beyond the headwaters of the eastward flowing rivers. Enforcing this proclamation was a large part of what we in the 60th Royal Americans had been attempting to do at Fort Pitt. It had proved impossible to check the western flood of settlers and so in 1768 at the treaty of Fort Stanwix, the Crown was suggesting to extend the line many hundreds of miles to the west, rather than admitting that it was not possible for the might of the British Army to maintain the rule of the October 1763 proclamation.

In the autumn of 1768 it was William Johnson's duty to explain all of this to the various tribes and attempt to map out a compromise that everyone might live with.

Many of the tribes had long trusted William Johnson. However, from Nick's stories it seemed that trust and honesty were missing at this treaty. The eastern tribes which had for so long been friends of William Johnson's were perfectly willing to give western tribal lands away. Especially since they were lands belonging to other tribes and were not theirs to give away. William Johnson was simply trying to cover over the fact that the Crown could not control its own settlers. At the same time he was personally benefiting from a vast tract of land that was to be set aside for him. As if this was not bad enough, religious missionaries had attempted to have parts of Pennsylvania, most of western New York, and parts of what would become the Ohio territory given to the Anglican Church as a religious haven. This movement was spearheaded by Eleazar Wheelock and backed by the Colony of Connecticut which had grand designs of its own, particularly regarding Pennsylvania lands in the Wyoming Valley. This part of Pennsylvania was being hotly disputed by claims of both Pennsylvania and Connecticut. The problem had been caused by earlier conflicting and overlapping land grants made to both Colonies by King Charles II. Eleazar Wheelock sent the Reverend Jacob Johnson, (no relation to William Johnson) to advocate that the Anita Tribe ought to hold their lands for such a religious haven. Jacob had arrived wearing a hair shirt and acting as if he was John the Baptist who had come to save the tribal lands. Throughout the conference and treaty negotiations, Jacob Johnson was a thorn in William Johnson's side. Fortunately, this religious land grab failed. Nick said that he guessed the Tribes thought the British gifts were a better deal than the Church's prayers for their souls. We both agreed that this new treaty would fail. It was simply one more step in driving the Indian Tribes farther and farther west as the ever increasing population of the Colonies demanded land.

Nick was in Philadelphia to receive a shipment of goods for a relative of his who lived in York, Pennsylvania. No one knew exactly when the ship might arrive, so he thought he would, as he put it, "fort up for the winter."

With little to occupy his time, he took to nearby hunting ventures. He had always been an excellent hunter and quickly proved that he had not lost any of his skills. That winter, he saved the Cooperage a great deal in costs of purchasing food. Venison was almost always on the menu along with squirrel, rabbit, and many types of fowl. Two days before Christmas, Nick returned with the largest turkey that any of us had ever seen. It weighed over fifty pounds. Nick insisted that I be allowed to touch it to see how large it was before it was consigned to Aunt Bronwyn's kitchen attentions. Christmas day that year, Will presented Nick with a beautiful example of one of his powder-horns. It was a large, mostly dark, nicely curved horn. The base fit excellently and was held in place by eight brass tacks. On one large light colored area, Ernie had engraved a turkey. The stopper peg, usually called a fiddle-peg, Will had carved to resemble a turkey feather. He had also fashioned a powder measure to be used with the horn made from the wing-bone of a large turkey. A brown leather strap finished off the look of this handsome powder horn. Nick was both touched and delighted. Forever after, this horn was referred to as Nick's Christmas turkey powder horn in honor of the huge turkey that Nick had brought to the Cooperage for Christmas dinner 1770.

Will had a good knowledge of tanning hides, as he had spent so much time at Jacob Snyder's tannery down on Dock Street. He helped Nick with the tanning and admitted that he had learned a few good tricks from Nick. Seth, Sarah, and Daniel's eldest were often found with these two, learning about tanning and the making of hides into good leather. That year, Nick made Christmas gifts for everyone of various furs and hides. He gave Lydia a beautiful fox pelt that she sewed onto one of her capes as a collar. He also gave us a bear skin that we used as a rug in the loft above the gun-shop.

Sarah again baked the traditional plum pudding. I had wondered who would find the shilling this year. A few days earlier, I had heard Sarah praising Molly for the great progress she had made with her school work. Listening to Sarah's words of encouragement, I wondered if Molly would be the recipient this year of the lucky silver shilling. When it turned out to be just so, I smiled and thought how proud of Sarah Mom would have been. When I hugged Sarah and told her so, she said, "Why Andrew, I have no idea what you are talking about." After a short pause, Sarah continued, "Oh Andrew, I am glad she has the shilling as I think she needs some good luck this year."

"What do you mean?"

Sarah took my sleeve and pulled me down the hall of the Cooperage and quietly said, "Do you not know she is pregnant?"

I seemed to be one of the last people in our growing family to know this. It was a topic everyone seemed to know about, but no one wanted to really discuss openly. Lydia told me later that night that she, Sarah, Cynthia, Gwynne, and Bronwyn had all known for a week or more. I commented that I had not known, and Lydia replied, "You are a man. You did not need to know."

Molly was now seventeen. I knew that because of her school work with Sarah, she had met and become quite friendly with Steven, although I had no idea that they had become quite that friendly. He would turn eighteen a few days into the new year of 1771, but still had three years of his apprenticeship to run. Generally apprentices were not allowed to marry, but Molly was already free and had been earning a small wage from Gwynne and John at the Cooperage. Steven was doing very well in the pottery. Since they both agreed that they wished to marry, and Steven already had a room above the pottery shop where they could live, no one saw any reason to not let their plans go ahead.

On January 4th, Steven's 18th birthday, they announced their plans to be married. As Sheila and Molly were very close as sisters, as well as in size, Sheila offered to let Molly be married in the wedding dress that Mom had made for Sheila's wedding. It only needed small alterations. Lydia made these alterations for Molly and before long all was ready. By the end of the month they were married and living together above the Pottery shop. This was only a half a square away from the Cooperage and about the same distance from Henry and Cynthia's home on Arch Street.

In late June, Molly gave birth to a healthy baby boy. They named him Patrick after the uncle who had helped them find a place in this new land.

A few days after the wedding, old Sadie Campbell, the neighborhood busybody was heard to say at the water pump that no good would come of such a marriage. Molly and Steven both seemed to have the same eye problem which had caused their blindness. The doctors had called it a kind of cataract. Their eyes looked very cloudy. As soon as the baby, Patrick, was born, it could be seen that he had very cloudy eyes as well. He was likely to have the same eye trouble that his parents had. Of course Sadie Campbell was crowing at the first opportunity and to anyone who would listen that she had been right, and this was a judgment of God. A little over two years later when this small baby died by drowning after falling into a well, Sadie was jubilant, proclaiming that the wrath of God had been made clear to everyone by this judgment of God.

By February 1771, Sarah gave birth to her third child. Another beautiful little girl, who they named Hannah. In March, Cynthia also had another child. This one was a boy who they named William. I was beginning to feel as if there were too many children for me to keep track of. When I expressed this thought to Lydia, she said that I had best be able to remember at least one more name as she was pregnant. It had been easy to think of my sister, or sister-in-law having children, but to learn that my wife was to have a child was a startling piece of news. Our lives were about to change.

Sarah's eldest son Seth had always shown an interest in the gun-shop. He had often visited when Sarah came over to help with the shop ledger book. He was now eleven and seemed to have adopted Nick as his hero. After speaking privately with Daniel, Nick invited Seth to accompany him on some of his short hunting trips. I decided that Ernie and I would start working on a rifle for him for his twelfth birthday in June.

Dad had always made a number of parts ahead. I had been able to find a very nice small flintlock mechanism that Dad must have made years earlier. Ernie agreed to make a rifled barrel. We agreed on 40 caliber, which would be very adequate for small game near the City area. I selected a nice curly maple stock blank and the project was begun. There was a fair amount of work in the shop just then, but we finished Seth's rifle in time for his June birthday.

Although it was to be a surprise for Seth, everyone else seemed to know about it. Nick made a beautiful hunting pouch from leather he had tanned himself. Lydia wove a wide linen shoulder strap for this pouch. Will made a very nice horn to go with the hunting bag. Seth's Uncle Henry engraved several animals on the horn for him.

Seth could not have been more pleased when he received this collection of gifts. He and Nick immediately went off for a day of shooting.

As soon as they had returned, Seth came into the gun-shop and asked Ernie if he would help him make a good hunting knife. Ernie laughed and said of course he would. He had helped make knives for people in the past. He did not elaborate, but I knew he was speaking of the one that he had made for Will. As the two of them walked out into the forge to look for the right piece of steel, I heard Ernie ask Seth if he had ever thought about wanting to join us in a few years as an apprentice and learn to make not only knives, but guns as well.

Ernie had not yet taken in any apprentices, but we both agreed that we would speak with Sarah and Daniel and determine if, in two years when Seth would become fourteen, he might wish to join us in the shop. I thought to myself that if this were to come about, Master Frederick would be pleased. By mid August, Nick's long awaited ship had finally arrived. He received the shipment of goods, as well as the two cousins who had traveled with the goods, and began making plans to transport the entire lot; relatives and goods, as well as all the supplies that he had been stock-piling as trade goods to sustain his own Tinker activities, out to York where others in his family had settled. This required purchasing a wagon, two oxen, and adequate food supplies for their journey.

Seth asked to be allowed to accompany Nick on this venture, but Sarah and Daniel thought him to young to be running off into the woods. Nick did not plan to return directly to Philadelphia and so Seth had to wave farewell to his hero on that day in September that the group slowly rolled out of town.

Lydia gave birth to our first child in October of 1771. We named her Margarete and began to think about where we might move if our family grew any larger. We would have to leave the loft of the gun-shop. For now we would get by. Christmas 1771 seemed especially fine. Perhaps it was little Margarete that brought increasing joy and warmth into our lives. Lydia and I seemed especially joyous. Even though the days when I told Ernie to go home early and I would close up the shop and mount the steps to pull Lydia's clothes off of her and romp about the loft with her in blissful abandon, seemed to have stopped, I hoped they would return. However, holding our little girl in my arms with Lydia beside us, I felt more at peace than I had since before the explosion.

That Christmas Will found the shilling in his piece of plum pudding. Later, in the kitchen of the Cooperage, I smiled remembering Sarah's words of the previous year that Molly might need the shilling as she was pregnant; I asked Sarah if she thought Will might have gotten anyone pregnant this year?

She laughed and replied, "I hope not."

Bronwyn rose from in front of the kitchen hearth and said, "I will skin him alive if the little devil has gotten some poor young girl with child." We all laughed and thought nothing more of it. As it turned out, Will had not gotten anyone with child, but he certainly did need the good luck of the shilling during the coming year.

# 27

## The Stable Fire

Will mostly lived in the attic of the Cooperage, but was often out and about for days at a time. He sometimes slept in Jacob Snyder's tannery on Dock Street where he got his horns. He might just as often be found at William Fall's stables on Locust Street. Despite the fact that he had lost his sight when a horse had kicked him in the head at age seven, Will loved horses. He was one of those people who seemed to have a natural ability to communicate with them. He had come to know William Fall through me and often helped out about the stable. William said he was a big help cleaning and repairing tack, rubbing down animals that folks had just returned, feeding and watering them and so forth.

The spring of 1772 found Will spending a lot of time in William Fall's stable and, in fact, living in the hay loft.

Later, I would learn that he had been sleeping there the night of May 16th, when the great stable fire had broken out. During the night Lydia and I heard folks running past the shop on Third Street, shouting "Put out your buckets! Put out your buckets!"

Once awake, we heard the double tolling of the bell from the State House. This bell ringing in the middle of the night signaled a fire. At first we had no idea where the fire was, but the double tolling signaled that the fire was south of Market Street. It was quite a distance away so we were not alarmed. I did run downstairs and place our two leather fire buckets on the step in front of the shop. All houses and shops had to have these fire buckets. Each one was marked with the owner's name so they could be reclaimed after the fire was out. Buckets that had been placed out in front of a home or shop would be gathered up by anyone running past on their way to fight the fire. They would be used to form a bucket brigade from the nearest pump or well to bring water to the fire.

Soon we heard the sound of the iron tires of one of the new pump carts from the Union Fire Company rumble by. I was certain that Ernie would be with this group as he always volunteered when a fire broke out. The Union Fire Company was the closest one to us, being on Grindstone alley which was but a half square away from our shop. Later in the morning, we learned from passersby, that the fire was in William Fall's stable at fourth and Locust Streets. This news filled me with dread. Stable fires were a very serious and terrible event. With the amount of hay that was always about, even the smallest fire grew and spread with terrifying effect. Once the fire got going and took hold, the heat and smoke became so intense that one could not even get close to a stable or any building that was engulfed in flames. There was no saving the building or anything much that had been in it. Add the presence of a number of terrified horses screaming and kicking while people tried to get them out through the rapidly increasing intense heat and smoke, and the dimensions of such a disaster begin to become clear. The best fire companies could hope for was to keep the fire from spreading to surrounding buildings while trying to save a few of the animals.

William Fall had come to be a good friend since that first time that I had met him when he had brought me home on the last leg of my journey from Fort Pitt. He was also, of course, a Brother Mason. I was very worried for him, but did not go down to Locust Street. Although I had helped fight many a fire when I had lived here as an apprentice, since the explosion I did not turn out when the fire-bells rang. I always felt as if I was in the way in large crowds of people. In the morning, Ernie did not appear at our shop for work. I was sure he was helping fight the fire. I was correct, but at that point I still did not know how bad it was. During the afternoon, Ernie appeared smelling of wood-smoke and completely exhausted. He told me the fire had been at William Fall's stable. It was completely destroyed. Of the twenty-four horses that had been there when the fire broke out, only seven had been saved. Ernie told me that without Will, even most of those would have been lost.

"Will was there?" I asked.

"Yes, he has been sleeping there in the hay loft of the Stable for a few weeks now. I don't know how the fire started. When we reached the fire, it was already terrible! The smoke was very dense. It had been a dark night anyway.

Men were shouting questions and orders, but you could hardly hear over the noise of the horses screaming in fright, the iron tires of the pump carts on the cobblestones, and the clanging of the fire-bells. Everything was very confusing with several fire companies arguing over who would do what.

"We got the new pump cart set up and went to work as soon as we reached the stable yard, but it was already too late," Ernie told me.

Ernie was one of the volunteers working the pump handles of the new pump cart made by Richard Mason. Richard Mason was a cousin of Daniel's. He was a mechanic who was always tinkering with some new idea. In 1769 he had designed and manufactured a pump cart for fighting fires. It was essentially a large rectangular trough on wheels. It was made of wood and lined with sheets of tin. The cart had a long shaft extending forward with cross-bar handles through it. Six men usually dragged this cart to the fire. The pump cylinder was set in the middle of the trough. The pump handles projected out over the cart ends in front and back, in what was becoming known as the Philadelphia style. Most pump carts had the handles projecting out of the sides of the carts. This allowed more men to stand shoulder to shoulder and pump the handles up and down in their see-saw like fashion. However, many of the streets in Philadelphia were quite narrow, and the front and back style pump handle placement was becoming increasingly popular. Two or three men would locate themselves on either end of the pump handles. They would begin pumping away as soon as the bucket brigade began dumping its water into the trough of the cart. The cart foreman called cadence for the men pumping by shouting through his fire-trumpet. A large long nozzle extended from the top of the pump. This could be turned in a complete circle so that it could be aimed at the fire.

Ernie continued, "I did not see Will at first, but then there he was leading a horse out of the stable. Will knows that stable like the back of his hand and led horse after horse out safely. The smoke was so thick you could not see anything. Will is really very good with horses you know. They trust him. Will kept going in after them and, horse after horse, he brought them safely out." Ernie went on to say that when Will had staggered out of the burning stable that final time, he did not look so good. "He had breathed in a lot of smoke. That last time he was not leading a horse, but was carrying a young black lad named Rufus Jackson over his shoulders. Will had certainly saved Rufus's life. Neither one of them looked too good. Rufus had blood all over his face and was clutching at his eye. William Fall had them both taken over to the Pennsylvania Hospital a few squares away, on Spruce Street. We could still hear horses whinnying and screaming inside. William should never have gone back in, but before anyone could stop him, he had disappeared back into the thick smoke. It was only a minute or two later that the entire burning loft and roof fell in."

Ernie placed his hand on my shoulder and said, "Andrew, William did not come out."

Ernie's words sent a chill through me. Hearing this news I felt sick. William must be dead. My good friend

William had been in the shop only yesterday and was so alive, standing here on this very spot, talking and laughing. We had been discussing a candidate for Free Masonry who William was acting for as his recommender. Suddenly now William was gone. Thoughts and memories of what a kind and generous man William Fall had been flashed through my mind.

Ernie went on to say that he had stopped at Pennsylvania Hospital on his way back here, but they could only tell him that Will had breathed a lot of smoke; they are not sure if he burned his lungs or not. Rufus is also in a bad way. Rufus had also been living in the loft and was helping bring the horses out. One of the terrified horses had kicked a rail of his stall so hard that he had shattered it. Rufus took a large splinter directly in his eye.

"I don't know Rufus, who is he?" I asked. Ernie told me that he did not know him well, but that Rufus Jackson was a young black teenage lad who had been working for William Fall. Like Will, he had also breathed in a lot of smoke, but the thing is, he only had one really useful eye, and he got the splinter in that eye.

"Oh my God," I said. Memories of my own sudden blindness came flooding back to me.

Ernie was exhausted and went home to rest. Later in the day, I closed the shop. Accompanied by Margarete, Sarah, and Lydia, Spark and I went over to the Pennsylvania Hospital to see if we could learn more about Will, or do anything for him.

When we found him, Will said he felt very sick and

kept coughing. He said he guessed he was doing better than Rufus. I told him that I did not really know Rufus, but heard that he had a bad eye injury.

"Bad? Yea, I guess you could say bad. You know he only had one good eye to start with, and now he sees about as well as we do." Between coughs, Will went on to tell me Rufus's story. Rufus was about half Will's age. He had been born on the Jackson plantation in South Carolina. He had no idea who his father was, but his mother worked as a cook in the kitchen of the big house. Rufus had always received good treatment, as well as whatever extra food he wanted by stopping by to visit his mother in the kitchen.

Rufus had worked in the stable and helped the coachman. When Rufus was about twelve or thirteen years old, Jeremiah Jackson, the plantation owner, had been thrown from a horse and died, having broken his neck. The plantation had been taken over by a new master who was rarely there. The new master had employed a very stern and often mean overseer. One day while walking past his mother's cabin, Rufus had heard her making sounds of great distress. Running to the cabin, and pushing the door open, he found that the overseer had just finished forcing himself upon his mother. The overseer turned on Rufus and told him to get out. As the overseer screamed this at him, he also struck Rufus in the face with his riding crop. The end of the crop had struck Rufus's left eye and he had never seen well again out of that eye. The overseer had ordered him out of the stable and sent him to work in the fields. Rufus had hated the field work and decided to run away. Months passed, but finally one day, he could not take it any longer and headed north. The next few months were miserable ones for him. He had only barely escaped from being caught and had nearly starved. After many months of struggle, he had reached Philadelphia and had stayed for a few weeks with a black family that had fed him and given him new clothes. As he had always liked working with the horses, he had asked for work at several stables. Finally he had asked a stable owner, who was a kindly looking man if he could work there. Later he learned this kind man was William Fall. William had liked him and had let him live in the loft. That is where Rufus met Will Davies.

Once he had been released from the Pennsylvania Hospital, he had been invited by Will to come and stay at the Cooperage until something could be found for him.

Rufus had completely lost all vision in his right eye from the splinter, but could still see shapes and shadows from his left eye. He, like Will, continued to cough, but by midsummer, he wanted to find something to do. John Cooper had worked on the docks for many years in a variety of jobs and knew many people. One of these individuals was a man named Robert Bridges.

# 28

# Robert Bridges Gives
# Rufus a Chance

By this time, Robert Bridges had become quite wealthy. John admitted that he had never really been close friends with Robert, but he knew him well enough and had done one or two favors for Robert in the past. Knowing that Robert had a large sailmaking loft on Willings' Wharf where he had employed many people, both black and white, John approached a free black man who he had worked beside for a time, named Thomas Fortune. John explained Rufus' circumstances and then introduced Rufus to Thomas. Thomas Fortune was a good and kindly man. He seemed to take a great liking to Rufus at their first meeting. John and Thomas both visited Robert Bridges. Thomas promised that if Robert would give Rufus a chance, he, Thomas, would teach him the sail sewing trade and generally get him off to a good start. Robert agreed and said that Rufus should be at his loft in the morning of the following day. There was a lot of smiling and good cheer at the Cooperage that evening, as Rufus was well liked and everyone wished him well in his new trade.

Thomas invited Rufus to live in his home located near the corner of Third and Walnut Streets. This arrangement would make it easier for them to walk to the sail loft together. Thomas treated Rufus as a member of his family. They would be accompanied by Thomas' eight year old son, James, who was also just then beginning to work and learn about sailmaking next to his father. This was a fortunate friendship for Rufus in future years. After Thomas died, young James, who later changed his name to Forton, was to become one of the wealthiest and most influential free black men in the City of Philadelphia. He never forgot learning sailmaking from his father next to Rufus who became something of a big brother to the younger lad. Throughout the rest of their lives, James Forton never forgot his friend Rufus Jackson, and was a great help to him.

Robert Bridges' loft was the upper floor above the warehouse of Thomas Willing & CO. When they reached Robert Bridges' loft on Willings' Wharf that first day, Rufus knew nothing of sailmaking, but he was soon to learn a great deal. Thomas explained to him that the first order of business was to make him a new set of clothing to work in. Bronwyn had made Rufus some presentable clothing after Gwynne had insisted on getting rid of all of Rufus's old things. Rufus told Thomas he already had better newer clothes than he had ever had in his life. Thomas laughed and told young James to show Rufus what he meant and explain about the need for these new clothes to him. James laughed and proudly showed Rufus the new suit of clothing that his father had just made for him. It consisted of a pullover canvas top and loose fitting canvas breeches that tied at the side.

"We will look like sailors," Rufus commented.

"Yes, but we need to wear these to protect the canvas that we are working on. We must always be concerned with the sail canvas that we are working on," Thomas explained. "We must not get it dirty from our street clothes and we must never walk on it or snag or tear it. We will start at once to make you your own suit of sailmakers clothes from some of the pieces of scrap canvas over there in the corner. While I measure you James will start sweeping the floor as we must always keep it clean."

As Rufus stood there being gently measured by Thomas, he breathed in the air. It was filled, as every sailmaking loft is, with the good smell of bee's wax, turpentine and tallow. This mixture was used on the thread which the sails were sewed together with. It made it easier to sew with and helped to prevent the stitching from rotting away. Soon Rufus came to love that good smell. There was much to learn, but he knew that a new life, a free life was opening to him and he reveled in it.

Robert Bridges appeared a bit later during the morning. Thomas was just finishing up cutting out Rufus' new suit.

"Well, is this our new lad?" he asked. "I see you are about to have a new suit of duck."

"Duck, sir?" Rufus inquired.

"Yes lad, duck comes from the old Dutch word

doek which means flax. Flax is the plant duck or canvas is made from."

Soon a voice was heard from the street below. "Ahoy there in the sail-loft!"

Addressing Rufus and James, Robert said, "Have a care there lads. We are about to sway up some old sails to be reworked. The brig 'Wanderer' is in port. She has newly arrived from the West Indies where she experienced a bad storm. Her Captain is sending her sails around for us to restore."

Robert stepped to a pair of large, floor to ceiling doors at the end of the loft and swung them open. The sounds and smells of the street which had both been muted now rushed in. As Robert released several ropes and pulleys, a large hook descended toward a cart which was positioned directly below. The hook and ropes were suspended from an enormous beam which extended well out over the street.

Two of the other sailmakers, Alex and Jonas positioned themselves around a capstan which was in line with the open doors, but located some distance away near the rear wall of the loft.

Taking Rufus by his sleeve and pulling him back against a side wall out of the way, imitating Robert, James said, "Have a care now."

As soon as the bundle of sails on the cart below had been secured to the hook, Robert signaled to these two men, and as they turned the capstan, the heavy bundle rose slowly into the air. When it was just above the level of the loft floor, two more workmen, using poles and ropes, hauled the bundle of sails into the loft. As Robert descended the stairway to speak with the Captain of the Wanderer, everyone moved quickly about the loft making the area ready to spread out the sails and carefully examine them. The large doors were closed and once again, the loft took on a warmer closer feeling. Thomas called Rufus and James over to his bench.

"Now let us get your new clothing sewed together. Laying the pieces out on the bench, Thomas made a few stitches along each seam to hold things together, showing Rufus how to sew. "This is how you work the needle in and out. You are going to start learning by sewing your own things. The thread is nice and heavy and the eyes in these needles are large. First use this wax to make the thread stiff. Then pinch the end flat so it can easily slide through the eye."

Rufus had no trouble waxing the thread, but struggled trying to get the thread through the eye of the needle.

"Here, try doing that with your mouth," Thomas advised. "I know you have trouble seeing it, but often it is dark in here and you will learn to use your mouth and lips to help guide the thread and needle together. There, now you have it."

Rufus was amazed that by midday he had a new sailmakers set of clothing that he had sewed together himself. Somehow he knew he had just begun a new life. A new free life, with people who cared about him and would help him. It was a great feeling!

# 29

# A Letter From Nick

During the summer of 1772, a letter arrived from Nick the Tinker.

To all of my good friends at the Cooperage,

I am hoping this note finds all of my friends there in good health and enjoying life.

After returning to my family's homestead last autumn, I spent a pleasant winter during which I met several people who have changed my life. A lady named Mary has taken my fancy. She has been earning her living by acting as a Scribner. In fact, she is putting this note on paper for me now. In the late spring we were married.

I also encountered a Dutch frontier trader named Otto Davenport. As you know, I brought many trade-goods back with me when I returned here to York. Otto and I have formed a partnership and will in a few days be heading north. We plan to establish a trading *post in the Fort Augusta area. He has filed a claim on what he tells me is a goodly piece of land not far from the Fort.*

*Although I do not know when, it seems certain that someday I will find myself in your City of Philadelphia to restock trade-goods. I will look forward to visiting all of you again at that time. Be well.*

*Nick the Tinker*

This letter was read repeatedly to anyone who had enjoyed Nick's company during the months that he had lived in the Cooperage. During my next few visits there, I observed that Bronwyn seemed rather short and generally a bit out of sorts. When I asked Gwynne about this she sighed and said, "Sometimes you men can be so dense. Did you not realize she was hoping Nick would return here?"

"Well, he said he would return sometime in the future," I replied.

"No silly, I mean she was hoping he would return for her."

"Oh!"

# 30

# Family Stress

Life moved quietly forward for the next year or so. Cynthia had another daughter named Charlotte. She now said that she had daughters all named after Queens of England, and a son named after one of the Kings. Daniel had asked Cynthia at a family gathering if that was such a good idea when there was so much unrest throughout the Colonies with growing bad feeling toward the British Royal Family.

"Why, Daniel, the unrest is largely in the minds of such as yourself who look for trouble at every turn. It is not the Royal Family that occasionally has made an error in judgment. It is the Parliament, made up of men such as yourself who keep the pot boiling." These words led to a very strained family discussion around the great table in the dining room of the Cooperage. It concluded when Daniel excused himself and after rising from the table left the room. Sarah was in tears, but she could not persuade him to stay.

There had been signs of strain throughout the family over the earlier Stamp Act, the Townshend Duties, and now the tax on tea. However, looking back on it, this was the first serious family disruption concerning what appeared to be a gathering political storm.

In the simplest terms, it all boiled down to the fact that the French & Indian War, although won by the British, had been very expensive. It had removed the threat of French domination of the westward expansion of the British Colonies. The British Crown had wished to find a way for the Colonists who had benefited from the removal of the French to help pay for the military costs. These costs continued to mount as it was necessary for England to maintain a standing army to govern and attempt to control the frontier. The Stamp Act had been the first major step in attempting to have the Colonies contribute to these costs. This had met with great resentment and resistance here in the Colonies. The Stamp Act had been repealed only to be replaced by a group of taxes known as the Townshend Duties. These Townshend Duties had been accompanied by a number of revisions in the Courts of Admiralty. This revision was aimed at an attempt to cut down on the widespread business of smuggling that was rampant throughout the Colonies. To give this Court teeth, the Writs of Assistance allowed for the Crown representatives to search property without written authority. As an additional regulation, the Crown demanded that the various cities having numerous dwellings provide winter quarters for British troops. New York City, for one, had refused this consideration. In Boston a mob has so harassed the soldiers that the crowd had been fired into and this had brought a loss of life. The Townshend Duties had been repealed, but as a compromise, as well as a face saving measure, the tax had been kept on the importation of tea. It was quite involved. As the British East India Company had been losing money, the Crown was allowing them to bring the tea directly to the Colonies for sale rather than making it be shipped to England, and then reshipped to the Colonies. Even with the tax imposed on the tea, it would be less costly here in the Colonies than the tea sold in England.

All in all, I felt the Crown had been quite tolerant toward her Colonies. This did not matter to the Colonists such as Daniel. They were quite certain that there was a principle at stake here. The Crown's willingness to back down in the past on the Stamp Act and the other Townshend Duties encouraged them to think they would also force the Crown to back down once again. However, this time the lines seemed to be firmly drawn. Anger was rising on both sides of the Atlantic Ocean.

What had been abstract tavern discussions had now become family issues. Having been a part of the British Military system, and observing it first hand, I had always felt that the taxes were not an unreasonable act on the part of the Crown. Other members of our family, such as Henry and his wife Cynthia agreed. Henry had been very close to his uncle Ebenezer who was proud to say he was a Royal Subject living in the British Empire. Cynthia had also come from a family whose loyalties were with the Crown. Mom and Dad had always believed that they had a good life here in Pennsylvania under the mantle of the British Empire. Daniel, although a very good man, seemed to have taken to his political stands as strongly as he had taken to making pottery.

Sarah was caught in the middle but of course would support her husband Daniel.

The family members attached to the Cooperage, which we had all come to think of as part of our extended family, were fairly neutral. John had always leaned toward supporting the Crown, but was willing to make a shilling on either side of the fence, as we would learn as time passed. Will was much the same way, although I think he was at heart more on the side of the Colonial viewpoint. He had said to me once, "Do you really think the Welsh love the English?"

My friend Michael was something of an enigma to me. In his lawyerlike way, he was able to represent both sides of the issue. He was very opposed to the unreasonable searches, but the other taxes did not seem to trouble him.

When I would try to discuss these political issues with Ernie, he would tell me that we were in the gun trade and no matter how folks felt, or whatever happened, people were going to be buying guns. I told him he sounded like Dad. He would reply, "I worked with Master Frederick for a long time. Do you think I learned nothing?"

When Seth was fourteen, in June of 1773, Ernie and I formally took him into the shop as an apprentice. Seth showed a good ability, and interest in learning. I was particularly touched when he said that he wished his grandfather was still here to teach him as well. Both Ernie and I laughed and agreed if Master Frederick had still been here that there would have been days when Seth might not have made that wish. Later, Ernie said quietly to me, "You know, he is really still here." I reached out and shook Ernie's hand and we said no more.

# 31

# A Great Little Schooner Named the Cyndia

## The Pennsylvania Gazette

September 22, 1773
TO BE SOLD, A NEW Schooner, built of red Cedar and Oak, 35 Feet Keel, 14 1/2 Beam, 6 1/2 Feet Hold, strong built, well found, and sails fast. For Terms, enquire of */ROBERT /**/BRIDGES /*. - Inventory to be seen at the London Coffee house. - The Vessel to be viewed at Mr. REESE MEREDITHWharff, who has likewise an Inventory of her Materials.

Henry brought this advertisement to me and asked if I had any interest in being a partner in buying this small vessel. He had visited the ship and thought it a fine one. I had met Robert Bridges earlier when Rufus Jackson had gone to work with James Fortune at Robert's sailmaking loft. He was a decent and respected man of business and I had no doubt that he would have had made a fine seaworthy vessel.

Offering to introduce Henry to Robert Bridges, I agreed to share the partnership with Henry if we could get the little ship at a good price.

Henry had always been interested in sailing ships. This interest had grown when he was with Uncle Ebenezer as Uncle had been a close friend of John Harris who had developed a ships chronometer, which made long ocean navigation possible. Henry thought this little ship would be a good investment. It was ideally suited for trade up and down the coast of the Colonies. He was offering me a chance to be a partner in the venture.

I visited the ship with Henry and John Cooper who had some sailing experience. After we met with Robert Bridges we came to an agreement and purchased the little vessel. We named her the "Cyndia," which was a combination of both Cynthia and Lydia, our wives' names.

Robert Bridges recommended both a captain and a mate who he said were honest men on the wharf at the time. The Captain was named Isaac Larson and the mate Jacob Castle. They would take on two or more hands as needed. Within days, I was not only an owner in a gunshop; I was a partner in a small two masted schooner designed for coastal trading. This little ship turned out to be a great investment. For many years, it transported light cargoes up and down the coast of North America. Good Pennsylvania hardwood as lumber went south to the Carolinas, Indigo, rice and cotton came north as well as hemp and pine tar. Folks always needed something brought from somewhere else to be used where it was less plentiful. Roads were still not what one might wish for and coastal trade flourished.

As none of us had ever been out on the water, Henry, Cynthia, Lydia and I all went out on the Delaware River after the Cyndia was fully rigged and ready to seek out a cargo. As we dropped down the river, we passed an inbound ship named the "Greyhound." We did not know it then, but one year later, The Greyhound would be part of a future event in Colonial history along the Delaware River.

# 32

The Tea Parties

As the year 1773 drew to a close, we learned of an event far to the north that would have a great and lasting effect upon the Colonies. This of course was what has come to be known as the Boston Tea Party.

With great enthusiasm, Daniel read an eyewitness account to us all in Mom's old kitchen one evening after dinner. It was written by a fellow named "George Hewes" and explained it in great detail. Eyewitness account...

The tea destroyed was contained in three ships, lying near each other at what was called at that time Griffin's wharf, and were surrounded by armed ships of war, the commanders of which had publicly declared that if the rebels, as they were pleased to style the Bostonians, should not withdraw their opposition to the landing of the tea before a certain day, the 17th day of December, 1773, they should on that day force it on shore, under the cover of their cannon's mouth.

On the day preceding the seventeenth, there was a meeting of the citizens of the county of Suffolk, convened at one of the churches in Boston, for the purpose of consulting on what measures might be considered expedient to prevent the landing of the tea, or secure the people from the collection of the duty. At that meeting a committee was appointed to wait on Governor Hutchinson, and request him to inform them whether he would take any measures to satisfy the people on the object of the meeting.

To the first application of this committee, the Governor told them he would give them a definite answer by five o'clock in the afternoon. At the hour appointed, the committee again repaired to the Governor's house, and on inquiry found he had gone to his country seat at Milton, a distance of about six miles. When the committee returned and informed the meeting of the absence of the Governor, there was a confused murmur among the members, and the meeting was immediately dissolved, many of them crying out, "Let every man do his duty, and be true to his country"; and there was a general huzza for Griffin's wharf.

It was now evening, and I immediately dressed myself in the costume of an Indian, equipped with a small hatchet, which I and my associates denominated the tomahawk, with which, and a club, after having painted my face and hands with coal dust in the shop of a blacksmith, I repaired to Griffin's wharf, where the ships lay that contained the tea. When I first appeared in the street after being thus disguised, I fell in with many who were dressed, equipped and painted as I was, and who fell in with me and marched in order to the place of our destination.

When we arrived at the wharf, there were three of our number who assumed an authority to direct our operations, to which we readily submitted.

They divided us into three parties, for the purpose of boarding the three ships which contained the tea at the same time. The name of him who commanded the division to which I was assigned was Leonard Pitt. The names of the other commanders I never knew.

We were immediately ordered by the respective commanders to board all the ships at the same time, which we promptly obeyed. The commander of the division to which I belonged, as soon as we were on board the ship appointed me boatswain, and ordered me to go to the captain and demand of him the keys to the hatches and a dozen candles. I made the demand accordingly, and the captain promptly replied, and delivered the articles; but requested me at the same time to do no damage to the ship or rigging.

We then were ordered by our commander to open the hatches and take out all the chests of tea and throw them overboard, and we immediately proceeded to execute his orders, first cutting and splitting the chests with our tomahawks, so as thoroughly to expose them to the effects of the water.

In about three hours from the time we went on board, we had thus broken and thrown overboard every tea chest to be found in the ship, while those in the other ships were disposing of the tea in the same way, at the same time. We were surrounded by British armed ships, but no attempt was made to resist us.

We then quietly retired to our several places of residence, without having any conversation with each other, or taking any measures to discover who were our associates; nor do I recollect of our having had the knowledge of the name of a single individual concerned in that affair, except that of Leonard Pitt, the commander of my division, whom I have mentioned. There appeared to be an understanding that each individual should volunteer his services, keep his own secret, and risk the consequence for himself. No disorder took place during that transaction, and it was observed at that time that the stillest night ensued that Boston had enjoyed for many months.

During the time we were throwing the tea overboard, there were several attempts made by some of the citizens of Boston and its vicinity to carry off small quantities of it for their family use. To effect that object, they would watch their opportunity to snatch up a handful from the deck, where it became plentifully scattered, and put it into their pockets.

One Captain O'Connor, whom I well knew, came on board for that purpose, and when he supposed he was not noticed, filled his pockets, and also the lining of his coat. But I had detected him and gave information to the captain of what he was doing. We were ordered to take him into custody, and just as he was stepping from the vessel, I seized him by the skirt of his coat, and in attempting to pull him back, I tore it off; but, springing forward, by a rapid effort he made his escape. He had, however, to run a gauntlet through the crowd upon the wharf nine each one, as he passed, giving him a kick or a stroke.

Another attempt was made to save a little tea from the ruins of the cargo by a tall, aged man who wore a large cocked hat and white wig, which was fashionable. He had slightly slipped a little into his pocket, but being detected, they seized him and, taking his hat and wig from his head, threw them, together with the tea, of which they had emptied his pockets, into the water. In consideration of his advanced age, he was permitted to escape, with now and then a slight kick.

The next morning, after we had cleared the ships of the tea, it was discovered that very considerable quantities of it were floating upon the surface of the water; and to prevent the possibility of any of its being saved for use, a number of small boats were manned by sailors and citizens, who rowed them into those parts of the harbor wherever the tea was visible, and by beating it with oars and paddles so thoroughly drenched it as to render its entire destruction inevitable.

— George Hewes

Daniel was glowing that such an event had taken place. However he was outraged that individuals had tried to pocket tea for their own use.

Sarah asked, "Oh Daniel, you get so worked up about these things. They were destroying good tea. What difference would it make for a few folks to take some tea to their wives and families?"

"What difference? Why it makes all the difference in the world," Daniel insisted. "Throwing the tea in the harbor is a political statement. Pocketing the tea for one's own use is theft."

"Well Daniel, should you ever be involved in such a political statement, I would hope you might be able to bring your wife a bit of tea," Sarah commented.

"My dear wife, why do you persist in failing to grasp the gravity of the situation?" Daniel continued.

I stood up and left the kitchen. I loved my sister Sarah and also had great respect and liking for Daniel, but listening to him reading, I knew that nothing good would come of this act. Other taxes, and events such as what had been called the "Boston Massacre" had distressed the Colonies, but this wanton destruction of tea, even at that early date, seemed to represent a line in the sand that could not be ignored.

When news of this event reached England, it immediately led to an order to close the port of Boston until the tea had been paid for. This was to bring great hardship down on the good people of that city. Letters flew back and forth between every large city requesting and offering support for this act. I felt as if things had rapidly gotten out of hand.

By now, Steven had completed his apprenticeship and in fact had taken over a great deal of the day to day operation of Daniel's pottery as Daniel was more and more being drawn into political meetings and letter writing. I felt the only people who were benefiting from all of this were the post-riders who were collecting their fees for carrying the news back and forth throughout the Colonies.

Sarah was very distressed and often in tears, as she wished to support her husband, but agreed with most of the family that this was a dangerous cause for Daniel to become so passionately involved in. In September of 1774, the First Continental Congress met at Carpenter's Hall in a session that would last for seven weeks. Although Daniel was not officially a member of that body he was well known to its members and was doing all that he could to be helpful to them.

There was a great deal of talk throughout the city concerning the tea tax. This issue over taxation was becoming quite wearisome. The colonists were more and more worked up. Many folks spoke of boycotting tea once their current pretaxed supply of tea ran out. Because of Daniel's strong opinions, Sarah was often heard to say with a smile, that she would certainly not touch a drop of the stuff; except of course for those times when she might need a cup to sooth some lady's complaint, or if she was perhaps just a bit under the weather. She told me on several occasions that Daniel was often provoked with her, but that he was a kind man and would never raise a hand to her or hurt her in any way.

Cynthia said she had no such need to prevent herself from enjoying a cup of tea whenever she wished. The daily custom of teatime which Mom had so enjoyed began to shift from Mom's old kitchen to Cynthia's. As a coffee-house, the Cooperage always had a pot of coffee brewing, but if one asked Bronwyn nicely with a bit of a wink, she could always produce a cup of strong tea which in those days she referred to as "Welsh coffee."

Every time the subject appeared to have quieted down, there seemed to be a new batch of letters from the north, in and around Boston, describing the cruel treatment that was being imposed upon, or more often suggesting what might be imposed upon, these loyal subjects of King George.

Ernie, Will and I still often frequented several of the local coffee-houses to learn of the news. The Cooperage was of course our favorite and safest place, but we also wanted a wider perspective. After its opening in December of 1773, a new coffee house named City Tavern, located on Second Street was becoming very popular.

# The Pennsylvania Gazette

February 16, 1774
CITY TAVERN, PHILADELPHIA.

DANIEL SMITH begs leave to inform the PUBLIC, that the Gentlemen Proprietors of the */CITY /**/TAVERN /* have been pleased to approve of him, as a proper person to keep said */tavern /*: in consequence of which he has compleatly furnished it, and, at a very great expence, has laid in every article of the first quality, perfectly in the stile of a London */tavern /*: And in order the better to accommodate strangers, he has fitted up several elegant bed rooms, detached from noise, and as private as in a lodging house. The best livery stables are quite convenient to the house. He has also fitted up a genteel Coffee Room, well attended, and properly supplied with English and American papers and magazines. He hopes his attention and willingness to oblige, together with the goodness of his wines and larder, will give the public entire satisfaction, and prove him not unworthy of the encouragement he has already experienced. The */City /**/ Tavern /* in Philadelphia was erected at a great expence, by a voluntary subscription of the principal gentlemen of the */city /*, for the convenience of the public, and is by much the largest and most elegant house occupied in that way in America.

Since my accident, I had learned to listen hard, but rarely offered my opinions. The opinions of blind people were neither sought out, nor welcomed. I did not wish to become involved in a tavern brawl in which I would certainly be the loser. Sadly enough, my opinion seemed to be falling out of favor. I had no doubt that there were those honest and decent individuals such as Daniel who seemed sincerely committed to this new cause. However, I also felt that there were many who were spinning the tales for their own personal gain or advantage.

In December the ship "The Greyhound" that we had seen the year before while sailing in the river on the Cyndia, was again in the news. It had brought a cargo of tea to Philadelphia. Ladened with the first consignment of East India tea to be taxed, it had been refused. The Captain, thinking he was very clever, had sought out a nearby port to land his cargo and had sailed across the Delaware River to the New Jersey port of Greenwich, located a short way up Cohansey Creek. This was a small, unarmed port and the Captain of the "Greyhound" met with no resistance unloading his cargo into a local warehouse belonging to a loyalist named Dan Bowen.

On the night of December 23rd, while the "Greyhound" was still lying at anchor in Cohansey Creek and most good folks were snug in their beds, a group of local citizens took matters into their own hands. In imitation of the Boston Tea Party of the year before, about forty individuals dressed as Indians, broke into Dan Bowen's warehouse and dragged all of the tea chests into the town square and set the lot ablaze. Not satisfied with this huge bonfire and the destruction it brought, they also set the "Greyhound" ablaze.

The Captain of the "Greyhound" no longer thought himself quite as clever as he watched his fine little ship burn to the waterline.

The Greenwich tea party was, of course, a major topic of conversation about our Christmas dinner that year in the dining room of the Cooperage. It was common knowledge amongst our family that Daniel had taken part in the destruction of tea in Greenwich. With a smile, I innocently inquired of Sarah if Daniel had been able to bring her any tea? In reply I received a vicious kick from her under the table. That year Sarah slipped the silver shilling into Daniel's plum pudding. I believed we all would have agreed that Daniel was charting a course where he well might need any luck the Christmas shilling might bring him. As the next few months passed, there was great anger over the destruction that had occurred in Greenwich, but it would all be overshadowed by the events in and around Boston, which took place during April of that year. There, a gathering storm was about to change the history of the Thirteen British Colonies forever.

# 33

# Lexington & Concord

April 27, 1775
POSTSCRIPT TO THE PENNSYLVANIA GAZETTE.
No. 2418. PHILADELPHIA, April 27.

By this DayBoston Mail we have received the following INTELLIGENCE, viz. Extract of a Letter from Boston, April 19. I HAVE taken up my pen to inform you, that last night, about eleven o, 1000 of the best troops in a very secret manner embarked on board a number of boats at the bottom of the Common, and went up Cambridge river, and landed. (In the mean time they stopped every person going over the Neck or any ferry; however we soon found a way to get some men to alarm the country.) From thence they marched to */Lexington /*, where they saw a number of men exercising; they ordered them to disperse, and immediately fired on them, killed eight men on the spot, and then marched to Concord. This alarmed the country, so that it seemed as if men came down from the clouds. This news coming to town the General sent out another thousand men, with a large train of artillery. In the mean time those troops at Concord had set fire to the Court house there. - We then had our men collected, so that an engagement immediately ensued, and the King's troops retreated very fast, till they were reinforced with the last 1000 that the General sent; but they did not stand long before the whole body gave way, and retreated very fast, and our men kept up at their heels, loading and firing till they got to Charlestown, where our men thought it not prudent to come any further, fearing the ships of war would be ordered to fire on Boston and Charlestown. They have gained a complete victory, and, by the best information I can get, most of the officers and soldiers are cut off. - There were two wagons, one loaded with powder and ball, the other with provisions, guarded by seventeen men and an officer, going to the army, when six of our men way laid them, shot two, wounded two, took the officer prisoner (the others took to the woods) and brought off the wagons. The engagement began about twelve o, and continued till seven, in the mean time they retreated 20 miles. I have endeavored to give you a few of the particulars, as near as I have been able, though I do not know whether I am wholly right. You must make allowances for bar writing and blunders, considering the situation we are in, not knowing but what the troops may have liberty to return the revenge on us. We have now at least ten thousand men round this town. It has been a most distressing day with us, but I pray God we may never have reason to be called to such another."

The coffee-houses and taverns were abuzz with talk and speculation. Although I had always had strong feelings of loyalty to the Crown, this attack upon the Colonial population of Massachusetts seemed harsh and unnecessary. Feeling ran high, with many folks not believing that the British Regulars would have fired on a small Colonial militia unit. Just as many believed that the Militia would never have fired upon the Regular Army. Yes, there had been that unfortunate scuffle in Boston five years earlier when a mob had harassed a British sentry and shots had been fired into a crowd. At least one man had been killed then, and more hurt. However, this was different. This was a case of the British Army attempting to seize the arms of the people, and in doing so had killed eight men who were not rioters, but rather good citizens of the Colony. Loyalists were very divided, but this act would go a long way to swinging the balance of popular support behind the Colonists. What was the truth concerning this dreadful affair near Boston? What had actually happened?

Pennsylvania is a large, centrally located, and influential Colony. Philadelphia is the largest and most prosperous city in the British North American Colonies. It had been chosen as the meeting place of the Continental Congress in part for that reason. It is also one of the freest Colonies with a wide diversity of religions. As a bustling port city it is the home to people from every corner of the world. Massachusetts and Virginia are both Colonies with strong American patriotic leanings, but for any cause advocating armed rebellion from Great Britain, it would be necessary to have Pennsylvania firmly behind such a movement. This would be no easy challenge with Pennsylvania's very strong Quaker influence in the governing body of the Pennsylvania Assembly. The Assembly had struggled against any form of armed militia. It was only with great reluctance that the Pennsylvania associators had been formed.

During May of 1775, the Assembly had quietly pushed aside the Proprietary Governor and formed the Pennsylvania

Committee of Safety. This committee would take the place of the Governor and many thought life could then calmly move ahead. One afternoon in early June, Michael Graham stormed into the shop, and although I had not seen him in a number of months, without any introduction, he announced his presence by saying,

"Have you read the letter published in this morning's *Gazette* from my old friend Reverend William Gordon? Finally we have a clear account of what happened outside of Boston last April. I know Reverend Gordon to be a fair and honest man. The *Gazette* has reprinted a long account describing the entire event in a letter that Reverend Gordon wrote to a friend in England. He has offered it to the *Gazette*. Let me read it to you."

# The Pennsylvania Gazette

June 7, 1775

An \*/ACCOUNT /\* of the Commencement of Hostilities between Great Britain and America, in the Province of Massachusetts Bay, by the Rev. William Gordon, of Roxbury, in a Latter to a Gentleman in England. (Published with the Consent of the Author.) MY DEAR SIR, I SHALL now give you a letter upon public affairs. This colony, judging itself possessed of an undoubted right to the charterprivileges which had been granted by our glorious deliverer King William III. and finding that the continent was roused by the measures and principles of administration, was determined upon providing the necessary requisites for self defense, in case there should be an attempt to support the late unconstitutional acts by the point of the sword, and upon making that resistance which the laws of God and nature justified, and the circumstances of the people would admit, and so to leave it with the righteous Judge of the world to settle the dispute. Accordingly the Provincial Congress, substituted by the inhabitants in lieu of the General Assembly, which could not convene but by the call of the Governor, prepared a quantity of stores for the service of an army, whenever the same might be brought into the field. These stores were deposited in various places; many of them at Concord, about 20 miles from Charlestown, which lies on the other side of the river, opposite to Boston, answering to Southwark, but without the advantage of a bridge. It was apprehended by numbers, from the attempt made to surprise some cannon at Salem on Feb. 26, that there would be something of the like kind in other places, and many were uneasy, after the resolutions of the Parliament were known, that any quantity of stores was within so small a distance of Boston, while there was no regular force established for the defense of them. Several were desirous of raising an army instantly upon hearing what had been determined at home, but it was judged best upon the whole not to do it, as that step might be immediately construed to the disadvantage of the colony by the enemies of it, and might not meet with the unanimous approbation of the Continental Congress. Here I must break off for a few minutes, to inform you, by way of episode, that on the 30th of March the Governor ordered out about 1100 men, to parade it for the distance of five miles to Jamaica Plains, and so round by the way of Dorchester back again; in performing which military exploit, they did considerable damage to the stone fences,... The Tories had been for a long while filing the officers and soldiers with the idea, that the Yankees would not fight, but would certainly run for it, whenever there was the appearance of hostilities on the part of the regulars. They had repeated the story so often, that they themselves really believed it, and the military were persuaded to think the same, in general, so that they held the country people in the utmost contempt....,: This cast of mind was much increased upon the news of what Parliament had resolved upon; the people however bore insults patiently, being determined that they would not be the aggressors. At length the General was fixed upon sending a detachment to concord to destroy the stores, having been, I apprehend, worried into it by the native tories that were about him, and confirmed in his design by the opinion of his officers, about ten of whom, on the 18th of April, passed over Charlestown ferry, and by the Neck through Roxbury, armed with swords and pistols, and placed themselves on different parts of the road in the night, to prevent all intelligence, and the countrybeing alarmed; they stopped various persons, threatening to blow their brains out, ordering them to dismount, &c. The grenadier and light infantry companies had been taken off duty some days, under pretence of learning a new exercise, which made the Bostonians jealous; one and another were confirmed in their suspicions by what they saw and heard on the 18th, so that expresses were forwarded to alarm the country, some of whom were secured by the officers on the road: the last had not got out of town more than about five minutes, ere the order arrived to stop all persons from leaving the town. An alarm was spread in many places (to some the number of officers on the road to Concord proved an alarm) however, as thee had been repeated false ones, the country was at a loss what to judge. On the first of the night, when it was very dark, the detachment, consisting of all the grenadiers and light infantry, the flower of the army, to the amount of 800 or better, officers included, the companies having been filled up, and several of the inimical torified [sic] natives, repaired to the boats, and got into them just as the moon rose, crossed the water, landed on Cambridge side, took through a private way to avoid discovery, and therefore had to go through some places up to their thighs in water. They made a quick march of it to */Lexington /*, about 13 miles from Charlestown, and got there by half an hour after four. Here I must pause again, to acquaint you that in the morning of the 19th , before we had breakfasted, between eight and nine, the whole neighbourhood was in alarm; the minute men (so called from their having agreed to turn out at a minutewarning) were collecting together; we had an */account /* that the regulars had killed six of our men at */Lexington /*; the country was in an uproar; another detachment was coming out of Boston; and I was desired to take care of myself and partner. I concluded that the brigade was intended to support the grenadiers and light infantry, and to cover their retreat, in which I was not mistaken. The brigade took out two cannon, the detachment had none. Having sent off my books, which I had finished packing up the day before, conjecturing what was coming on from the moment I had heard of the resolutions of Parliament, tho'I did not expect it till the reinforcement arrived, we got into our chaise, and went to Dedham. At night we had it confirmed to us, that the regulars had been roughly handled by the Yankees, a term of reproach for the New Englanders, when applied by the regulars. The Brigade under Lord Percy marched out, playing, by way of contempt, Yankee Doodle; they were afterwards told, they had been made to dance to it. Soon after the affair, knowing what untruths are propagated by each party in matters of this nature, I concluded that I would ride to Concord, enquire for myself, and not rest upon the depositions that might be taken by others; accordingly I went the last week. The Provincial Congress have taken dispositions, which they have forwarded to Great Britain; but the Ministry and pretended friends to government will cry them down, as being evidence from party persons and rebels; the like may be objected against the present */account /*, as it will materially contradict what has been published in Boston, though not expressly, yet as is commonly supposed, by authority; however with the impartial world, and those who will not imagine me capable of sacrificing honesty to the old, at present heretical, principles of the revolution, it may have some weight. Before Major Pitcairn arrived at */Lexington /* signal guns had been fired, and the bells had been rung to give the alarm; but let not the sound of bells lead you to think of a ring of bells like what you hear in England; for they are only small sized bells, one in a parish, just sufficient to notify to the people the time for attending worship, &c. */Lexington /* being alarmed, the train band or militia, and the alarm men (consisting of the aged and others exempted from turning out, excepting upon an alarm) repaired in general to the common, close in with the Meeting house, the usual place of parade; and there were present when the roll was called over about one hundred and thirty of both, as I was told by Mr. Daniel Harrington, Clerk to the company, who further said, that the night being chilly, so as to make it uncomfortable being upon the parade, they having received no certain intelligence of the regulars being upon their march, and being waiting for the same, the men were dismissed, to appear again at the beat of drum. Some who lived near went home, others to the public house at the corner of the common. Upon information being received about half an hour after, that the troops were not far off, the remains of the company who were at hand collected together, to the amount of 60 or 70, by the time the regulars appeared, but were chiefly in a confused state, only a few of them being drawn up, which accounts for other witnesses making the number less, about 30. There were present, as spectators, about 40 more, scarce any of whom had arms. The printed */account /* tells is, indeed, that they observed about 200 armed men. Possibly the intelligence they had before received had frightened those that gave the */ account /* to the General, so that they saw more than double. The said */account /*, which has little truth in it, says, that Major Pitcairn galloping up to the head of the advanced companies, two officers informed him, that a man (advanced from those that were assembled) had presented his musquet, and attempted to shoot them, but the piece flashed in the pan. The simple truth I take to be this, which I received from one of the prisoners at Concord in free conversation, one James Marr, a native of Aberdeen, in Scotland, of the 4th regiment, who was on the advanced guard, consisting of six, besides a serjeant and corporal. They were met by three men on horseback before they got to the meeting house a good way; an officer bid them stop; to which it was answered, you had better turn back, for you shall not enter the town; when the said three persons rode back again, and at some distance one of them offered to fire, but the piece flashed in the pan, without going off. I asked Marr, whether he could tell if the piece was designed at the soldiers, or to give an alarm? he could not say which. The said Marr further declared, that when they and the others were advanced, Major Pitcairn said to the */Lexington /* company, (which, by the by, was the only one there) stop you rebels! and he supposed that the design was to take away their arms; but upon seeing the regulars they dispersed, and a firing commenced, but who fired first he could not say. The said Marr, together with Evan

Davies, of the 23d, George Cooper, of the 23d, and William McDonald, of the 38th, respectively assured me in each otherpresence, that being in the room where John Bateman, of the 52d, was (he was in an adjoining room, too ill to admit of my conversing with him) they heard the said Bateman say, that the regulars fired first, and saw him go thro'the solemnity of confirming the same by an oath on the bible. Samuel Lee, a private in the 18th regiment, Royal Irish, acquainted me, that it was the talk among the soldiers that Major Pitcairn fired his pistol, then drew his sword, and ordered them to fire; which agrees with what Levi Harrington, a youth of 14 last November, told me, that being upon the common, and hearing the regulars were coming up, he went to the meeting house, and saw them down the road, on which he returned to the */ Lexington /* company —- that a person on horseback rode round the meeting, and came towards the company that way, said something aloud, but could not tell what, rode a little further, then stopt and fired a pistol, which was the first report he heard, then another on horseback fired his pistol, then 3 or 4 regulars fired their guns, upon which, hearing the bullets whistle, he ran off, and saw no more of the affair. Mr. Paul Revere, who was sent express, was taken and detained some time by the officers, being afterwards upon the spot, and finding the regulars at hand, passed thro'the */Lexington /* company with another, having between them a box of papers belonging to Mr. Hancock, and went down across road, till there was a house so between him and the company, as that he could not see the latter; he told me likewise, that he had not got half a gun shot from them before the regulars appeared; that they halted about three seconds; that upon hearing the report of a pistol or gun, he looked round, and saw the smoke in front of the regulars, our people being out of view because of the house; then the regulars huzzaand fired, first two more guns, then the advanced guard, and so the whole body; the bullets flying thick about him, and he having nothing to defend himself, ran into a wood, where he halted, and heard the firing about a quarter of an hour. James Brown, one of the */ Lexington /* militia, informed me, that he was upon the common, that two pistols were fired from the party of the soldiers towards the militia men, as they were getting over the wall to be out of the way, and that immediately upon it the soldiers began to fire their guns; that being got over the wall, and seeing the soldiers fire pretty freely, he fired upon them, and some others did the same. Simon Winship, of */Lexington /*, declared, that being upon the road about four o, two miles and an half on this side of the meeting house, he was stopt by the regulars, and commanded by some of the officers to dismount, or he was a dead man; that he was obliged to march with the said troops until he came within about half a quarter of a mile of the said meeting house, when an officer commanded the troops to halt, and then to prime and load, which being done, the troops marches on till they came within a few rods of Capt. ParkerLexington company, who were partly collected on the place of parade, when said Winship observed an officer at the head of said troops flourishing his sword round his head in the air, and with a loud voice giving the word FIRE; the said Winship is positive that there was no discharge of arms on either side, until the word FIRE was given by the said officer as above. I shall not trouble you with more particulars, but give you the substance as it lies in my own mind, collected from the persons whom I examined for my own satisfaction. The */Lexington /* company, upon seeing the troops, and being themselves so unequal a match for them, were deliberating for a few moments what they should do, when several dispersing of their own heads, the Captain soon ordered the rest to disperse for their own safety. Before the order was given, three or four of the regular Officers, seeing the company as they came up on the rising ground on this side the meeting, rode forward, one or more, round the Meeting house, leaving it on the right hand, and so came upon them that way; upon coming up, one cryout, damnrebels lay down your arms;"another, you rebels;"a third, you rebels;"&c. Major Pitcairn, I suppose, thinking himself justified by parliamentary authority to consider them as rebels, perceiving that they did not actually lay down their arms, observing that the generality were getting off, while a few continued in their military position, and apprehending there could be no great hurt in killing a few such Yankees, which might probably, according to the notions that had been instilled into him by the tory party, of the Americans being poltroons, end all the contest, gave the command to fire, then fired his own pistol, and so set the whole affair a going. The printed */account /* says very different, but whatever the General may have sent home in support of that */account /*, the public have nothing but bare assertions, and I have such valid evidence of the falshood of several matters therein contained, that with me it has very little weight. The same */account /*tells us, that several shots were fired from a meeting house on the left, of which I heard not a single syllable, either from the prisoners or others, and the mention of which it would have been almost impossible to have avoided, had it been so, by one or another among the numbers with whom I freely and familiarly conversed. There is a curious note at the bottom of the */account /*, telling us, that notwithstanding the fire from the meeting house, Col. Smith and Major Pitcairn with the greatest difficulty kept the soldiers from forcing into the meeting house, and putting all those in it to death. Would you not suppose that there was a great number in the meeting house, while the regulars were upon the common on the right of it, between that and the \*/ Lexington /\* company? Without doubt. And who do you imagine they were? One Joshua Simonds, who happened to be getting powder there as the troops arrived; besides whom I believe there were not two, if so much as one, for by reason of the position of the meeting house, none would have remained in it thro'choice, but fools and madmen. However, Col. Smith and Major Pitcairnhumanity prevented the soldiers putting all those persons to death, their military skill should certainly have made some of them prisoners, and the \*/account /\* should have given us their names. To what I have wrote respecting Major Pitcairn, I am sensible his general character may be objected. But character must not be allowed to overthrow positive evidence when good, and the conclusions fairly deduced therefrom. Besides, since hearing from Mr. Jones in what shameful abusive manner, with oaths and curses, he was treated by the Major at Concord, for shutting the doors of his tavern against him and the troops, and in order to terrify him to make discoveries of stores; and the manner in which the Major crowover the two four and twenty pounders found in the yard, as a mighty acquisition, worthy the expedition on which the detachment was employed, I have no such great opinion of the Majorcharacter, tho when he found that nothing could be done of any great importance, by bullying, blustering and threatening, he could alter his tone, begin to coax, and offer a reward. It may be said this Jones was a goaler. Yes, and such a goaler as I would give credit to, sooner than the generality of those officers, that will degrade the British arms, by employing their swords in taking away the rights of a free people, when they ought to be devoted to a good cause only. There were killed at \*/Lexington /\* eight persons; one Parker, of the same name with the captain of the company, and two or three more, on the common; the rest on the other side of the walls and fences while dispersing. The soldiers fired at persons who had no arms. Eight hundred of the best British troops in America having thus nobly vanquished a company of non-resisting Yankees while dispersing and slaughtered a few of them by way of experiment, marched forward in the greatness of their might to Concord. The Concord people had received the alarm, and had drawn themselves up in order for defence; upon a messengercoming and telling them that the regulars were three times their number, they prudently changed their situation, determining to wait for reinforcements from the neighbouring towns, which were now alarmed; but as to the vast numbers of armed people seen assembling in all the heights, as related in the */account /*, 'tis mostly fiction. The Concord company retired over the North bridge, and when strengthened returned to it, with a view of dislodging Capt. Laurie, and securing it for themselves. They knew not what had happened at */Lexington /*, and therefore orders were given by the commander not to give the first fire; they boldly marched towards it, though not in great numbers (as told in the */account /*) and were fired upon the regulars, by which fire a Captain belonging to Acton was killed, and I think a private. The Rev. Mr. Emerson, of Concord, living in the neighbourhood of the bridge, who gave me the */account /*, went near enough to see it, and was nearer the regulars than the killed. He was very uneasy till he found that the fire was returned, and continued till the regulars were drove off. Lieut. Gould, who was at the bridge, was wounded and taken prisoner, has deposed that their regulars gave the first fire there, tho'the printed narrative asserts the contrary; and the soldiers, that knew any thing of the matter, with whom I conversed, made no scruple of owning the same that Mr.

Gould deposed. After the engagement began, the whole detachment collected together as fast as it could. The narrative tells us that as Capt. Parsons returned with his three companies over the bridge, they observed three soldiers on the ground, one of them scalped, his head much mangled, and his ears cut off, tho'not quite dead; all this is not fiction, tho'the most is. The Rev. Mr. Emerson informed me how the matter was, with great concern for its having happened. A young fellow coming over the bridge in order to join the country people, and seeing the soldier wounded and attempting to get up, not being under the feelings of humanity, very barbarously broke his scull and let out his brains, with a small axe (apprehend of the tomahawk kind) but as to his being scalped and having his ears cut off, there was nothing in it. The poor object lived an hour or two before he expired. The detachment, when joined by Capt. Parsons, made a hasty retreat, finding by woeful experience that the Yankees would fight, and that their numbers would be continually encreasing. The regulars were pushed with vigour by the country people, who took the advantage of walls, fences, &c. but those that could get up to engage were not upon equal terms with the regulars in point of number any part of the day, tho'the country was collecting together from all quarters, and had there been two hours more for it, would probably have cut off both detachment and brigade, or made them prisoners. The soldiers being obliged to retreat with haste to */Lexington /*, had no time to do any considerable mischief. But a little on this side */Lexington /* meeting house, where they were met by the brigade, with cannon, under Lord Piercy, the scene changed. The inhabitants had quitted their houses in general upon the road, leaving almost everything behind them, and thinking themselves well off in escaping with their lives. The soldiers burnt in */Lexington /* three houses, one barn and two shops, one of which joined to the house, and a mill house adjoining to the barn: Other houses and buildings were attempted to be burnt, and narrowly escaped. You would have been shockat the destruction which has been made by the regulars, as they are miscalled, had you been present with me to have beheld it. many houses were plundered of every thing valuable that could be taken away, and what could not be carried off was destroyed; looking glasses, pots, pans, &c. were broke all to pieces; doors when not fastened, sashes and windows wantonly damaged and destroyed. The people say that the soldiers are worse than the Indians; in short, they have given the country such an early specimen of their brutality as will make the inhabitants dread submission to the power of the British ministry, and determine them to fight desperately rather than have such cruel masters to lord it over them. The troops at length reached Charleston, where there was no attacking them with safety to the town, and that night and the next day crossed over in boats to Boston, where they continue to be shut up; for the people poured down in so amazing a manner from all parts, for scores of miles round, even the grey-headed came to assist their countrymen, the General was obliged to set about further fortifying the town immediately at all points and places. The proceedings of April 19th have united the colony and continent, and brought in New York to act as vigorously as any other place whatsoever; and has raised an army in an instant, which are lodged in the several houses of the town round Boston till their tents are finished, which will be soon. All that is attended to, besides plowing and planting, &c. is making ready for fighting. The non-importations and non- exportations will now take place from necessity, and traffic give place to war. We have a fine spring, prospects of great plenty; there was scarce

ever known such a good fall of lambs; we are in no danger
of starving, thro'the cruel acts against the New England
governments; and the men who had been used to the fishery,
a hardy generation of people, Lord North has undesignedly
kept in the country to give strength to our military
operations, and to assist as occasion may require: Thanks
to a superior wisdom for his blunders. The General is
expecting reinforcements, but few have arrived as yet; the
winds, contrary to the common run at this season, instead
of being easterly, have been mostly the reverse. When the
reinforcement arrives, and is recovered of the voyage, the
General will be obliged in honour to attempt dislodging
the people, and penetrating into the country; both soldiers
and inhabitants are in want of fresh provisions, and will
be like to suffer much, should the provincial army be able
to keep the town shut up on all sides, excepting by water,
as at present. The General engaged with the Selectmen of
Boston, that if the townpeople would deliver up their
arms into their custody, those that chose it should be
allowed to go out with their effects; the townsmen
complied, and the General forfeited his word, for which
there will be an after reckoning, should they ever have it
in their power to call him to an */account /*. A few have
been allowed to come out with many of their effects;
numbers are not permitted to come out, and the chief of
those who have been, have been obliged to leave their
merchandize and goods (linen and houshold stuff, cash and
plate excepted) behind them. You must look back to the
origin of the united provinces, that you may have an idea
of the resolution of this people. May the present struggle
end as happily in favour of American Liberty, without
proving the destruction of Great Britain. We are upon
a second edition of King Charles the Firstreign, enlarged.
May the dispute be adjusted, before the times are too
tragical to admit of it. Both officers and privates have

altered their opinion of the Yankees very much since the 18th of April. The detachment, while at Concord, disabled two 24 pounders, destroyed their two carriages, and seven wheels for the same, with their limbers; sixteen wheels for brass 3 pounders, and two carriages, with limber and wheels for two 4 pounders; 500 pounds of ball thrown into the river, wells and other places; and broke in pieces about 60 barrels of flour, half of which was saved. Cannot be certain of the numbers that were killed. Apprehend upon the whole the regulars had more than 100 killed, and 150 wounded, besides about 50 taken prisoners. The country people had about 40 killed, 7 or 8 taken prisoners, and a few wounded. N.B. I never saw the printed */account /* till Monday, so that I was not directed by it in any of my enquiries when at */Lexington /* and Concord. —— The General, I am persuaded, gave positive orders to the detachments not to fire first, or I am wholly mistaken in my opinion of him. The prisoners at Worcester, Concord and */Lexington /*, all agreed in their being exceedingly well used. The policy of the people would determine them thereto, if their humanity did not.

May 17, 1775.

Michael dropped the paper on my bench and began to pace about the shop.

I commented that demonstrations over a few taxes or the writs of assistances had been one thing. That showed a certain spirit; a determination to be a hearty people. But now, I could hardly believe the good folks in and about Boston had taken up arms against the Crown. "I wish it had not come to this."

Michael stopped pacing and faced my bench. "Andrew my good friend, I know you have always held a special place in your heart for the British Army because you served with the 60th Royal Americans, but you served fifteen to twenty years ago. You must let it go. Things are very different today in 1775 than they were in 1755. Now things have gone too far. If this fellow Pitcairn actually fired his pistols and ordered the King's troops to fire into the lads on Lexington Green, well, this will lead to no good. This is not a case of the Army controlling an unruly mob as it was during what they called the Boston Massacre No my friend, this is the Army directly firing upon the people of the land! This has gone a long way toward turning me against the Crown. I must be off now, but I shall return later." With that he turned and quickly left the shop.

# 34

# The Committee of
# Safety Contract

A few minutes later Ernie walked over to my bench. "Andrew, I am glad Michael stopped by and read that article to us. I have been meaning to speak with you for some time. Thomas Palmer down on Market street has been advertising in the *Gazette* that he wishes to employ stock makers and lock filers for a large contract that he has obtained. I believe he has contracted to make muskets for the Committee of Safety. Listen to his advertisement:

EXTRAORDINARY Wages will be given to two or three Journeymen Gunsmiths, who are skilled in Stocking of Muskets and Rifles. Likewise good Encouragement will be given to a Gunlock Filer, that can make Musket Locks. — Apply to */THOMAS /**/PALMER /*, the North Side of Market street, between Fourth and Fifth streets, Philadelphia.

N.B. Any person that has Skill to accomplish either of the aforesaid Branches, may, if they choose, work Piece work, and receive their Cash every Saturday Afternoon; or a Sum of Money will be advanced to them, by giving Security for the Delivery of their Work.

"We have always gotten on well with Thomas as there has been plenty of work for all of us. I feel certain we could contract with him for some of his Committee of Safety work. Your support for the British is well known. If we could take on some Committee of Safety work, well, it would show that we are fair. Besides, we could use a bit more work at this time."

I knew that both Michael and Ernie were correct in their assessment of the time and were offering sound advice.

"Well, Ernie, I believe you make a very good point. Shall we step around the corner and discuss matters with Mr. Palmer?"

Thomas Palmer was glad to see us and we quickly worked out an agreement to take on a substantial part of his contract. One day in late June, while I was at my bench filing parts for one of the musket locks that we were doing for Thomas Palmer, our shop door swung open and the sound of booted feet came across the floor to my bench. As I looked up, I heard a voice that was familiar, but that I had not heard in a very long time.

"Good morning Andrew! It has been a long time since we have spoken. I was very saddened to learn of your accident. However, I am glad to see that you are still working at your trade."

Suddenly the strong yet quiet voice jogged a cord in my memory. Smiling I stood and saluted. "Greetings Colonel Washington," I replied.

George Washington placed his hand on my shoulder. "Thank you Andrew, it is General now. The Continental

Congress has just showed enough faith in me to grant me a General's commission and appoint me to command the new Continental Army gathered outside of Boston. I will be leaving Philadelphia shortly to take up that command."

"Congratulations General. I know you will provide good leadership to what I hear is currently little more than a mob," I replied.

"Yes, I believe it will be a challenge."

I remembered George Washington well from The Campaign of General Forbes to open a road west through the Pennsylvania frontier to take Fort Duquesne. The then Colonel Washington had had many discussions with General Forbes at Headquarters in which he had tried to convince General Forbes that the road should be cut through Virginia rather than Pennsylvania.

"I was in Philadelphia last autumn during the First Continental Congress, but did not have a chance to stop by to speak with you. This time before leaving to travel North, I find myself in need of some good gunflints for my pistols. I have been told you always keep a good stock of fine flints on hand."

"Yes indeed we do," I replied showing him the same drawer that Nick the Tinker had made his selection from. Remembering that the General would have known Nick from the same military campaign now so many years ago, I told him of Nick's visit a few years earlier.

"We do have a way of turning up old friends from time to time," General Washington replied. An hour passed pleasantly before the General took his leave. I saluted once again and he was gone.

The door had hardly closed before Seth came to my bench.

"Master Andrew, I have wished to speak with you and Master Ernie."

"Yes Lad what is it?"

"Sir I wish to ask you and Master Ernie if you would release me from my apprenticeship in order that I might join the Continental Army."

"Why Seth, are you unhappy with the work here?" I asked.

"Oh no sir! But an army has formed outside of Boston and I thought if you would let me go and join it, I could serve in the Army and then return and finish my apprenticeship afterwards."

I sat at my bench for several minutes remembering my own wish to join The British Army when the French & Indian War had broken out. I also remembered Master Frederick's words and had always been glad that he had made me finish learning my trade before I went off on my great adventure: An adventure that had turned out so badly.

I was about to reply in the negative and make him finish his apprenticeship, when Seth said, "You know how strongly Father feels about this cause. He has been insisting that I should speak with you and then join the Army."

Suddenly I could imagine the pressure that Seth had been under as I was sure that Daniel would be a powerful influence on the lad.

"Do you not think you might do better to finish learning your trade before running off to war?"

"If you allow me, I really think I would like to go now Sir. Perhaps I could go North with your friend General Washington."

I laughed. "I have a great deal of respect for Colonel, I mean General Washington, but I would not presume to be so familiar as to address him as my friend. Let me think about it a bit and speak with Ernie."

"Thank you sir!" Sending Seth out of the shop on an errand, I went out into the forge where Ernie was working and asked him if we could have a few words. We both agreed that it would be better if Seth stayed on and finished learning his trade. Having just accepted all of this Committee of Safety work from Thomas Palmer, we would be hard pressed to complete it on time without Seth's extra pair of hands working in the shop. However, we also understood what pressure he would be under from Daniel.

Ernie asked, "Could you get the Lad a position on General Washington's staff?"

"Ernie, I could not guarantee that. It has been close to twenty years ago that I served with General Washington. I am certain that there are many people currying his favor for any new staff positions there might be. Seth certainly does not merit an officer level staff position. The lad is hardly sixteen and has no military experience."

"But even so, you could try and put in a word for him?" Ernie pressed.

"Yes, I could try. However, I do not believe that would be the right thing to do. Is it your thinking that we should release him?"

A long silence followed, leaving my question hanging in the air. I could feel Ernie carefully thinking it through. Finally he answered:

"No Andrew, it is not. It certainly would not be what Master Frederick would have wished. In fact he would not even be having this discussion. He would simply say 'No!' and return to his work. I do feel badly for the lad as you know Daniel is going to make it very hard on him if he does not enlist in the new Continental Army. I believe he would encourage him to go whether or not we agree. Keeping him will certainly cause a lot of family issues for you."

"Alright, I think you are correct."

When Seth returned from the errand that I had sent him on, I told him of our discussion. His only comment was that his father would not be pleased with him.

Ernie said, "Seth, you are your father's son, but you are also our apprentice. You have signed your apprenticeship papers and we are all trying to honor them. You will learn a good trade in this shop and we believe you should stay and learn."

Seth returned to his bench and continued filing a musket lock-plate.

Later in the afternoon, Daniel entered the shop.

"A good day to all!" he said. "I understand you are considering releasing Seth from his apprenticeship to join the Continental Army."

"Daniel, we have listened to Seth's request and denied it," I replied.

Daniel stood there for a moment seeming surprised.

"I thought you would let him go. I had hoped my son would join this cause."

"Daniel, this 'cause' as you put it is tearing the people of this, and I suspect every other Colony, apart. I know there is an army gathering outside of Boston and that Colonel, I mean General, Washington is leaving to take command of it. One would hope that these differences with the Crown could be resolved, but if not, and this land is torn apart by an armed rebellion, it will not end tomorrow. Let the lad finish his trade and if there is still a conflict at that time, he will be free to do whatever he wishes. In the meantime, are you aware that he is at this moment making a musket lock for a Committee of Safety contract? If he were to leave suddenly, we would be hard pressed to complete it on time. So in a very significant way, your son is helping to support the Continental Army."

"Yes, he has told me of this contract and I am glad of it. I guess for now that must be enough. Your sister Sarah will certainly be glad of your decision."

"I have no doubt of that Daniel," I laughed. Before leaving the shop, Daniel touched me on the shoulder to let me know that our shop decision would not lead to family trouble.

One evening, not long after this, while Ernie and I were enjoying a glass of Madeira at City Tavern and listening to the latest news, a large hand clapped me on the shoulder.

"Would you be remembering an old friend Master Andrew?"

I knew I had heard that voice before, but at first could not place it.

"Would you be remembering the time we served together at Fort Pitt?"

Suddenly it came to me. It was old Ian Duncan, Sergeant in the 42$^{nd}$ Highlanders.

"Of course Ian. Greetings! What brings you to Philadelphia? Are you here on the King's business?"

"Andrew, I tend to no one's business these days but my own. I am no longer with the 42nd." Knowing that service for the enlisted ranks was for life in the British service, I asked what had happened.

Ian told me that his left foot had been crushed by a military supply wagon. He had collected his back pay and had been invalided out. He had come to Philadelphia as he had had quite enough of the wilderness and was now employed here at City Tavern tending the bar.

"Ian, you are too smart a Sergeant to have your foot run over by a supply wagon," I commented.

"Why, Andrew, placing my foot in front of that wagon wheel was the smartest thing I ever did. You know our service is for life. I believe another war is coming and I will fight no more wars for King George or any other man. Life here in this tavern suits me just fine. These Americans have a point you know.

As Ian limped back to the bar, I sat there thinking about Ian's words. It seemed as if there would in fact be a war. However, unlike all of the previous Colonial wars in which we had fought for the Empire, with the might of the

British Army behind us, if war was to come we would be fighting both against the British as well as between ourselves. God help this poor Colony. Would Pennsylvania, like me, prove to be one of the Fortunate Ones? Only time would tell.

Tick, tick, tick, tick, tick: closing the cover of my large silver watch, which still rested in the palm of my right hand, I rubbed my face with my left hand as if I had just awakened from a deep sleep.

## The End

City Tavern 1776

# Acknowledgements

In his famous quotation, John Donne (1572-1631), wrote that "No man is an island unto himself." In the same way, creative endeavors are not forged in a vacuum. Any writer setting out to craft a tale is inspired, influenced, and aided by countless others. This is certainly true in my case. Colonial History has always drawn my interest. As a totally blind person, the idea of how blind people lived during other times has never been far from my thoughts. Over the last five years, working seasonally as a Colonial Person for Historic Philadelphia, as well as several visits to Colonial Williamsburg and Mount Vernon, has given me the opportunity to put these thoughts and observations together. The result has been the writing of *The Fortunate Ones*.

Over a ten month period of time, while working at my desk, the characters bubbled out of the antique items that I surrounded myself with, to tell their own stories. However, the journey from the telling of the tale, to the publishing of a book is a long and arduous one. Without the kindly offered help of many friends, this book would never have become the book that you are now holding in your hands.

A comprehensive list of all those who deserve thanks is beyond the scope of this small volume. However, a few individuals and organizations do stand out and must be mentioned.

Michael P. Marotta is a good friend of many decades with whom I have shared similar interests. He devoted countless hours to finding the many Philadelphia Gazette articles that help to shore up the historic fabric of this work. His advice and good council during the writing has been very appreciated. The character of Michael Graham in the book was loosely based on my old friend Michael.

Nick Padulo is a fascinating individual. I first met Nick while I was lecturing on the history of flintlock weapons in the Independence Visitor's Center. Nick stopped to chat. Before he walked away over three hours later, a friendship was forged. Over the years, this friendship has grown and strengthened as Nick is a wonderful source of historic information, particularly about the French & Indian War as well as the American Revolutionary period. He has tirelessly dug out facts and stories that I wanted to know more about. He has introduced me to countless historic friends whose knowledge has been a great help. The character of Nick the Tinker is loosely based on my good friend Nick.

Although Hilary Ward did an initial proofreading, the lion's share of editing has been done by Ron DiFonzo, who is another good friend of many years. Ron has been a volunteer copyholder for a non-profit Braille publishing house for many decades. Knowing that my written work needed formatting, punctuation, and spelling editing, when I asked him to take on this major task, Ron agreed without a moment's hesitation. Without his thorough, painstaking effort, this book would never have made it to the printer.

My wife Margarete A. Noesner, who is an artist and certificate Student at the Pennsylvania Academy of the Fine Arts, provided the art-work. She has always been supportive of my interest in Colonial history. This included marrying me in a completely colonial wedding held at City Tavern. She has encouraged me along every step of the way.

My brother Robert F. Noesner has been all one could ever wish for in a brother. From early childhood he has tried to include me in and give me every opportunity to experience things that sighted children might be learning. From playing soldiers with his friends in the woods behind our home, to putting baseball cards in the spokes of the wheels of his bicycle so I could follow the sound on another bicycle, to trips to a shooting range so I could enjoy firing antique weapons, to working on our houses, he has always been there for me.

My daughter Lynn served as my youngest research aid. Her eager willingness to accompany me to libraries and museums for research has always been very much appreciated. We have shared an enchantment with the written word. Over mugs of coffee, we have enjoyed many hours discussing books that we have read. We both dreamed of the day when we would write books. I look forward to reading her work in the future as I know it will be great.

Donald R. Toppel is the greatest antiquarian, historian and raconteur whom I have ever known. By telling me an elaborate story about every antique that he would show me, he taught me to appreciate their history and by doing so, learn to listen to the stories that every antique has to tell.

"Uncle Don" as he asked me to call him has sadly now passed on to handle the antiquarian concerns in heaven. However, when listening to antiques speak, I always feel he is there with me.

Jean and Don Toppel, thru their generous gift to me of my first talking computer and scanning reading system, opened the door for me to read, research, and begin writing my first published magazine article.

Tom Groninger has been a good friend since high school. His quiet steady friendship has always made him a good person to discuss the chapters in the book, or even life issues with. His experience of many years as a volunteer fire fighter as well as his personal interest in antique fire-fighting equipment made him a good person to review those portions of the book that deal with 18th century fire-fighting efforts.

John McGovern has taught and retaught me most of what I know about using computers. He has always been very patient reviewing many of the same computer questions that my 18th Century mind never seems to retain.

Doug Wakefield has been extremely helpful in helping me set up my newest talking computer and scanner. He has made it all talk and work smoothly. Without this computer, I would not have been able to write *The Fortunate Ones*.

Anne Arietta and Joseph Langton have been steady friends and cheerleaders. Their thoughtful gifts of antique inkwells have served to inspire my writing. When one holds an antique inkwell in one's hands, one can not help but wonder how many thousands of words may have flowed from its depths.

World class Chef Walter Staib of City Tavern has been very helpful in creating a colonial environment for us to enjoy many dinners, meetings, and yes, even as I have said, our colonial wedding. For one day, December 26th 2004, (December 26th, 1774), he transformed the City Tavern into our home for our glorious celebration where every guest was offered a researched 18th century identity. Ah, but therein lies a tale for another day. Soon after the publication of this work, I look forward to a book signing at City Tavern.

Lukas Franck of The Seeing Eye was very helpful in educating me to the early historic use of dogs by blind people as guides. This is of particular interest as it is a point so little known or understood by the general public.

Barbara Shaputis of Yesteryer has done a beautiful job making Colonial clothing for me. Clothing that has helped me slip back into the 18th Century.

When writing the chapter concerning the small sailing vessel that the Annaler Brothers purchased from Robert Bridges and named the "Cyndia," I wanted to learn what a small sailing vessel of that size would have felt like. Nick Fry invited Margarete and me to spend a wonderful afternoon sailing with him aboard his sailboat the "Cirrus." Although the Cirrus is a modern vessel, it is approximately the same size as the Cyndia. Nick was able to give me a good understanding as to what a sailing vessel of that size and period would have felt like and what it could have been used for.

Ed Weintraut, a Philadelphia jeweler who I have known for many years was very helpful concerning finding, and teaching me about, 18th century key wound pocket watches. Ed seems to be one of the last old time jewelers who understands how to make these fine old watches tick.

M. Richard Tully, Esq. Editor & publisher of *The Society of 18th–Century Gentlemen's Magazine*, typifies an 18th Century gentleman. He has encouraged my writing and added to my understanding of a time that we and others are so fascinated by.

Glenys A. Waldman, Librarian at the Masonic library and Museum has tirelessly helped me find and understand many Masonic facts and dates. She is that rare and wonderful kind of person who tries to help one find whatever one wants to know no matter how obscure it might seem to others.

Samuel C. Williamson, Past Grand Master, must be remembered for his enlightened 1983 decision to wave the ruling that a person must have no physical disability to become a Mason. It required great courage for him to make this change as it had stood as a requirement in Free Masonry for well over two-hundred and fifty years. As Past Grand Master Williamson said during a recent interview, "The wheels of Free Masonry grind slowly."

The good folks at the Philadelphia Fire Museum spent, what was for me, a very interesting afternoon teaching me about 18th century fire-fighting equipment.

Nancy Gibbs at the historic Friends Meeting House on Arch Street was very helpful in making clear to me the fine points of 18th century Quaker etiquette.

Nicole Joniec, Print Department Assistant & Digital Collections Manager, Library Company of Philadelphia, has been helpful in finding, and obtaining permission for me to print in this work a historic Philadelphia Map from 1756.

Tom Nagy, Vice-President of Operations, Accessible Archives, Inc. has graciously allowed me to quote extensively from the newspaper, *The Philadelphia Gazette.* This has brought the actual history of that time into the book.

Historic Philadelphia, Inc. (HPI), has given me the opportunity to live, dress like, and walk the streets of Old City Philadelphia as a colonial person. I must particularly thank David Holland for having enough faith in me to hire me as a colonial person; to Sandra Mackenzie Lloyd H.P.I., historian for discussing many historic points; and to Jennifer Hoffmaster, my supervisor who believed in my character as a powder horn maker. John Morrison helped me to clearly understand the character of John Cooper through many hours spent with him in the 18th century, both on and off the job. There are too many individual colonials to list by name, however, every one of them has been a joy to work with and learn from. They have all added greatly to my understanding of that long ago time.

Finally, in closing, I must thank you, the reader for taking the time to visit with these 18th Century characters to appreciate how they lived. I hope that you will enjoy being with them as much as I have enjoyed telling you about them.

Frederick W. Noesner
fwnoesner@verizon.net

2010

$$\frac{63}{1947}$$